D0641308

WOMEN WITH MEN

A Note on the Author

Richard Ford was born in Jackson, Mississippi, in 1944. He has published six novels and three collections of stories, including *The Sportswriter*, *Independence Day*, *Wildlife*, *A Multitude of Sins* and most recently *The Lay of the Land*. *Independence Day* was awarded the Pulitzer Prize and the PEN/Faulkner Award for Fiction.

By the Same Author

Richard Ford

WOMEN WITH MEN

THREE STORIES

BLOOMSBURY

First published in Great Britain by the Harvill Press 1997
This paperback edition published 2006

Copyright © Richard Ford 1992, 1997

The moral right of the author has been asserted

The Womanizer first appeared in *Granta* 1992
Jealous first appeared in the *New Yorker* 1992

Bloomsbury Publishing Plc, 36 Soho Square, London
W1D 3QY

A CIP catalogue record for this book
is available from the British Library

ISBN 0 7475 8527 X
9780747585275

10 9 8 7 6 5 4 3 2

Printed and bound by CPI Group (UK) Ltd, Croydon, CR0 4YY

All papers used by Bloomsbury Publishing are natural,
recyclable products made from wood grown in well-man-
aged forests. The manufacturing processes conform to
the environmental regulations of the country of origin

www.bloomsbury.com/richardford

Kristina

I wish to thank my friends Bill Buford, Charles McGrath and most especially Gary Fisketjon, who read these stories and gave me indispensable editorial advice. I wish also to thank my friends Michel Fabre and Suzanne Mayoux for their unique counsel. And finally, I wish to record my debt of gratitude to the stories and novels of Richard Yates, a writer too little appreciated.

CONTENTS

The Womanizer

1

MARTIN AUSTIN turned up the tiny street—rue Sarrazin—at the head of which he hoped he would come to a larger one he knew, rue de Vaugirard, possibly, a street he could take all the way to Joséphine Belliard's apartment by the Jardin du Luxembourg. He was on his way to sit with Joséphine's son, Léo, while Joséphine visited her lawyers to sign papers divorcing her husband. Later in the evening, he was taking her for a romantic dinner. Joséphine's husband, Bernard, was a cheap novelist who'd published a scandalous book in which Joséphine figured prominently; her name used, her parts indelicately described, her infidelity put on display in salacious detail. The book had recently reached the stores. Everybody she knew was reading it.

"Okay. Maybe it is not so bad to *write* such a book," Joséphine had said the first night Austin had met her, only the week before, when he had also taken her to dinner. "It is his choice to write it. I cause him unhappiness. But to publish this? In Paris? No." She had shaken her head absolutely. "I'm sorry. This is too much. My husband—he is a shit. What can I do? I say goodbye to him."

Austin was from Chicago. He was married, with no children, and worked as a sales representative for an old family-owned company that sold expensive specially treated paper to foreign textbook publishers. He was forty-four and had worked for the same company, the Lilienthal Company of Winnetka, for fifteen years. He'd met Joséphine Belliard at a cocktail party given by a publisher he regularly called on, for one of its important authors. He'd been invited only as a courtesy, since his company's paper had not been used for the author's book, a sociological text that calculated the suburban loneliness of immigrant Arabs by the use of sophisticated differential equations. Austin's French was lacking—he'd always been able to speak much more than he could understand—and as a consequence he'd stood by himself at the edge of the party, drinking champagne, smiling pleasantly and hoping he'd hear English spoken and find someone he could talk to instead of someone who would hear him speak a few words of French and then start a conversation he could never make sense of.

Joséphine Belliard was a sub-editor at the publishing house. She was a small, slender dark-haired Frenchwoman in her thirties and of an odd beauty—a mouth slightly too wide and too thin; her chin soft, almost receding; but with a smooth caramel skin and dark eyes and dark eyebrows that Austin found appealing. He had caught a glimpse of her earlier in the day when he'd visited the publisher's offices in the rue de Lille. She was sitting at her desk in a small, shadowy office, rapidly and animatedly speaking English into the telephone. He'd peered in as he passed but had forgotten about her until she came up to him at the party and smiled and asked in English how he liked Paris. Later that night they had gone to dinner, and at the end of the evening he'd taken her home in a taxi, then returned to his hotel alone and gone to sleep.

The next day, though, he'd called her. He had nothing special in mind, just an aimless, angling call. Maybe he could sleep with her—not that he even thought that. It was just a possibility, an inevitable thought. When he asked if she would like to see him again, she said she would if he wanted to. She didn't say she'd had a good time the night before. She didn't mention that at all—almost, Austin felt, as if that time had never happened. But it was an attitude he found attractive. She was smart. She judged things. It wasn't an American attitude. In America a woman would have to seem to care—more, probably, than she did or could after one harmless encounter.

That evening they had gone to a small, noisy Italian restaurant near the Gare de l'Est, a place with bright lights and mirrors on the walls and where the food was not very good. They'd ordered light Ligurian wine, gotten a little drunk and engaged in a long and in some ways intimate conversation. Joséphine told him she had been born in the suburb of Aubervilliers, north of Paris, and couldn't wait to leave home. She had gone to a university and studied sociology while living with her parents, but now had no relationship with her mother, or with her father, who had moved to America in the late seventies and not been heard from. She said she had been married eight years to a man she once liked and had had one child with but did not especially love, and that two years ago she had begun an affair with another man, a younger man, which lasted only a short time, then ended, as she had expected it might. Afterwards she had believed she could simply resume married life more or less as she'd left it, a lifelong bourgeois muddle of continuance. But her husband had been shocked and incensed by his wife's infidelity and had moved out of their apartment, quit his job at an advertising firm, found a woman to live with and gone to work writing a novel which had as its only subject his wife's supposed indiscretions—some of which, she told Austin, he'd obviously made up, though others, amusingly enough, were surprisingly accurate.

"It's not so much I blame him, you know?" Joséphine had said and laughed. "These things come along. They happen. Other people do what they please." She looked out the restaurant window at the row of small parked cars along the street. "So?"

"But what's happening now?" Austin said, trying to find a part of the story that would allow him into it. A phrase, a niche that could be said to invite his closer interest— though there didn't seem to be such a phrase.

"Now? Now I am living with my child. Alone. That is all of my life." She unexpectedly looked up at Austin, her eyes opened wide, as though to say, What else is there? "What more else?" she in fact did say.

"I don't know," Austin said. "Do you think you'll go back with your husband?" This was a question he was quite happy to ask.

"Yes. I don't know. No. Maybe," Joséphine said, extending her lower lip slightly and raising one shoulder in a gesture of carelessness Austin believed was typical of French women. He didn't mind it in Joséphine, but he usually disliked people for affecting this gesture. It was patently false and always came at the service of important matters a person wished to pretend were not important.

Joséphine, though, did not seem like a woman to have an affair and then talk about it matter-of-factly to someone she barely knew; she seemed more like an unmarried woman looking for someone to be interested in. Obviously she was more complicated, maybe even smarter, than he'd thought, and quite realistic about life, though slightly disillusioned. Probably, if he wanted to press the matter of intimacy, he could take her back to his room—a thing he'd done before on business trips, and even if not so many times, enough times that to do so now wouldn't be extraordinary or meaningful, at least not to him. To share an unexpected intimacy might intensify both their holds on life.

Yet there was a measure of uncertainty surrounding that very thought—a thought he was so used to having he couldn't keep from it. Maybe it was true that even though he liked her, liked the frankness and direct nature of her conduct toward him, intimacy was not what he wanted. She appealed to him in a surprising way, but he was not physically attracted to her. And maybe, he thought, looking at her across the table, an intimacy with him was the last thing on earth *she* was interested in. She was French. He didn't know anything about them. An illusion of potential intimacy was probably what all French women broadcast, and everyone knew it. Probably she had no interest in him at all and was just passing the time. It made him feel pleased even to entertain such a multilayered view.

They finished dinner in thoughtful, weighted silence. Austin felt ready to begin a discourse on his own life—his marriage, its length and intensity, his feelings about it and himself. He was willing to talk about the uneasy, unanchored sensation he'd had lately of not knowing exactly how to make the next twenty-five years of life as eventful and important as the previous twenty-five, a sensation buttressed by the hope that he wouldn't fail of courage if courage was required, and by the certainty that everybody had his life entirely in his hands and was required to live with his own terrors and mistakes, etc. Not that he was unhappy with Barbara or lacked anything. He was not the conventionally desperate man on the way out of a marriage that had grown tiresome. Barbara, in fact, was the most interesting and beautiful woman he'd ever known, the person he admired most. He wasn't looking for a better life. He wasn't looking for anything. He loved his wife, and he hoped to present to Joséphine Belliard a different human perspective from the ones she might be used to.

"No one thinks your thoughts for you when you lay your head on the pillow at night" was a sobering expression Austin often used in addressing himself, as well as when he'd addressed the few women he'd known since being married—including Barbara. He was willing to commence a frank discussion of this sort when Joséphine asked him about himself.

But the subject did not come up. She didn't ask about his thoughts, or about himself. And not that she talked about *her*self. She talked about her job, about her son, Léo, about her husband and about friends of theirs. He had told her he was married. He had told her his age, that he had gone to college at the University of Illinois and grown up in the small city of Peoria. But to know no more seemed fine to her. She was perfectly nice and seemed to like him, but she was not very responsive, which he felt was unusual. She seemed to have more serious things on her mind and to take life seriously—a quality Austin liked. In fact, it made her appealing in a way she had not seemed at first, when he was only thinking about how she looked and whether he wanted to sleep with her.

But when they were walking to her car, down the sidewalk at the end of which were the bright lights of the Gare de l'Est and the Boulevard Strasbourg, swarming with taxis at eleven o'clock, Joséphine put her arm through his arm and pulled close to him, put her cheek against his shoulder and said, "It's all confusion to me."

And Austin wondered: *what* was all confusion? Not him. He was no confusion. He'd decided he was a good-intentioned escort for her, and that was a fine thing to be under the circumstances. There was already plenty of confusion in her life. An absent husband. A child. Surviving alone. That was enough. Though he took his arm from her grip and reached it around her shoulder and pulled her close to him until they reached her little black Opel and got in, where touching stopped.

When they reached his hotel, a former monastery with a walled-in courtyard garden, two blocks from the great lighted confluence of St.-Germain and the rue de Rennes, she stopped the car and sat looking straight ahead as if she were waiting for Austin to get out. They had made no mention of another meeting, and he was scheduled to leave in two days.

Austin sat in the dark without speaking. A police station occupied the next corner down the shadowy street. A police van had pulled up with blinking lights, and several uniformed officers in shiny white Sam Browne belts were leading a line of handcuffed men inside, the prisoners' heads all bowed like penitents. It was April, and the street surface glistened in the damp spring air.

This was the point, of course, to ask her to come inside with him if such a thing was ever to be. But it was clearly the furthest thing from possibility, and each of them knew it. And apart from privately acknowledging that much, Austin had no real thought of it. Although he wanted to do *something* good, something unusual that would please her

and make them both know an occurrence slightly out of
the ordinary had taken place tonight—an occurrence they
could both feel good about when they were alone in bed,
even if in fact nothing much had taken place.

His mind was working on what that extra-ordinary
something might be, the thing you did if you didn't make
love to a woman. A gesture. A word. What?

All the prisoners were finally led into the police station,
and the officers had gotten back in their van and driven it
straight up rue de Mézières, where Austin and Joséphine
Belliard were sitting in the silent darkness. Obviously she
was waiting for him to get out, and he was in a quandary
about what to do. Though it was a moment he relished,
the exquisite moment before anything is acted on and
when all is potential, before life turns this way or that—
toward regret or pleasure or happiness, toward one kind of
permanence or another. It was a wonderful, tantalizing,
important moment, one worth preserving, and he knew
she knew it as well as he did and wanted it to last as long
as he wanted it to.

Austin sat with his hands in his lap, feeling large and cum-
bersome inside the tiny car, listening to himself breathe, con-
scious he was on the verge of what he hoped would be the
right—rightest—gesture. She hadn't moved. The car was
idling, its headlights shining weakly on the empty street, the
dashboard instruments turning the interior air faintly green.

Austin abruptly—or so it felt to him—reached across the
space between them, took Joséphine's small, warm hand off
the steering wheel and held it between his two large equally
warm ones like a sandwich, though in a way that would also
seem protective. He would be protective of her, guard her
from some as yet unnamed harm or from her own con-
cealed urges, though most immediately from himself, since

he realized it was her reluctance more than his that kept them apart now, kept them from parking the car and going inside and spending the night in each other's arms.

He squeezed her hand tightly, then eased up.

"I'd like to make you happy somehow," he said in a sincere voice, and waited while Joséphine said nothing. She did not remove her hand, but neither did she answer. It was as if what he'd said didn't mean anything, or that possibly she wasn't even listening to him. "It's just human," Austin said, as though she *had* said something back, had said, "Why?" or "Don't try," or "You couldn't possibly," or "It's too late."

"What?" She looked at him for the first time since they'd stopped. "It's what?" She had not understood him.

"It's only human to want to make someone happy," Austin said, holding her warm, nearly weightless hand. "I like you very much, you know that." These were the right words, as ordinary as they sounded.

"Yes. Well. For what?" Joséphine said in a cold voice. "You are married. You have a wife. You live far away. In two days, three days, I don't know, you will leave. So. For what do you like me?" Her face seemed impenetrable, as though she were addressing a cab driver who'd just said something inappropriately familiar. She left her hand in his hand but looked straight ahead.

Austin wanted to speak again. He wished to say something—likewise absolutely correct—into this new void she'd opened between them, words no one could plan to say or even know in advance, but something that admitted to what she'd said, conceded his acquiescence to it, yet allowed another moment to occur during which the two of them would enter onto new and uncharted ground.

Though the only thing that Austin could say—and he had no idea why, since it sounded asinine and ruinous—

was: *People have paid a dear price for getting involved with me*. Which were definitely the wrong words, since to his knowledge they weren't particularly true, and even if they were, they were so boastful and melodramatic as to cause Joséphine or anyone else to break out laughing.

Still, he could say that and immediately have it all be over between them and forget about it, which might be a relief. Though relief was not what he wanted. He wanted something to go forward between them, something definite and realistic and in keeping with the facts of their lives; to advance into that area where nothing actually seemed possible at the moment.

Austin slowly let go of Joséphine's hand. Then he reached both of his hands to her face and turned it toward him, and leaned across the open space and said, just before he kissed her, "I'm at least going to kiss you. I feel like I'm entitled to do that, and I'm going to."

Joséphine Belliard did not resist him at all, though she did not in any way concur. Her face was soft and compliant. She had a plain, not in the least full, mouth, and when Austin put his lips against hers she did not move toward him. She let herself be kissed, and Austin was immediately, cruelly aware of it. This is what was taking place: he was forcing himself on this woman, and a feeling came over him as he pressed his lips more completely onto hers that he was delusionary and foolish and pathetic—the kind of man he would make fun of if he heard himself described using only these facts as evidence. It was an awful feeling, like being old, and he felt his insides go hollow and his arms become heavy as cudgels. He wanted to disappear from this car seat and remember none of the idiotic things he had just an instant before been thinking. *This* had now been the first permanent move, when potentiality ended, and it had been the wrong one, the worst one possible. It was ludicrous.

Though before he could move his lips away, he realized Joséphine Belliard was saying something, speaking with her lips against his lips, faintly, and that by not resisting him she was in fact kissing him, her face almost unconsciously giving up to his intention. What she was saying all the while Austin was kissing her thin mouth was—whisperingly, almost dreamily—*"Non, non, non, non, non.* Please. I can't. I can't. *Non, non."*

Though she didn't stop. *No* was not what she meant exactly—she let her lips slightly part in a gesture of recognition. And after a moment, a long suspended moment, Austin inched away, sat back in his seat and took a deep breath. He put his hands back in his lap, and let the kiss fill the space between them, a space he had somehow hoped to fill with words. It was the most unexpected and enticing thing that could've come of his wish to do right.

She did not take an audible breath. She merely sat as she'd sat before he'd kissed her, and did not speak or seem to have anything in her mind to say. Things were mostly as they had been before he'd kissed her, only he *had* kissed her—*they* had kissed—and that made all the difference in the world.

"I'd like to see you tomorrow," Austin said very resolutely.

"Yes," Joséphine said almost sorrowfully, as if she couldn't help agreeing. "Okay."

And he was satisfied then that there was nothing else to say. Things were as they should be. Nothing would go wrong.

"Good night," Austin said with the same resolution as before. He opened the car door and hauled himself out onto the street.

"Okay," she said. She didn't look out the door, though he leaned back into the opening and looked at her. She had her hands on the steering wheel, staring straight ahead, appearing no different really from when she'd stopped to let him out five minutes before—only slightly more fatigued.

He wanted to say one more good word that would help balance how she felt at that moment—not that he had the slightest idea how she felt. She was opaque to him, completely opaque, and that was not even so interesting. Though all he could think to say was something as inane as the last thing had been ruinous. *Two people don't see the same landscape.* These were the terrible words he thought, though he didn't say them. He just smiled in at her, stood up, pushed the door closed firmly and stepped slowly back so Joséphine could turn and start down rue de Mézières. He watched her drive away and could tell that she did not look at him in the rearview mirror. It was as though in a moment he did not exist.

2

WHAT AUSTIN HOPED would be the rue de Vaugirard, leading around and up to Joséphine's apartment, turned out instead to be the rue St.-Jacques. He had walked much too far and was now near the medical college, where there were only lightless shop windows containing drab medical texts and dusty, passed-over antiques.

He did not know Paris well—only a few hotels he'd stayed in and a few restaurants he didn't want to eat in again. He couldn't keep straight which arrondissement was which, what direction anything was from anything else, how to take the metro, or even how to leave town, except by airplane. All the large streets looked the same and traveled at confusing angles to one another, and all the famous landmarks seemed to be in unexpected locations when they peeked up into view above the building tops. In the two days he'd been back in Paris—after leaving home in a fury and taking the plane to Orly—he'd tried to make a point of remembering in which direction on the Boulevard St.-Germain the numbers got larger. But he couldn't keep it straight, and in fact he couldn't always find the Boulevard St.-Germain when he wanted to.

At rue St.-Jacques he looked down toward where he thought would be the river and the Petit Pont bridge, and there they were. It was a warm spring day, and the sidewalks along the river banks were jammed with tourists cruising the little picture stalls and gaping at the vast cathedral on the other side.

The prospect down the rue St.-Jacques seemed for an instant familiar—a pharmacy front he recognized, a café with a distinctive name. Horloge. He looked back up the street he'd come down and saw that he was only half a block away from the small hotel he'd once stayed in with his wife, Barbara. The Hôtel de la Tour de Notre Dame, which had advertised a view of the cathedral but from which no such view was possible. The hotel was run by Pakistanis and had rooms so small you couldn't have your suitcase open and also reach the window. He'd brought Barbara with him on business—it was four years ago—and she had shopped and visited museums and eaten lunch along the Quai de la Tournelle while he made his customer calls. They had stayed out of the room as long as possible until fatigue dumped them in bed in front of the indecipherable French TV, which eventually put them to sleep.

Austin remembered very clearly now, standing on the busy sidewalk on his way to Joséphine Belliard's apartment, that he and Barbara had left Paris on the first of April—intending to take a direct flight back to Chicago. Though, once they'd struggled their heavy luggage out of the room, crammed themselves into the tiny, airless elevator and emerged into the lobby, looking like beleaguered refugees but ready to settle their bill and depart, the Pakistani room clerk, who spoke crisp British English, looked across the reception desk in an agitated way and said, "Oh, Mr. Austin, have you not heard the bad news? I'm sorry."

"What's that?" Austin had said, out of breath. "What bad news?" He looked at Barbara, who was holding a garment bag and a hatbox, not wanting to hear any bad news now.

"There is a quite terrible strike," the clerk said and looked very grave. "The airport's closed down completely. No one can leave Paris today. And, I'm sorry to say, we have already booked your room for another guest. A Japanese. I'm so, so sorry."

Austin had stood amid his suitcases, breathing in the air of defeat and frustration and anger he felt certain it would be useless to express. He stared out the lobby window at the street. The sky was cloudy and the wind slightly chilled. He heard Barbara say behind him, as much to herself as to him, "Oh well. We'll do something. We'll find another place. It's too bad. Maybe it'll be an adventure."

Austin looked at the clerk, a little beige man with neat black hair and a white cotton jacket, standing behind his marble desk. The clerk was smiling. This was all the same to him, Austin realized: that they had no place to go; that they were tired of Paris; that they had brought too much luggage and bought too much to take home; that they had slept badly every night; that the weather was inexplicably changing to colder; that they were out of money and sick of the arrogant French. None of this mattered to this man—in some ways, Austin sensed, it may even have pleased him, pleased him enough to make him smile.

"What's so goddamned funny?" Austin had said to the smug little subcontinental. "Why's my bad luck a source of such goddamned amusement to you?" This man would be the focus of his anger. He couldn't help himself. Anger couldn't make anything worse. "Doesn't it matter that we're guests of this hotel and we're in a bit of a bad situation here?" He heard what he knew was a pleading voice.

"April fool!" the clerk said and broke out in a squeaking little laughter. "Ha, ha, ha, ha, ha, ha, ha. It is only a joke, *monsieur*," the man said, so pleased with himself, even more than when he'd told Austin the lie. "The airport is perfectly fine. It is open. You can leave. There is no trouble. It's fine. It was only a joke. *Bon voyage*, Mr. Austin. *Bon voyage*."

3

FOR THE TWO DAYS after she had left him standing in the street at midnight, after he had kissed her the first time and felt that he had done something exactly right, Austin saw a great deal of Joséphine Belliard. He'd had plans to take the TGV to Brussels and then go on to Amsterdam, and from there fly to Chicago and home. But the next morning he sent messages to his customers and to the office, complaining of "medical problems" which had inexplicably "recurred," although he felt it was "probably nothing serious." He would conclude his business by fax when he was home the next week. He told Barbara he'd decided to stay in Paris a few extra days—to relax, to do things he'd never taken the time to do. Visit Balzac's house, maybe. Walk the streets like a tourist. Rent a car. Drive to Fon-tainebleau.

As to Joséphine Belliard, he decided he would spend every minute he could with her. He did not for an instant think that he loved her, or that keeping each other's company would lead him or her to anything important. He was married; he had nothing to give her. To get deluded about such a thing was to bring on nothing but trouble—the kind of trouble that when you're younger you glance away from, but when you're older you ignore at risk. Hesitancy in the face of trouble, he felt, was probably a virtue.

But short of that he did all he could. Together they went to a movie. They went to a museum. They visited Notre Dame and the Palais Royal. They walked together in the narrow streets of the Faubourg St.-Germain. They looked in store windows. They acted like lovers. Touched. She allowed him to hold her hand. They exchanged knowing looks. He discovered what made her laugh, listened carefully for her small points of pride. She stayed as she had been—seemingly uninterested, but willing—as if it was all his idea and her duty, only a duty she surprisingly liked. Austin felt this very reluctance in her was compelling, attractive. And it caused him to woo her in a way that made him admire his own intensity. He took her to dinner in two expensive places, went with her to her apartment, met her son, met the country woman she paid to care for him during the week, saw where she lived, slept, ate, then stood gazing out her apartment windows to the Jardin du Luxembourg and down the peaceful streets of her neighborhood. He saw her life, which he found he was curious about, and once he'd satisfied that curiosity he felt as though he'd accomplished something, something that was not easy or ordinary.

She told him not much more about herself and, again, asked nothing about him, as if his life didn't matter to her. She told him she had once visited America, had met a musician in California and decided to live with him in his small wooden house by the beach in Santa Cruz. This was in the early seventies. She had been a teenager. Only one morning—it was after four months—she woke up on a mattress on the floor, underneath a rug made out of a tanned cowhide, got up, packed her bag and left.

"This was too much," Joséphine said, sitting in the window of her apartment, looking out at the twilight and the street where children were kicking a soccer ball. The musician had been disturbed and angry, she said, but she had come back to France and her parents' house. "You cannot live a long time where you don't belong. It's true?" She looked at him and elevated her shoulders. He was sitting in a chair, drinking a glass of red wine, contemplating the rooftops, enjoying how the tawny light burnished the delicate scrollwork cornices of the apartment buildings visible from the one he was in. Jazz was playing softly on the stereo, a sinuous saxophone solo. "It's true, no?" she said. "You can't."

"Exactly right," Austin said. He had grown up in Peoria. He lived on the northwest side of Chicago. He'd attended a state U. He felt she was exactly right, although he saw nothing wrong in being here at this moment, enjoying the sunlight as it gradually faded then disappeared from the rooftops he could see from this woman's rooms. That seemed permissible.

She told him about her husband. His picture was on the wall in Léo's room—a bulbous-faced, dark-skinned Jew, with a thick black mustache that made him look like an Armenian. Slightly disappointing, Austin had thought. He'd imagined Bernard as being handsome, a smooth-skinned Louis Jourdan type with the fatal flaw of being boring. The real man looked like what he was—a fat man who once wrote French radio jingles.

Joséphine said that her affair had proved to her that she did not love her husband, although perhaps she once had, and that while for some people to live with a person you did not love was possible, it was not possible for her. She looked at Austin as if to underscore the point. This was not, of course, how she had first explained her feelings for her husband, when she said she'd felt she could resume their life after her affair but that her husband had left her flat. This was how she felt now, Austin thought, and the truth certainly lay somewhere in the middle. In any case, it didn't matter to him. She said her husband gave her very little money now, saw his son infrequently, had been seen with a new girlfriend who was German, and of course had written the terrible book, which everyone she knew was reading, causing her immense pain and embarrassment.

"But," she said, and shook her head as if shaking the very thoughts out of her mind. "What I can do, yes? I live

my life now, here, with my son. I have twenty-five more
years to work, then I'm finished."

"Maybe something better'll come along," Austin said.
He didn't know what that might be, but he disliked her
being so pessimistic. It felt like she was somehow blaming
him, which he thought was very French. A more hopeful,
American point of view, he thought, would help.

"What is it? What will be better?" Joséphine said, and
she looked at him not quite bitterly, but helplessly. "What
is going to happen? Tell me. I want to know."

Austin set his wineglass carefully on the polished floor,
climbed out of his chair and walked to the open window
where she sat, and below which the street was slowly being
cast into grainy darkness. There was the bump of the soccer ball still being kicked aimlessly against a wall over and
over, and behind that the sound of a car engine being
revved down the block. Austin put his arms around her
arms and put his mouth against her cool cheek and held
her to him tightly.

"Maybe someone will come along who loves you," he
said. He was offering encouragement, and he knew she
knew that and would take it in a good spirit. "You wouldn't
be hard to love. Not at all." He held her more tightly to
him. "In fact," he said, "you'd be very easy to love."

Joséphine let herself be pulled, be gathered in. She let
her head fall against his shoulder. It was perilous to be
where she was, Austin thought, in the window, with a man
holding her. He could feel the cool outside air on the backs
of his hands and against his face, half in, half out. It was
thrilling, even though Joséphine did not put her arms
around him, did not reciprocate his touch in any way, only
let him hold her as if pleasing him was easy but did not
matter to her a great deal.

THAT NIGHT he took her to dinner at the Closerie des Lilas, a famous bistro where writers and artists had been frequenters in the twenties—a bright, glassy and noisy place where the two of them drank champagne, held hands, but did not talk much. They seemed to be running out of things to say. The next most natural things would be subjects that connected them, subjects with some future built in. But Austin was leaving in the morning, and those subjects didn't seem to interest either of them, though Austin could feel their pull, could imagine below the surface of unyielding facts that there could be a future for them. Certainly under different, better circumstances they would be lovers, would immediately begin to spend more time together, discover what there was to discover between them. Austin had a strong urge to say these very things to her as they sat silently over their champagne, just to go ahead and put that much on the table from his side and see what it called forth from hers. But the restaurant was too noisy. Once he tried to begin, the words sounded too loud. And these were not that kind of words. These were important words and needed to be said respectfully, even solemnly, with their inevitable sense of loss built in.

The words, though, had stayed in his mind as Joséphine again drove the short distance back to rue de Mézières and to the corner where she'd left him the first night. The words seemed to have missed their moment. They needed another context, a more substantial setting. To say them in the dark, in a crummy Opel with the motor running, at the moment of parting, would give them a sentimental weightiness they didn't mean to have, since they were, for all their built-in sorrow, an expression of optimism.

When Joséphine stopped the car, the gate into the hotel only a few steps away, she kept her hands on the steering wheel and stared straight ahead, as she had two nights before. She did not offer him anything, a word, a gesture, even a look. To her, this night, their last one, the night before Austin left for Chicago and home and his wife, possibly never to come back again, never to try to pick up from where they were at that moment—this night was just like their first, one Joséphine would forget as soon as the door slammed shut and her headlights swung onto the empty street toward home.

Austin looked out her window at the hotel's rustic wooden gate, beyond which was a ferny, footlit courtyard, a set of double glass doors, the lobby and the stairs up two flights to his small room. What he wanted was to take her there, lock the door, close the curtains and make sorrowful love until morning, until he had to call a cab to leave for the airport. But that was the wrong thing to do, having gotten this far without complication, without greater confusion or harm being caused to either of them. Harm *could* be caused by getting involved with him, Austin thought. They both knew it, and it didn't require saying. She wouldn't think of sleeping with him in any case. *No* did mean *no* to her. And that was the right way to play this.

Austin sat with his hands in his lap and said nothing. It was the way he'd known this moment of leaving would occur. Somberly on his part. Coldly on hers. He didn't think he should reach across and take her hands again as he had before. That became playacting the second time you did it, and he had already touched her that way plenty of times—sweetly, innocently, without trying anything more except possibly a brief, soft kiss. He would let this time—the last time—go exactly according to her wishes, not his.

He waited. He thought Joséphine might say something, something ironic or clever or cold or merely common-place, something that would break her little rule of silence and that he could then reply to and perhaps have the last good word, one that would leave them both puzzled and tantalized and certain that a small but important moment had not entirely been missed. But she did not speak. She was intent on there being nothing that would make her do anything different from what she did naturally. And Austin knew if he had simply climbed out of the car right then, without a goodbye, she would've driven straight away. Maybe this was why her husband had written a book about her, Austin thought. At least he'd known he'd gotten her attention.

Joséphine seemed to be waiting for the seat beside her to become empty. Austin looked across at her in the car dark-ness, and she for an instant glanced at him but did not speak. This was annoying, Austin thought; annoying and stupid and French to be so closed to the world, to be so un-willing to let a sweet and free moment cause you happi-ness—when happiness was in such short supply. He realized he was on the verge of being angry, of saying nothing else, of simply getting out of the car and walking away.

"You know," he said, more irritably than he wanted to sound, "we could be lovers. We're interested in each other. This isn't a sidetrack for me. This is real life. I like you. You like me. All I've wanted to do is take advantage of that in some way that makes you glad, that puts a smile on your face. Nothing else. I don't need to sleep with you. That would cause me as much trouble as it would cause you. But that's no reason we can't just like each other." He looked at her intently, her silhouette softened against the lights above the hotel gate across the street. She said nothing. Though he thought he heard a faint laugh, hardly more than an exhaled breath, intended, he presumed, to express what she'd thought of all he'd just said. "Sorry," Austin said, angry now, swiveling his knees into the doorway to get out. "Really, I am."

But Joséphine put her hand on his wrist and held him back, not looking at him, but speaking toward the cold windshield. "I am not so strong enough," she whispered, and squeezed his wrist.

"For what?" Austin said, also whispering, one foot already on the paving stones, but looking back at her in the darkness.

"I am not so strong enough to have something with you," she said. "Not now." She looked at him, her eyes soft and large, her one hand holding his wrist, the other in her lap, half curled.

"Do you mean you don't feel strongly enough, or you aren't strong enough in yourself?" Austin said, overassertive but feeling good about it.

"I don't know," Joséphine said. "It is still very confusing for me now. I'm sorry."

"Well, that's better than nothing," Austin said. "At least you gave me that much. That makes me glad." He reached across and squeezed her wrist where she was holding his tightly. Then he got out of the car into the street. She put her hand on the gearshift and pushed it forward with a loud rasp.

"If you come back," she said in a husky voice through the doorway, "call me."

"Sure," Austin said, "I'll call you. I don't know what else I'd do in Paris."

He closed the door firmly, and she drove away, spinning her tires on the slick stones. Austin walked across the street to the hotel without looking back at her taillights as they disappeared.

AT ONE A.M., when it was six p.m. in Chicago, he had called Barbara, and they had come close to having a serious argument. It had made Austin angry, because when he had dialed the number, his own familiar number, and heard its reassuring ring, he'd felt happy—happy to be only hours away from leaving Paris, happy to be coming home and to have not just a wife to come home to but this wife—Barbara, whom he both loved and revered. And happy, also, to have effected his "contact" with Joséphine Belliard (that was the word he was using; at first it had been "rapprochement," but that had given way). Happy that there were no bad consequences to rue—no false promises inspiring false hopes, no tearful partings, no sense of entrapping obligations or feelings of being in over your boot tops. No damage to control.

Which was not to say nothing had taken place, because plenty had—things he and Joséphine Belliard both knew about and that had been expressed when she held his wrist in the car and admitted she wasn't strong enough, or that something was too strong for her.

What does one want in the world? Austin thought, propped against the headboard of the bed that night, having a glass of warm champagne from the minibar. He was in his blue pajama bottoms, on top of the covers, barefoot, staring across the room at his own image in the smoky mirror that occupied one entire wall—a man in a bed with a lighted bed lamp beside him, a glass on his belly. What does one want most of all, when one has experienced much, suffered some, persevered, tried to do good when good was within reach? What does this experience teach us that we can profit from? That the memory of pain, Austin thought, mounts up and lays a significant weight upon the present—a sobering weight—and the truth one has to discover is: exactly what's possible but also valuable and desirable between human beings, on a low level of event.

No easy trick, he thought. Certainly not everyone could do it. But he and Joséphine Belliard had in an admittedly small way brought it off, found the point of contact whose consequences were only positive for each of them. No hysteria. No confusion. Yet not insignificant, either. He realized, of course, that if he'd had his own way, Joséphine would be in bed beside him right now; though in God knows what agitated state of mind, the late hours ticking by, sex their sole hope of consolation. It was a distasteful thought. *There* was trouble, and nothing would've been gained—only something lost. But the two of them had figured out a better path to take, which had eventuated in his being alone in his room and feeling quite good about everything. Even virtuous. He almost raised his glass to himself in the mirror, only it seemed ridiculous.

He waited a while before phoning Barbara, because he thought Joséphine might call—a drowsy late-night voice from bed, an opportunity for her to say something more to him, something interesting, maybe serious, something she hadn't wanted to say when they were together in the car and could reach each other.

But she didn't call, and Austin found himself staring at the foreign-looking telephone, willing it to ring. He'd had a lengthy conversation between himself and Joséphine playing in his mind for several minutes: he wished she was here now—that's what he wanted to say to her, even though he'd already decided that was distasteful. Still, he thought of her lying in bed asleep, alone, and it gave him a hollow, almost nauseated feeling. Then, for some reason, he thought of her meeting the younger man she'd had the calamitous affair with, the one that had ended her marriage. He picked up the receiver to see if the telephone was working. Then he put it down. Then he picked it up again and called Barbara.

"What did you do tonight, sweetheart? Did you have some fun?" Barbara was in jolly spirits. She was in the kitchen, fixing dinner for herself. He heard pots and pans rattling. He pictured her in his mind, tall and beautiful, confident about life.

"I took a woman to dinner," he said bluntly. There was no delay on the line—it was as if he were calling from the office. Something, though, was making him feel irritated. The sound of the pans, he thought; the fact that Barbara considered fixing her dinner to be important enough to keep doing it as she was talking to him. His feeling of virtue was fading.

"Well, that's wonderful," Barbara said. "Anybody special, or just somebody you met on a street corner who looked hungry?" She wasn't serious.

"A woman who works at Éditions Périgord," Austin said sternly. "An editor."

"That's nice," Barbara said, and what seemed like a small edge rose in her voice. He wondered if there was a signal in *his* voice, something that alerted her no matter how hard he tried to seem natural, something she'd heard before over the years and that couldn't be hidden.

"It *was* nice," Austin said. "We had a good time. But I'm coming home tomorrow."

"Well, we're waiting for you," Barbara said brightly.

"Who's we?" Austin said.

"Me. And the house. And the plants and the windows. The cars. Your life. We're all waiting with big smiles on our faces."

"That's great," Austin said.

"It *is* great," Barbara said. Then there was silence on the line—expensive, transoceanic silence. Austin felt the need to reorganize his good mood. He had nothing to be mad about. Or uncomfortable. All was well. Barbara hadn't done anything, but neither had he. "What time is it there?" she said casually. He heard another pot clatter, then water turn on in the sink. His champagne glass had gotten warmer, the champagne flat and sweet.

"After one," he said. "I'm sleepy now. I've got a long day tomorrow."

"So go to sleep," Barbara said.

"Thanks," Austin said.

There was more silence. "Who *is* this woman?" Barbara said somewhat brittlely.

"Just a woman I met," Austin said. "She's married. She has a baby. It's just *la vie moderne*."

"*La vie moderne*," Barbara said. She was tasting something now. Whatever she was cooking she was tasting.

"Right," Austin said. "Modern life."

"I understand," Barbara said. "*La vie moderne*. Modern life." She tapped a spoon hard on the rim of a pan.

"Are you glad I'm coming home?"

"Of course," Barbara said, and paused again while Austin tried to particularize for himself the look that was on her face now. All the features in her quite beautiful face seemed to get thinner when she got angry. He wondered if they were thin now. "Do you think," Barbara said, trying to sound merely curious, "that you might just possibly have taken me for granted tonight?" Silence. She was going on cooking. She was alone in their house, cooking for herself, and he was in a nice hotel in Paris—a former monastery—drinking champagne in his pajamas. There was some discrepancy. He had to admit that. Though it finally wasn't very important, since each of them was well fixed. But he felt sorry for her, sorry that she thought he took her for granted, when he didn't think he did; when in fact he loved her and was eager to see her. He was sorry she didn't know how he felt right now, how much regard he had for her. If she did, he thought, it would make her happy.

"No," Austin said, finally answering her question. "I don't think I do. I really don't think so. Do you think I ever do?"

"No? It's fine, then," Barbara said. He heard a cabinet door close. "I wouldn't want you to think that you took me for granted, that's all."

"Why do we have to talk about this now?" Austin said plaintively. "I'm coming home tomorrow. I'm eager to see you. I'm not mad about anything. Why are you?"

"I'm not," Barbara said. "Never mind. It doesn't matter. I just think things and then they go away." More spoon banging.

"I love you," Austin said. The rim of his ear had begun to ache from the receiver being pressed into it with his shoulder.

"Good," Barbara said. "Go to sleep loving me."

"I don't want to argue."

"Then don't argue," Barbara said. "Maybe I'm just in a bad mood. I'm sorry."

"Why are you mad?" Austin said.

"Sometimes," Barbara said. Then she stopped. "I don't know. Sometimes you just piss me off."

"Well, shit," Austin said.

"Shit is right. Shit," Barbara said. "It's nothing. Go to sleep."

"Fine. I will," Austin said.

"I'll see you tomorrow, sweetheart."

"Sure," Austin said, wanting to sound casual. He started to say something else. To tell her he loved her, again in the casual voice. But Barbara had hung up the phone.

Austin sat in bed in his pajamas, staring at himself in the smoky mirror. It was a different picture from before. He looked grainy, displeased, the light beside his bed harsh, intrusive, his champagne glass empty, the night he'd just spent unsuccessful, unpromising, vaguely humiliating. He looked like he was on drugs. That was the true picture, he thought. Later, he knew, he would think differently, would see events in a kinder, more flattering light. His spirits would rise as they always did and he would feel very, very encouraged by something, anything. But now was the time to take a true reading, he thought, when the tide was out and everything exposed—including himself—as it really, truly was. *There* was the real life, and he wasn't deluded about it. It was this picture you had to act on.

He sat in bed and felt gloomy, drank the rest of his champagne and thought about Barbara in the house alone, probably doing something to prepare for his arrival the next afternoon—arranging some fresh flowers or preparing to cook something he especially liked. Maybe that's what she was doing when they were talking, in which case he was certainly wrong to have been annoyed. After thinking along these lines for a while, he reached over and began to dial Joséphine's number. It was two a.m. He would wake her up, but that was all right. She'd be glad he had. He would tell her the truth—that he couldn't keep from calling her, that she was on his mind, that he wished she was here with him, that he already missed her, that there was more to this than seemed. But when he'd dialed her number the line was busy. And it was busy in five minutes. And in fifteen. And in thirty. So that after a while he dispiritedly turned off the light beside the bed, put his head on the crisp pillow and passed quickly into sleep.

4

IN THE SMALL suburban community of Oak Grove, Illinois, Austin meant to take straight aim on his regular existence—driving to and from the Lilienthal office in nearby Winnetka; helping coach a Little League team sponsored by a friend's Oak Grove linoleum company; spending evenings at home with Barbara, who was a broker for a big firm that sold commercial real estate and who was herself having an excellent selling season.

Austin, however, could sense that something was wrong, which bewildered him. Although Barbara had decided to continue everyday life as if that were not true, or as if whatever was bothering him was simply outside her control and because she loved him, eventually his problem would either be solved privately or be carried away by the flow of ordinary happy life. Barbara's was a systematically optimistic view: that with the right attitude, everything works out for the best. She possessed this view, she said, because her family had all been Scottish Presbyterians. And it was a view Austin admired, though it was not always the way he saw things. He thought ordinary life had the potential to grind you into dust—his parents' life in Peoria, for instance, a life he couldn't have stood—and sometimes unusual measures were called for. Barbara said this point of view was typically shanty Irish.

On the day Austin returned—into a hot, springy airport sunshine, jet-lagged and forcibly good-spirited— Barbara had cooked venison haunch in a rich secret fig sauce, something she'd had to sleuth the ingredients for in a Hungarian neighborhood on West Diversey, plus Brabant potatoes and roasted garlics (Austin's favorite), plus a very good Merlot that Austin had drunk too much of while earnestly, painstakingly lying about all he'd done in Paris. Barbara had bought a new spring dress, had her hair restreaked and generally gone to a lot of trouble to orchestrate a happy homecoming and to forget about their unpleasant late-night phone conversation. Though Austin felt it should be his responsibility to erase that uncomfortable moment from memory and see to it his married life of long standing was once again the source of seamless, good-willed happiness.

Late that night, a Tuesday, he and Barbara made brief, boozy love in the dark of their thickly curtained bedroom, to the sound of a neighbor's springer spaniel barking unceasingly one street over. Theirs was practiced, undramatic lovemaking, a set of protocols and assumptions lovingly followed like a liturgy which points to but really has little connection with the mysteries and chaos that had once made it a breathless necessity. Austin noticed by the digital clock on the chest of drawers that it all took nine minutes, start to finish. He wondered bleakly if this was of normal or less than normal duration for Americans his and Barbara's age. Less, he supposed, though no doubt the fault was his.

Lying in the silent dark afterwards, side by side, facing the white plaster ceiling (the neighbor's dog had shut up as if on cue from an unseen observer of their act), he and Barbara sought to find something to say. Each knew the other's mind was seeking it; an upbeat, forward-sounding subject that conjured away the past couple or maybe it was three years, which hadn't been so wonderful between the two of them—a time of wandering for Austin and patience from Barbara. They wished for something unprovoking that would allow them to go to sleep thinking of themselves the way they assumed they were.

"Are you tired? You must be pretty exhausted," Barbara said matter-of-factly into the darkness. "You poor old thing." She reached and patted him on his chest. "Go to sleep. You'll feel better tomorrow."

"I feel fine now. I'm not tired," Austin said alertly. "Do I seem tired?"

"No. I guess not."

They were silent again, and Austin felt himself relaxing to the sound of her words. He was, in fact, corrosively tired. Yet he wanted to put a good end to the night, which he felt had been a nice one, and to the homecoming itself, and to the time he'd been gone and ridiculously infatuated with Joséphine Belliard. That encounter—there *was* no encounter, of course—but in any case those pronouncements and preoccupations could be put to rest. They could be disciplined away. They were not real life—at least not the bedrock, real*est* life, the one everything depended on—no matter how he'd briefly felt and protested. He wasn't a fool.

He wasn't stupid enough to lose his sense of proportion. He was a survivor, he thought, and survivors always knew which direction the ground was.

"I just want to see what's possible now," Austin said unexpectedly. He was half asleep and had been having two conversations at once—one with Barbara, his wife, and one with himself about Joséphine Belliard—and the two were getting mixed up. Barbara hadn't asked him anything to which what he'd just mumbled was even a remotely logical answer. She hadn't, that he remembered, asked him anything at all. He was just babbling, talking in his near sleep. But a cold, stiffening fear gripped him, a fear that he'd said something, half asleep and half drunk, that he'd be sorry for, something that would incriminate him with the truth about Joséphine. Though in his current state of mind, he wasn't at all sure what that truth might be.

"That shouldn't be hard, should it?" Barbara said out of the dark.

"No," Austin said, wondering if he was awake. "I guess not."

"We're together. And we love each other. Whatever we want to make possible we ought to be able to do." She touched his leg through his pajamas.

"Yes," Austin said. "That's right." He wished Barbara would go to sleep now. He didn't want to say anything else. Talking was a minefield, since he wasn't sure what he would say.

Barbara was silent, while his insides contracted briefly, then slowly began to relax again. He resolved to say nothing else. After a couple of minutes Barbara turned and faced the curtains. The streetlight showed palely between the fabric closings, and Austin wondered if he had somehow made her cry without realizing it.

"Oh well," Barbara said. "You'll feel better tomorrow, I hope. Good night."

"Good night," Austin said. And he settled himself help-lessly into sleep, feeling that he had not pleased Barbara very much, and that not only was he a man who probably pleased no one very much now, but that in his own life—among the things that should and always had made him happy—very little pleased him at all.

IN THE NEXT DAYS Austin went to work as he usually did. He made make-up calls to his accounts in Brussels and Am-sterdam. He told a man he'd known for ten years and deeply respected that doctors had discovered a rather "mysterious inflammation" high in the upper quadrant of his stomach but that there was reasonable hope surgery could be averted with the aid of drugs. He tried to think of the name of the drug he was "taking" but couldn't. Afterwards he felt gloomy about having told such a pointless falsehood and worried that the man might mention something to his boss.

He wondered, staring at the elegantly framed azimuth map Barbara had given him when he'd been awarded the prestigious European accounts, and which he'd hung be-hind his desk with tiny red pennants attached, denoting where he'd increased the company's market share—Brus-sels, Amsterdam, Düsseldorf, Paris—wondered if his life, his normal carrying-on, was slipping out of control, yet so gradually as not to be noticed. But he decided it wasn't, and as proof he offered the fact that he was entertaining this idea in his office, on an ordinary business day, with every-thing in his life arrayed in place and going forward, rather than entertaining it in some Parisian street café in the blear aftermath of calamity: a man with soiled lapels, in need of a shave and short of cash, scribbling his miserable thoughts into a tiny spiral notebook like all the other morons he'd seen who'd thrown their lives away. This feeling now, this sensation of heaviness, of life's coming unmoored, was actually, he believed, a feeling of vigilance, the weight of responsibility accepted, the proof that carrying life to a successful end was never an easy matter.

On Thursday, the moment he arrived in the office he put in a call to Joséphine at work. She'd been on his mind almost every minute: her little oddly matched but inflaming features, her boyish way of walking with her toes pointed out like a country bumpkin. But also her soft, shadowy complexion and soft arms, her whispered voice in his memory: *"Non, non, non, non, non."*

"Hi, it's me," Austin said. This time a bulky delay clogged his connection, and he could hear his voice echo on the line. He didn't sound like he wanted to sound. His voice was higher pitched, like a kid's voice.

"Okay. Hi," was all Joséphine said. She was rustling papers, a sound that annoyed him.

"I was just thinking about you," he said. A long pause opened after this announcement, and he endured it uncomfortably.

"Yes," she said. Another pause. "Me, too. How are you?"

"I'm fine," Austin said, though he didn't want to stress that. He wanted to stress that he missed her. "I miss you," he said, and felt feeble hearing his voice inside the echo.

"Yeah," she said finally though flatly. "Me, too."

He wasn't sure if she'd actually heard what he'd said. Possibly she was talking to someone else, someone in her office. He felt disoriented and considered hanging up.

Though he knew how he'd feel if that happened. Wretched beyond imagining. In fact, he needed to persevere now or he'd end up feeling wretched anyway.

"I'd like to see you very much," Austin said, his ear pressed to the receiver.

"Yeah," Joséphine said. "Come and take me to dinner tonight." She laughed a harsh, ironic laugh. He wondered if she was saying this for someone else's benefit, someone in her office who knew all about him and thought he was stupid. He heard more papers rustle. He felt things spinning.

"I mean it," he said. "I would."

"When are you coming back to Paris?"

"I don't know. But very soon, I hope." He didn't know why he'd said that, since it wasn't true, or at least wasn't in any plans he currently had. Only in that instant it seemed possible. Anything was possible. And indeed *this* seemed imminently possible. He simply had no idea how. You couldn't decide to go for the weekend. France wasn't Wisconsin.

"So. Call me, I guess," Joséphine said. "I would see you."

"I will," Austin said, his heart beginning to thump. "When I come I'll call you."

He wanted to ask her something. He didn't know what, though. He didn't know anything to ask. "How's Leo?" he said, using the English pronunciation.

Joséphine laughed, but not ironically. "How is Leo?" she said, using the same pronunciation. Léo is okay. He is at home. Soon I'm going there. That's all."

"Good," Austin said. "That's great." He swiveled quickly and stared at Paris on the map. As usual, he was surprised at how much nearer the top of France it was instead of perfectly in the middle, the way he always thought of it. He wanted to ask her why she hadn't called him the last night he'd seen her, to let her know he'd hoped she would. But then he remembered her line had been busy, and he wanted to know who she'd been talking to. Although he couldn't ask that. It wasn't his business.

"Fine," he said. And he knew that in five seconds the call would be over and Paris would instantly be as far from Chicago as it ever was. He almost said "I love you" into the receiver. But that would be a mistake, and he didn't say it, though part of him furiously wanted to. Then he nearly said it in French, thinking possibly it might mean less than it meant in English. But again he refrained. "I want to see you very much," he said as a last, weak, compromise.

"So. See me. I kiss you," Joséphine Belliard said, but in a strange voice, a voice he'd never heard before, almost an emotional voice. Then she quietly hung up.

Austin sat at his desk, staring at the map, wondering what that voice had been, what it meant, how he was supposed to interpret it. Was it the voice of love, or some strange trick of the phone line? Or was it a trick of his ear to confect something he wanted to hear and so allow him not to feel as wretched as he figured he'd feel but in fact didn't feel. Because how he felt was wonderful. Ebullient. The best he'd felt since the last time he'd seen her. Alive. And there was nothing wrong with that, was there? If something makes you feel good for a moment and no one is crushed by it, what's the use of denying yourself? Other people denied. And for what? The guys he'd gone to college with, who'd never left the track once they were on it, never had a moment of ebullience, and maybe even never knew the difference. But he *did* know the difference, and it was worth it, no matter the difficulties you endured living with the consequences. You had one life, Austin thought. Use it up. He'd heard what he'd heard.

THAT EVENING HE picked Barbara up at the realty offices
and drove them to a restaurant. It was a thing they often
did. Barbara frequently worked late, and they both liked a
semi-swanky Polynesian place in Skokie called Hai-Nun, a
dark, teak-and-bamboo hideaway where the drinks were all
doubles and eventually, when you were too drunk to nego-
tiate your way to a table, you could order a platter of fried
specialties and sober up eating dinner at the bar.

For a while an acquaintance of Austin's, a commodities
trader named Ned Coles, had stood beside them at the bar
and made chitchat about how the salad days on the Board
of Trade were a thing of the past, and then about the big
opportunities in Europe after 1992 and how the U.S. was
probably going to miss the boat, and then about how the
Fighting Illini were sizing up at the skilled positions during
spring drills, and finally about his ex-wife, Suzie, who was
moving to Phoenix the next week so she could participate
more in athletics. She was interested, Ned Coles said, in
taking part in iron-woman competitions.

"Can't she be an iron woman in Chicago?" Barbara said.
She barely knew Ned Coles and was bored by him. Ned's
wife was also "kidnapping" their two kids to Arizona, which
had Ned down in the dumps but not wanting to make a fuss.

"Of course she can," Ned said. Ned was a heavy, beet-
faced man who looked older than forty-six. He had gone to
Harvard, then come home to work for his old man's company and quickly become a drunk and a nuisance. Austin
had met him in MBA night school fifteen years ago. They
didn't see each other socially. "But that's not the big problem," Ned went on.

"What's the big problem?" Austin said, muddling an ice
cube in his gin.

"Moi-même," Ned said, and looked grim about it. "She contends I'm a force field of negativism that radiates into all the north suburbs. So I have to move to Indiana for her to stay. And that's way too big a sacrifice." Ned laughed humorlessly. He knew a lot of Indiana jokes that Austin had already heard. Indiana, to Ned Coles, was the place where you caught sight of the flagship of the Polish navy and visited the Argentine war heroes memorial. He was old Chicago, and also, Austin thought, an idiot. He wished Ned's wife a good journey to Arizona.

When Ned wandered off into the restaurant, leaving them alone at the lacquered teak bar, Barbara grew quiet. Both of them were drinking gin, and in silence they let the bartender pour them another two on the rocks. Austin knew he was a little drunk now and that Barbara was probably more drunk than he was. He sensed a problem could be lurking—about what he wasn't sure. But he longed for the feeling he'd had when he put the phone down with Joséphine Belliard that morning. Ebullience. To be fiercely alive. It had been a temporary feeling, he understood perfectly well. But he longed for it now all the more achingly on account of its illusory quality, its innocent smallness. Even realists, he thought, needed a break now and then.

"Do you remember the other night?" Barbara began as if she were choosing her words with extreme precision. "You were in Paris, and I was back here at home. And I asked you if you thought you might be taking me for granted?" She focused on the rim of her glass, but unexpectedly her eyes cast up and found his. There was one other couple in the bar, and the bartender had seated himself on a stool at the end and was reading a newspaper. This was the dinner hour, and many people were in the restaurant section. Someone had ordered a dish that required fire to be brought from the kitchen to their table, and Austin could see the yellow flame lick up at the ceiling, hear the loud *ssss* and the delighted diners say, "Oooo."

"I didn't think that was true," Austin said resolutely in answer to her question.

"I know you didn't," Barbara said and nodded her head slowly. "And maybe that's exactly right. Maybe I was wrong." She stared at her glass of gin again. "What *is* true, though, Martin, and what's worse—about you, anyway— is that you take *yourself* for granted." Barbara kept nodding her head without looking at him, as if she'd discovered an interesting but worrisome paradox in philosophy. When Barbara got mad at him, particularly if she was a little drunk, she nodded her head and spoke in this overly meticulous way, as if she'd done considerable thinking on the subject at hand and wished to illuminate her conclusions as a contribution to common sense. Austin called this habit "reading the ingredients on the Molotov cocktail," and he hated it and wished Barbara wouldn't do it, though there was never a good moment to bring the subject up.

"I'm sorry, but I don't think I know what you mean by that," he said in the most normal voice he could manufacture.

Barbara looked at him curiously, her perfect Lambda Chi beauty-queen features grown as precise and angular as her words. "What I mean is that you think—about yourself—that you can't be changed, as if you're *fixed*. On your insides, I mean. You think of yourself as a given, that what you go off to some foreign country and do won't have any effect on you, won't leave you different. But that isn't true, Martin. Because you *are* different. In fact, you're unreachable, and you've been becoming that way for a long time. For two or three years, at least. I've just tried to get along with you and make you happy, because making you happy has always made me happy. But now it doesn't, because you've changed and I don't feel like I can reach you or that you're even aware of what you've become, and frankly I don't even much care. All this just occurred to me while I was ordering a title search this afternoon. I'm sorry it's such a shock."

Barbara sniffed and looked at him and seemed to smile. She wasn't about to cry. She was cold-eyed and factual, as if she were reporting the death of a distant relative neither of them remembered very well.

"I'm sorry to hear that," Austin said, wanting to remain as calm as she was, though not as cold. He didn't exactly know what this meant or what could've brought it about, since he didn't think he'd been doing anything wrong. Nothing had happened two or three years ago that he could remember. Joséphine Belliard had had a small effect on him, but it would pass the way anything passed. Life seemed to be going on. He thought, in fact, that he'd been acting about as normal as he could hope to act.

But did this mean that she had taken all she intended to and was through with him? That would be a shock, he thought, something he definitely didn't want. Or did she only mean to say he needed to shape up and become more reachable, go back to some nice way he'd been that she approved of—some way he would've said he still was. Or maybe she was saying she intended to make her own changes now, be less forgiving, less interested in him, less loving, take more interest in herself; that their marriage was going to start down a new, more equitable road—something else he didn't like the sound of.

He sat thoughtfully in the silence she was affording him for just this purpose. He certainly needed to offer a response. He needed intelligently and forthrightly to answer her charges and demonstrate sympathy for her embattled position. But also he needed to stand up for himself, while offering a practical way out of this apparent impasse. Much, in other words, was being asked of him. He was, it seemed, expected to solve everything: to take *both* positions—hers and his—and somehow join them so that everything was either put back to a way it had been or else made better so that both of them were happier and could feel that if life was a series of dangerous escarpments you scaled with difficulty, at least you eventually succeeded, whereupon the plenteous rewards of happiness made all the nightmares worthwhile.

It was an admirable view of life, Austin thought. It was a sound, traditional view, absolutely in the American grain, and one that sent everybody to the altar starry-eyed and certain. It was a view Barbara had always maintained and he'd always envied. Barbara was in the American grain. It was one of the big reasons he'd been knocked out by her years ago and why he knew she would be the best person he or anyone else could ever love. Only he didn't see at that moment what he could do to make her wishes come true, if he in fact knew anything about what her wishes were. So that what he said, after admitting he was sorry to hear what she'd already said, was: "But I don't think there's anything I can do about it. I wish there was. I'm really sorry."

"Then you're just an asshole," Barbara said and nodded again very confidently, very conclusively. "And you're also a womanizer and you're a creep. And I don't want to be married to any of those things anymore. So." She took a big emptying swig out of her glass of gin and set the thick tumbler down hard on its damp little napkin coaster. "So," she said again, as if appreciating her own self-assured voice, "fuck you. And goodbye." With that, she got up and walked very steadily and straight out of the Hai-Nun (so straight that Austin didn't wonder about whether she was in any condition to drive) and disappeared around the bamboo corner just as another fat lick of yellow flame swarmed into the dark dining-room air and another hot, loud sizzling sound went up, and another "Oooo" was exhaled from the dazzled diners, a couple of whom even clapped.

This was certainly an over-response on Barbara's part, Austin felt. In the first place, she knew nothing about Joséphine Belliard, because there was nothing to know. No incriminating facts. She was only guessing, and unfairly. In all probability she was just feeling bad about herself and hoping to make him responsible for it. In the second place, it wasn't easy to tell the truth about how you felt when it wasn't what someone you loved wanted to be the truth. He'd done his best by saying he wasn't sure what he could do to make her happy. That had been a place to start. He'd sensed her opening certitude had just been a positioning strategy and that while a big fight might've been brewing, it would've been one they could settle over the course of the evening, ending with apologies, after which they could both feel better, even liberated. It had gone like that in the past when he'd gotten temporarily distracted by some woman he met far from home. Ordinary goings-on, he thought.

Though women were sometimes a kind of problem. He enjoyed their company, enjoyed hearing their voices, knowing about their semi-intimate lives and daily dramas. But his attempts at knowing them often created a peculiar feeling, as if on the one hand he'd come into the possession of secrets he didn't want to keep, while on the other, some other vital portion of life—his life with Barbara, for instance—was left not fully appreciated, gone somewhat to waste.

But Barbara had stepped out of all bounds with this leaving. Now they were both alone in separate little cocoons of bitterness and self-explanation, and that was when matters did not get better but worse. Everyone knew that. She had brought this situation into existence, not him, and she would have to live with the outcome, no matter how small or how large. Drinking had something to do with it, he thought. His and hers. There was a lot of tension in the air at the moment, and drinking was a natural response. He didn't think either of them had a drinking problem per se—particularly himself. But he resolved, sitting at the teak bar in front of a glass of Beefeater's, that he would quit drinking as soon as he could.

When he walked outside into the dark parking lot, Barbara was nowhere in sight. A half hour had gone by. He thought he might find her in the car, mad or sleeping. It was eight-thirty. The air was cool, and Old Orchard Road was astream with automobiles.

When he drove home, all the lights were off and Barbara's car, which she'd left at her office when he picked her up, was not in the garage. Austin walked in through the house, turning on lights until he got to their bedroom. He opened the door gingerly, so as not to wake Barbara if she was there, flung across the top covers, asleep. But she wasn't there. The room was dark except for the digital clock. He was alone in the house, and he didn't know where his wife was, only that she was conceivably leaving him. Certainly she'd been angry. The last thing she had said was "fuck you." Then she'd walked out—something she hadn't done before. Someone, he understood, might conclude she was leaving him.

Austin poured himself a glass of milk in the brightly lit kitchen and considered testifying to these very moments and facts, as well as to the unpleasant episode in the Hai-Nun and to the final words of his wife, in a court of law. A divorce court. He featured himself sitting at a table with his lawyer, and Barbara at a table with her lawyer, both of them, eyes straight ahead, facing a judge's bench. In her present state of mind Barbara wouldn't be persuaded by his side of the story. She wouldn't have a change of heart or decide just to forget the whole thing in the middle of a courtroom once he'd looked her square in the eye and told only the truth. Still, divorce was certainly not a good solution, he thought.

Austin walked up to the sliding glass door that gave on to the back yard and to the dark and fenceless yards of his neighbors, their soft house lights and the reflection of his own kitchen cabinets and himself holding his glass of milk and of the breakfast table and chairs, all combined in a perfect half-lit diorama.

On the other hand, he thought (the first being a messy divorce attempt followed by sullen reconciliation once they realized they lacked the nerve for divorce), *he was out.*

He hadn't left. *She* had. *He* hadn't made any threats or complaints or bitter, half-drunk, name-calling declarations or soap-operaish exits into the night. *She* had. *He* hadn't wanted to be alone. *She* had wanted to be alone. And as a result *he* was free. Free to do anything he wanted, no questions asked or answered, no suspicions or recriminations. No explanatory half-truths. It was a revelation.

In the past, when he and Barbara had had a row and he had felt like just getting in the car and driving to Montana or Alaska to work for the forest service—never writing, never calling, though not actually going to the trouble of concealing his identity or whereabouts—he'd found he could never face the moment of actual leaving. His feet simply wouldn't move. And about himself he'd said, feeling quietly proud of the fact, that he was no good at departures. There was in leaving, he believed, the feel of betrayal—of betraying Barbara. Of betraying himself. You didn't marry somebody so you could leave, he'd actually said to her on occasion. He could never in fact even seriously think about leaving. And about the forest service he could only plot as far as the end of the first day—when he was tired and bruised from hard work, his mind emptied of worries. But after that he was confused about what would be happening next—another toilsome day like the one before. This had meant, he understood, that he didn't want to leave; that his life, his love for Barbara, were simply too strong. Leaving was what weak people did. Again his college classmates were called upon to be the bad examples, the cowardly leavers. Most of them had been divorced, strewn kids of all ages all over the map, routinely and grimly posted big checks off to Dallas and Seattle and Atlanta, fed on regret. They had left and now they were plenty sorry. But his love for Barbara was simply worth more. Some life force was in him too strongly, too fully, to leave—which meant something, something lasting and important. This force, he felt, was what all the great novels ever written were about.

Of course, it had occurred to him that what he might be was just a cringing, lying coward who didn't have the nerve to face a life alone; couldn't fend for himself in a complex world full of his own acts' consequences. Though that was merely a conventional way of understanding life, another soap-opera view—about which he knew better. He was a stayer. He was a man who didn't have to do the obvious thing. He would be there to preside over the messy consequences of life's turmoils. This was, he thought, his one innate strength of character.

Only now, oddly, he was in limbo. The "there" where he'd promised to stay seemed to have suddenly separated into pieces and receded. And it was invigorating. He felt, in fact, that although Barbara had seemed to bring it about, he may have caused all this himself, even though it was probably inevitable—destined to happen to the two of them no matter what the cause or outcome.

He went to the bar cart in the den, poured some scotch into his milk, and came back and sat in a kitchen chair in front of the sliding glass door. Two dogs trotted across the grass in the rectangle of light that fell from the window. Shortly after, another two dogs came through—one the springer spaniel he regularly heard yapping at night. And then a small scruffy lone dog, sniffing the ground behind the other four. This dog stopped and peered at Austin, blinked, then trotted out of the light.

Austin had been imagining Barbara checked into an expensive hotel downtown, drinking champagne, ordering a Cobb salad from room service and thinking the same things he'd been thinking. But what he was actually beginning to feel now, and grimly, was that when push came to shove, the aftermath of almost anything he'd done in a very long time really *hadn't* given him any pleasure. Despite good intentions, and despite loving Barbara as he felt few people ever loved anybody and feeling that he could be to blame for everything that had gone on tonight, he considered it unmistakable that he could do his wife no good now. He was bad for her. And if his own puny inability to satisfy her candidly expressed and at least partly legitimate grievances was not adequate proof of his failure, then her own judgment certainly was: "You're an asshole," she'd said. And he concluded that she was right. He *was* an asshole. And he was the other things too, and hated to think so. Life didn't veer—

you discovered it *had* veered, later. Now. And he was as sorry about it as anything he could imagine ever being sorry about. But he simply couldn't help it. He didn't like what he didn't like and couldn't do what he couldn't do.

What he *could* do, though, was leave. Go back to Paris. Immediately. Tonight if possible, before Barbara came home, and before he and she became swamped all over again and he had to wade back into the problems of his being an asshole, and their life. He felt as if a fine, high-tension wire strung between his toes and the back of his neck had been forcefully plucked by an invisible finger, causing him to feel a chilled vibration, a bright tingling that radiated into his stomach and out to the ends of his fingers.

He sat up straight in his chair. He was leaving. Later he would feel awful and bereft and be broke, maybe homeless, on welfare and sick to death from a disease born of dejection. But now he felt incandescent, primed, jittery with excitement. And it wouldn't last forever, he thought, probably not even very long. The mere sound of a taxi door closing in the street would detonate the whole fragile business and sacrifice his chance to act.

He stood and quickly walked to the kitchen and telephoned for a taxi, then left the receiver dangling off the hook. He walked back through the house, checking all the doors and windows to be certain they were locked. He walked into his and Barbara's bedroom, turned on the light, hauled his two-suiter from under the bed, opened it and began putting exactly that in one side, two suits, and in the other side underwear, shirts, another pair of shoes, a belt, three striped ties, plus his still-full dopp kit. In response to an unseen questioner, he said out loud, standing in the bedroom: "I really didn't bring much. I just put some things in a suitcase."

He closed his bag and brought it to the living room. His passport was in the secretary. He put that in his pants pocket, got a coat out of the closet by the front door—a long rubbery rain jacket bought from a catalog—and put it on. He picked up his wallet and keys, then turned and looked into the house.

He was leaving. In moments he'd be gone. Likely as not he would never stand in this doorway again, surveying these rooms, feeling this way. Some of it might happen again, okay, but not all. And it was so easy: one minute you're completely in a life, and the next you're completely out. Just a few items to round up.

A note. He felt he should leave a note and walked quickly back to the kitchen, dug a green Day-Glo grocery-list pad out of a drawer, and on the back scribbled, "Dear B," only then wasn't sure what to continue with. Something meaningful would take sheets and sheets of paper but would be both absurd and irrelevant. Something brief would be ironic or sentimental, and demonstrate in a completely new way what an asshole he was—a conclusion he wanted this note to make the incontrovertible case against. He turned the sheet over. A sample grocery list was printed there, with blank spaces provided for pencil checks.

Pain ....
Lait......................
Cereal ....
Oeufs...................
Veggies.................
Hamburger...........
Lard.....................
Fromage ....
Les Autres ....

He could check "Les Autres," he thought, and write "Paris" beside it. Paris was certainly *autres*. Though *only* an asshole would do that. He turned it over again to the "Dear B" side. Nothing he could think of was right. Everything wanted to stand for their life, but couldn't. Their life was their life and couldn't be represented by anything but their life, and not by something scratched on the back of a grocery list.

His taxi honked outside. For some reason he reached up and put the receiver back on the hook, and almost instantly the phone started ringing—loud, brassy, shrill, unnerving rings that filled the yellow kitchen as if the walls were made of metal. He could hear the other phones ringing in other rooms. It was suddenly intolerably chaotic inside the house. Below "Dear B" he furiously scribbled, "I'll call you. Love M," and stuck the note under the jangling phone. Then he hurried to the front door, grabbed his suitcase, and exited his empty home into the soft spring suburban night.

5

DURING HIS FIRST few dispiriting days back in Paris, Austin did not call Joséphine Belliard. There were more pressing matters: to arrange, over terrible phone connections, to be granted a leave of absence from his job. "Personal problems," he said squeamishly to his boss, and felt certain his boss was concluding he'd had a nervous breakdown. "How's Barbara?" Fred Carruthers said cheerfully, which annoyed him.

"Barbara's great," he said. "She's just fine. Call her up yourself. She'd like to hear from you." Then he hung up, thinking he'd never see Fred Carruthers again and didn't give a shit if he didn't, except that his own voice had sounded desperate, the one way he didn't want it to sound.

He arranged for his Chicago bank to wire him money— enough, he thought, for six months. Ten thousand dollars. He called up one of the two people he knew in Paris, a for- mer Lambda Chi brother who was a homosexual and a would-be novelist, living someplace in Neuilly. Dave, his old frat bro, asked him if he was a homosexual himself now, then laughed like hell. Finally, though, Dave remembered he had a friend who had a friend—and eventually, after two unsettled nights in his old Hôtel de la Monastère, during which he'd worried about money, Austin had been given the keys to a luxurious, metal-and-velvet faggot's lair with enormous mirrors on the bedroom ceiling, just down rue Bonaparte from the Deux Magots, where Sartre was sup- posed to have liked to sit in the sun and think.

Much of these first days—bright, soft mid-April days— Austin was immensely jet-lagged and exhausted and looked sick and haunted in the bathroom mirror. He didn't want to see Joséphine in this condition. He had been back home only three days, then in the space of one frenzied evening had had a big fight with his wife, raced to the airport, waited all night for a flight and taken a middle-row standby to Orly seated between two French children. It was crazy. A large part of this was definitely crazy. Probably he *was* hav- ing a nervous breakdown and was too out of his head even to have a hint about it, and eventually Barbara and a psychiatrist would have to bring him home heavily sedated and in a straitjacket. But that would be later.

"Where are you?" Barbara said coldly, when he'd finally reached her at home.

"In Europe," he said. "I'm staying a while."

"How nice for you," she said. He could tell she didn't know what to think about any of this. It pleased him to baffle her, though he also knew it was childish.

"Carruthers might call you," he said.

"I already talked to him," Barbara said.

"I'm sure he thinks I'm nuts."

"No. He doesn't think that," she said, without offering what he did think.

Outside the apartment the traffic on rue Bonaparte was noisy, so that he moved away from the window. The walls in the apartment were dark red-and-green suede, with glistening tubular-steel abstract wall hangings, thick black carpet and black velvet furniture. He had no idea who the owner was, though he realized just at that moment that in all probability the owner was dead.

"Are you planning to file for divorce?" Austin said. It was the first time the word had ever been used, but it was inescapable, and he was remotely satisfied to be the first to put it into play.

"Actually I don't know what I'm going to do," Barbara said. "I don't have a husband now, apparently."

He almost blurted out that it was she who'd walked out, not him, she who'd actually caused this. But that wasn't entirely true, and in any case saying anything about it would start a conversation he didn't want to have and that no one *could* have at such long distance. It would just be bickering and complaining and anger. He realized all at once that he had nothing else to say, and felt jittery. He'd only wished to announce that he was alive and not dead, but was now ready to hang up.

"You're in France, aren't you?" Barbara said.

"Yes," Austin said. "That's right. Why?"

"I supposed so." She said this as though the thought of it disgusted her. "Why not, I guess. Right?"

"Right," he said.

"So. Come home when you're tired of whatever it is, whatever her name is." She said this very mildly.

"Maybe I will," Austin said.

"Maybe I'll be waiting, too," Barbara said. "Miracles still happen. I've had my eyes opened now, though."

"Great," he said, and he started to say something else, but he thought he heard her hang up. "Hello?" he said. "Hello? Barbara, are you there?"

"Oh, go to hell," Barbara said, and then she did hang up.

FOR TWO DAYS Austin took long, exhausting walks in completely arbitrary directions, surprising himself each time by where he turned up, then taking a cab back to his apartment. His instincts still seemed all wrong, which frustrated him. He thought the Place de la Concorde was farther away from this apartment than it was, and in the wrong direction. He couldn't always remember which way the river ran. And unhappily he kept passing the same streets and movie theater playing *Cinema Paradiso* and the same news kiosk, over and over, as if he continually walked in a circle.

He called his other friend, a man named Hank Bullard, who'd once worked for Lilienthal but had decided to start an air-conditioning business of his own in Vitry. He was married to a Frenchwoman and lived in a suburb. They made plans for a lunch, then Hank canceled for business reasons—an emergency trip out of town. Hank said they should arrange another date but didn't specifically suggest one. Austin ended up having lunch alone in an expensive brasserie on the Boulevard du Montparnasse, seated behind a glass window, trying to read *Le Monde* but growing discouraged as the words he didn't understand piled up. He would read the *Herald Tribune,* he thought, to keep up with the world, and let his French build gradually.

There were even more tourists than a week earlier when he'd been here. The tourist season was beginning, and the whole place, he thought, would probably change and become unbearable. The French and the Americans, he decided, looked basically like each other; only their language and some soft, almost effeminate quality he couldn't define distinguished them. Sitting at his tiny, round boulevard table, removed from the swarming passersby, Austin thought this street was full of people walking along dreaming of doing what he was actually doing, of picking up and leaving everything behind, coming here, sitting in cafés, walking the streets, possibly deciding to write a novel or paint watercolors, or just to start an air-conditioning business, like Hank Bullard. But there was a price to pay for that. And the price was that doing it didn't feel the least romantic. It felt purposeless, as if he himself had no purpose, plus there was no sense of a future now, at least as he had always experienced the future—as a palpable thing you looked forward to confidently even if what it held might be sad or tragic or unwantable. The future was still there, of course; he simply didn't know how to imagine it. He didn't know, for instance, exactly what he was in Paris for, though he could perfectly recount everything that had gotten him here, to this table, to his plate of *moules meunières,* to this feeling of great fatigue, observing tourists, all of whom might dream whatever he dreamed but in fact knew precisely where they were going and precisely why they were here. Possibly they were the wise ones, Austin thought, with their warmly lighted, tightly constructed lives on faraway landscapes. Maybe he had reached a point, or even gone far beyond a point now, when he no longer cared what happened to himself—the crucial linkages of a good life, he knew, being small and subtle and in many ways just lucky things you hardly even noticed. Only you could fuck them up and never know quite how you'd done it. Everything just started to go wrong and unravel. Your life could be on a track to ruin, to your being on the street and disappearing from view entirely, and you, in spite of your best efforts, your best hope that it all go differently, you could only stand by and watch it happen.

For the next two days he did not call Joséphine Belliard, although he thought about calling her all the time. He thought he might possibly bump into her as she walked to work. His garish little roué's apartment was only four blocks from the publishing house on rue de Lille, where, in a vastly different life, he had made a perfectly respectable business call a little more than a week before.

He walked down the nearby streets as often as he could—to buy a newspaper or to buy food in the little market stalls on the rue de Seine, or just to pass the shop windows and begin finding his way along narrow brick alleys. He disliked thinking that he was only in Paris because of Joséphine Belliard, because of a woman, and one he really barely knew but whom he nevertheless thought about constantly and made persistent efforts to see "accidentally." He felt he was here for another reason, too, a subtle and insistent, albeit less specific one he couldn't exactly express to himself but which he felt was expressed simply by his being here and feeling the way he felt.

Not once, though, did he see Joséphine Belliard on the rue de Lille, or walking along the Boulevard St.-Germain on her way to work, or walking past the Café de Flore or the Brasserie Lipp, where he'd had lunch with her only the week before and where the sole had been full of grit but he hadn't mentioned it.

Much of the time, on his walks along strange streets, he thought about Barbara; and not with a feeling of guilt or even of loss, but normally, habitually, involuntarily. He found himself shopping for her, noticing a blouse or a scarf or an antique pendant or a pair of emerald earrings he could buy and bring home. He found himself storing away things to tell her—for instance, that the Sorbonne was actually named after somebody named Sorbon, or that France was seventy percent nuclear, a headline he deciphered off the front page of *L'Express* and that coursed around his mind like an electron with no polarity other than Barbara, who, as it happened, was a supporter of nuclear power. She occupied, he recognized, the place of final consequence—the destination for practically everything he cared about or noticed or imagined. But now, or at least for the present time, that situation was undergoing a change, since being in Paris and waiting his chance to see Joséphine lacked any customary destination, but simply started and stopped in himself. Though that was how he wanted it. And that was the explanation he had not exactly articulated in the last few days: he wanted things, whatever things there were, to be for him and only him.

On the third day, at four in the afternoon, he called Joséphine Belliard. He called her at home instead of her office, thinking she wouldn't be at home and that he could leave a brief, possibly inscrutable recorded message, and then not call her for a few more days, as though he was too busy to try again any sooner. But when her phone rang twice she answered.

"Hi," Austin said, stunned at the suddenness of Joséphine being on the line and only a short distance from where he was standing, and sounding unquestionably like herself. It made him feel vaguely faint. "It's Martin Austin," he managed to say feebly.

He heard a child scream in the background before Joséphine could say more than hello. *"Nooooon!"* the child, certainly Léo, screamed again.

"Where are you?" she said in a hectic voice. He heard something go crash in the room where she was. "Are you in Chicago now?"

"No, I'm in Paris," Austin said, grappling with his composure and speaking very softly.

"Paris? What are you doing *here*?" Joséphine said, obviously surprised. "Are you on business again now?"

This, somehow, was an unsettling question. "No," he said, still very faintly. "I'm not on business. I'm just here. I have an apartment."

"Tu as un appartement!" Joséphine said in even greater surprise. "What for?" she said. "Why? Is your wife with you?"

"No," Austin said. "I'm here alone. I'm planning on staying for a while."

"Oooo-laaa," Joséphine said. "Do you have a big fight at home? Is that the matter?"

"No," Austin lied. "We didn't have a big fight at home. I decided to take some time away. That's not so unusual, is it?"

Léo screamed again savagely. *"Ma-man!"* Joséphine spoke to him patiently. *"Doucement, doucement,"* she said. *"J'arrive.*

Une minute. Une minute. "One minute didn't seem like very much time, but Austin didn't want to stay on the phone long. Joséphine seemed much more French than he remembered. In his mind she had been almost an American, only with a French accent. "Okay. So," she said, a little out of breath. "You are here now? In Paris?"

"I want to see you," Austin said. It was the moment he'd been waiting for—more so even than the moment when he would finally see her. It was the moment when he would declare himself to be present. Unencumbered. Available. Willing. That mattered a great deal. He actually slipped his wedding ring off his finger and laid it on the table beside the phone.

"Yes?" Joséphine said. "What . . ." She paused, then resumed. "What do you like to do with me? When do you like? What?" She was impatient.

"Anything. Anytime," Austin said, and suddenly felt the best he'd felt in days. "Tonight," he said. "Or today. In twenty minutes."

"In twenty minutes! Come on. No!" she said and laughed, but in an interested way, a pleased way—he could tell. "No, no, no," she said. "I have to go to my lawyer in one hour. I have to find my neighbor now to stay with Léo. It is impossible now. I'm divorcing. You know this already. It's very upsetting. Anyway."

"I'll stay with Léo," Austin said rashly.

Joséphine laughed. "*You'll* stay with him! You don't have children, do you? You said this." She laughed again.

"I'm not offering to adopt him," Austin said. "But I'll stay with him for an hour. Then you can have your neighbor come, and I'll take you to dinner. How's that?"

"He doesn't like you," Joséphine said. "He likes only his father best. He doesn't even like me."

"I'll teach him some English," Austin said. "I'll teach him to say 'Chicago Cubs.' " He could feel enthusiasm already leaching off. "We'll be great friends."

"What is Chicago Cubs?" Joséphine said.

"It's a baseball team." And he felt, just for an instant, bleak. Not because he wished he was home, or wished Barbara was here, or wished really anything was different. Everything was how he'd hoped it would be. He simply wished he hadn't mentioned the Cubs. This was over-confident, he thought. It was the wrong thing to say. A mistake.

"So. Well," Joséphine said, sounding businesslike. "You come here, then? I go to my lawyers to sign my papers. Then maybe we have a dinner together, yes?"

"Absolutely," Austin said, bleakness vanished. "I'll come right away. I'll start in five minutes." On the dark suede wall, under a little metal track light positioned to illuminate it, was a big oil painting of two men, naked and locked in a strenuous kiss and embrace. Neither man's face was visible, and their bodies were weight lifters' muscular bodies, their genitals hidden by their embroiled pose. They were seated on a rock, which was very crudely painted in. It was like Laocoön, Austin thought, only corrupted. He'd wondered if one of the men was the one who owned the apartment, or possibly the owner was the painter or the painter's lover. He wondered if either one of them was alive this afternoon. He actually hated the painting and had already decided to take it down before he brought Joséphine here. Which was what he meant to do—bring her here, tonight if possible, and keep her with him until morning, when they could walk up and sit in the cool sun at the Deux Magots and drink coffee. Like Sartre.

"Martin?" Joséphine said. He was about to put down the phone and go move the smarmy Laocoön painting. He'd almost forgotten he was talking to her.

"What? I'm here," Austin said. Though it might be fun to leave it up, he thought. It could be an ice-breaker, something to laugh about, like the mirrors on the ceiling, before things got more serious.

"Martin, what are you doing here?" Joséphine said oddly. "Are you okay?"

"I'm here to see you, darling," Austin said. "Why do you think? I said I'd see you soon, and I meant it. I guess I'm just a man of my word."

"You are a very silly man, though," Joséphine said and laughed, not quite so pleased as before. "But," she said, "what I can do?"

"You can't do anything," Austin said. "Just see me tonight. After that you never have to see me again."

"Yes. Okay," Joséphine said. "That's a good deal. Now. You come to here. *Ciao*."

"*Ciao*," Austin said oddly, not really being entirely sure what *ciao* meant.

6

NEAR THE ODÉON, striding briskly up the narrow street that ended at the Palais du Luxembourg, Austin realized he was arriving at Joséphine's apartment with nothing in his hands—a clear mistake. Possibly some bright flowers would be a good idea, or a toy, a present of some minor kind which would encourage Léo to like him. Léo was four, and ill-tempered and spoiled. He was pale and had limp, wispy-thin dark hair and dark, penetrating eyes, and when he cried—which was often—he cried loudly and had the habit of opening his mouth and leaving it open for as much of the sound to come out as possible, a habit which accentuated the simian quality of his face, a quality he on occasion seemed to share with Joséphine. Austin had seen documentaries on TV that showed apes doing virtually the same thing while sitting in trees—always it seemed just as daylight was vanishing and another long, imponderable night was at hand. Possibly that was what Léo's life was like. "It is because of my divorce from his father," Joséphine had said matter-of-factly the one time Austin had been in her apartment, the time they had listened to jazz and he had sat and admired the golden sunlight on the building cornices. "It is too hard on him. He is a child. But." She'd shrugged her shoulders and begun to think about something else.

Austin had seen no store selling flowers, so he crossed rue Regnard to a chic little shop that had wooden toys in its window: bright wood trucks of ingenious meticulous design, bright wood animals—ducks and rabbits and pigs in preposterous detail, even a French farmer wearing a red neckerchief and a black beret. An entire wooden farmhouse was painstakingly constructed with roof tiles, little dormer windows and Dutch doors, and cost a fortune—far more than he intended to pay. Kids were fine, but he'd never wanted any for himself, and neither had Barbara. It had been their first significant point of agreement when they were in college in the sixties—the first reason they'd found to think they might be made for each other. Years ago now, Austin thought—twenty-two. All of it past, out of reach.

The little shop, however, seemed to have plenty of nice things inside that Austin *could* afford—a wooden clock whose hands you moved yourself, wooden replicas of the Eiffel Tower and the Arc de Triomphe. There was a little wood pickaninny holding a tiny red-and-green wood watermelon and smiling with bright painted-white teeth. The little pickaninny reminded Austin of Léo—minus the smile—and he thought about buying it as a piece of Americana and taking it home to Barbara.

Inside, the saleslady seemed to think he would naturally want that and started to take it out of the case. But there was also a small wicker basket full of painted eggs on the countertop, each egg going for twenty francs, and Austin picked up one of those, a bright-green enamel and gold paisley one made of perfectly turned balsa that felt hollow. They were left over from Easter, Austin thought, and had probably been more expensive. There was no reason Léo should like a green wooden egg, of course. Except *he* liked it, and Joséphine would like it too. And once the child pushed it aside in favor of whatever he liked better, Joséphine could claim it and set it on her night table or on her desk at work, and think about who'd bought it.

Austin paid the clerk for the nubbly-sided little egg and started for the door—he was going to be late on account of being lost. But just as he reached the glass door Joséphine's husband came in, accompanied by a tall, beautiful, vivacious blond woman with a deep tan and thin, shining legs. The woman was wearing a short silver-colored dress that encased her hips in some kind of elastic fabric, and she looked, Austin thought, standing by in complete surprise, rich. Joséphine's husband—short and bulgy, with his thick, dark Armenian-looking mustache and soft, swart skin—was at least a head shorter than the woman, and was dressed in an expensively shapeless black suit. They were talking in a language which sounded like German, and Bernard—the husband who had written the salacious novel about Joséphine and who provided her little money and his son precious little attention, and whom Joséphine was that very afternoon going off to secure a divorce from—Bernard was seemingly intent on buying a present in the store.

He glanced at Austin disapprovingly. His small, almost black eyes flickered with some vague recognition. Only there couldn't be any recognition. Bernard knew nothing about him, and there was, in fact, nothing to know. Bernard had certainly never laid eyes on him. It was just the way he had of looking at a person, as though he had your number and didn't much like you. Why, Austin wondered, would that be an attractive quality in a man? Suspicion. Disdain. A bullying nature. Why marry an asshole like that?

Austin had paused inside the shop door, and now found himself staring down into the display window from behind, studying the miniature Eiffel Tower and Arc de Triomphe. They were, he saw, parts of a whole little Paris made of wood, a kit a child could play with and arrange any way he saw fit. A wooden Notre Dame, a wooden Louvre, an Obélisque, a Centre Pompidou, even a little wooden Odéon, like the one a few steps down the street. The whole set of buildings was expensive as hell—nearly three thousand francs—but you could also buy the pieces separately. Austin thought about buying something to accompany the egg—give the egg to Joséphine and miniature building to Léo. He stood staring down at the little city in wood, beyond which out the window the real city of metal and stone went on unmindful.

Bernard and his blond friend were laughing at the little pickaninny holding his red-and-green watermelon. The clerk had it out of the case, and Bernard was holding it up and laughing at it derisively. Once or twice Bernard said, "a leetle neeger," then said, *"voilà, voilà,"* then the woman said something in German and both of them burst out laughing. Even the shopkeeper laughed.

Austin fingered the green egg, a lump against his leg. He considered just going up and buying the whole goddamned wooden Paris and saying to Bernard in English, "I'm buying this for *your* son, you son of a bitch," then threatening him with his fist. But that was a bad idea, and he didn't have the stomach for a row. It was remotely possible, of course, that the man might not be Bernard at all, that he only looked like the picture in Léo's room, and he would be a complete idiot to threaten him.

He slipped his hand in his pocket, felt the enamel paint of the egg and wondered if this was an adequate present, or would it be ludicrous? The German woman turned and looked at him, the smile of derisive laughter still half on her lips. She looked at Austin's face, then at his pocket where his hand was gripping the little egg. She leaned and said something to Bernard, something in French, and Bernard turned and looked at Austin across the shop, narrowed his eyes in a kind of disdainful warning. He raised his chin slightly and turned back. They both said something else, after which they both chuckled. The proprietress looked at Austin and smiled in a friendly way. Then Austin changed his mind about buying the wooden city and opened the glass door and stepped out onto the sidewalk, where the air was cool and he could see up the short hill to the park.

7

JOSÉPHINE'S APARTMENT block was an unexceptional one on a street of similar older buildings with white modernistic fronts overlooking the Jardin du Luxembourg. In the tiny, shadowy lobby, there was an elegant old Beaux Arts grillework elevator. But since Joséphine lived on the third level, Austin walked up, taking the steps two at a time, the little green paisley egg bumping against his leg with each stride.

When he knocked, Joséphine immediately threw open the door and flung her arms around his neck. She hugged him, then held her hands on his cheeks and kissed him hard on the mouth. Little Léo, who'd just been running from one room to another, waving a wooden drumstick, stopped stock-still in the middle of the floor and stared, shocked by his mother's kissing a man he didn't remember seeing before.

"Okay. Now I must go," Joséphine said, releasing his face and hurrying to the open window which overlooked the street and the park. She was putting on her eye shadow, using a tiny compact mirror and the light from outside.

Joséphine was dressed in a simple white blouse and a pair of odd, loose-fitting pants that had pictures of circus animals all over them, helter-skelter in loud colors. They were strange, unbecoming pants, Austin thought, and they fit in such a way that her small stomach made a noticeable round bulge below the waistband. Joséphine looked slightly fat and a little sloppy. She turned and smiled at him as she fixed her face. "How do you feel?" she said.

"I feel great," Austin said. He smiled at Léo, who had not stopped staring at him, holding up his drumstick like a little cigar-store Indian. The child had on short trousers and a white T-shirt that had the words BIG-TIME AMERICAN LUXURY printed across the front above a huge red Cadillac convertible which seemed to be driving out from his chest.

Léo uttered something very fast in French, then looked at his mother and back at Austin, who hadn't gotten far into the room since being hugged and kissed.

"Non, non, Léo," Joséphine said, and laughed with an odd delight. "He asks me if you are my new husband. He thinks I need a husband now. He is very mixed up." She went on darkening her eyes. Joséphine looked pretty in the window light, and Austin wanted to go over right then and give her a much more significant kiss. But the child kept staring at him, holding the drumstick up and making Austin feel awkward and reluctant, which wasn't how he thought he'd feel. He thought he'd feel free and completely at ease and on top of the world about everything.

He reached in his pocket, palmed the wooden egg and knelt in front of the little boy, showing two closed fists.

"J'ai un cadeau pour toi," he said. He'd practiced these words and wondered how close he'd come. "I have a nice present for you," he said in English to satisfy himself. *"Choisez le main."* Austin tried to smile. He jiggled the correct

hand, his right one, trying to capture the child's attention. *"Choissez le main, Léo,"* he said again and smiled, this time, a little grimly. Austin looked at Joséphine for encouragement, but she was still appraising herself in her mirror. She said something very briskly to Léo, who beetled his dark little brow at the two presented fists. Reluctantly he pointed his drumstick at Austin's right fist, the one he'd been jiggling. And very slowly—as though he were opening a chest filled with gold—Austin opened his fingers to reveal the bright little green egg with gold paisleys and red snowflakes. Some flecks of the green paint had already come off on his palm, which surprised him. *"Voilà,"* Austin said dramatically. *"C'est une jolie oeuf!"*

Léo stared intently at the clammy egg in Austin's palm. He looked at Austin with an expression of practiced inquisitiveness, his thin lips growing pursed as though something worried him. Very timidly he extended his wooden drumstick and touched the egg, then nudged it, with the shaped tip, the end intended to strike a drum. Austin noticed that Léo had three big gravelly warts on his tiny fingers, and instantly a cold wretchedness from his own childhood opened in him, making Léo for an instant seem frail and sympathetic. But then with startling swiftness Léo raised the drumstick and delivered the egg—still in Austin's proffered palm—a fierce downward blow, hoping apparently to smash it and splatter its contents and possibly give Austin's fingers a painful lashing for good measure.

But the egg, though the blow chipped its glossy green enamel and Austin felt the impact like a shock, did not break. And little Léo's pallid face assumed a look of controlled fury. He quickly took two more vengeful back-and-forth swipes at it, the second of which struck Austin's thumb a stinging then numbing blow, then Léo turned and fled out of the room, down the hall and through a door which he slammed behind him.

Austin looked up at Joséphine, who was just finishing at the window.

"He is very mixed up. I tell you before," she said, and shook her head.

"That didn't work out too well," Austin said, squeezing his throbbing thumb so as not to have to mention it.

"It's not important," she said, going to the couch and putting her compact in her purse. "He is angry all the time. Sometimes he hits *me*. Don't feel bad. You're sweet to bring something to him."

But what Austin felt, at that moment, was that he wanted to kiss Joséphine, and not to talk about Léo. Now that they were alone, he wanted to kiss her in a way that said he was here and it wasn't just a coincidence, that he'd had her on his mind this whole time, and wanted her to have him on her mind, and that this whole thing that had started last week in discretion and good-willed restraint was rising to a new level, a level to be taken more seriously. She could love him now. He could conceivably even love her. Much was possible that only days ago was not even dreamed of.

He moved toward where she was, repocketing the egg, his injured thumb pulsating. She was leaned over the couch in her idiotic animal pants, and he rather roughly grasped her hips—covering the faces of a yellow giraffe and a gray rhino with his hands—and pulled, trying to turn her toward him so he could give her the kiss he wanted to give her, the authoritative one that signaled his important arrival on the scene. But she jumped, as though he'd startled her, and she shouted, "Stop! What is it!" just as he was negotiating her face around in front of his. She had a lipstick tube in her hand, and she seemed irritated to be so close to him. She smelled sweet, surprisingly sweet. Like a flower, he thought.

"There's something important between us, I think," Austin said directly into Joséphine's irritated face. "Important enough to bring me back across an ocean and to leave my wife and to face the chance that I'll be alone here."

"What?" she said. She contorted her mouth and, without exactly pushing, exerted a force to gain a few inches from him. He still had her by her hips, cluttered with animal faces. A dark crust of eye shadow clung where she had inexpertly doctored her eyelids.

"You shouldn't feel under any pressure," he said and looked at her gravely. "I just want to see you. That's all. Maybe have some time alone with you. Who knows where it'll go?"

"You are very fatigued, I think." She struggled to move backward. "Maybe you can have a sleep while I'm going."

"I'm not tired," Austin said. "I feel great. Nothing's bothering me. I've got a clean slate."

"That's good," she said, and smiled but pushed firmly away from him just as he was moving in to give her the important kiss. Joséphine quickly kissed him first, though, the same hard, unpassionate kiss she'd greeted him with five minutes before and that had left him dissatisfied.

"I want to kiss you the right way, not that way," Austin said. He pulled her firmly to him again, taking hold of her soft waist and pushing his mouth toward hers. He kissed her as tenderly as he could with her back stiff and resistant, and her mouth not shaped to receive a kiss but ready to speak when the kiss ended. Austin held the kiss for a long moment, his eyes closed, his breath traveling out his nose,

trying to feel his own wish for tenderness igniting an answering tenderness in her. But if there was tenderness, it
was of an unexpected type—more like forbearance. And
when he had pressed her lips for as many as six or eight seconds, until he had breathed her breath and she had relaxed
her resistance, he stood back and looked at her—a woman
he felt he might love—and took her chin between his
thumb and index finger and said, "That's really all I
wanted. That wasn't all that bad, was it?"

She shook her head in a perfunctory way and very softly,
almost compliantly, said, "No." Her eyes were cast down,
though not in a way he felt confident of, more as if she were
waiting for something. He felt he should let her go; that was
the thing to do. He'd forced her to kiss him. She'd relented.
Now she could be free to do anything she wanted.

Joséphine hurriedly turned back toward her purse on
the couch, and Austin walked to the window and surveyed
the vast chestnut trees of the Jardin du Luxembourg. The
air was cool and soft, and the light seemed creamy and rich
in the late afternoon. He heard music, guitar music from
somewhere, and the faint sound of singing. He saw a jog-
ger running through the park gate and out into the street
below, and he wondered what anyone would think who
saw him standing in this window—someone glancing up a
moment out of the magnificent garden and seeing a man
in an apartment. Would it be clear he was an American? Or
would he possibly seem French? Would he seem rich?
Would his look of satisfaction be visible? He thought almost certainly that would be visible.

"I have to go to the lawyer now," Joséphine said behind
him.

"Fine. Go," Austin said. "Hurry back. I'll look after little Gene Krupa. Then we'll have a nice dinner."

Joséphine had a thick sheaf of documents she was forcing into a plastic briefcase. "Maybe," she said in a distracted voice.

Austin, for some reason, began picturing himself talking to Hank Bullard about the air-conditioning business. They were in a café on a sunny side street. Hank's news was good, full of promise about a partnership.

Joséphine hurried into the hall, her flat shoes scraping the boards. She opened the door to Léo's room and said something quick and very soft to him, something that did not have Austin's name in it. Then she closed the door and entered the WC and used the toilet without bothering to shut herself in. Austin couldn't see down the hall from where he stood by the window, but could hear her pissing, the small trickle of water hitting more water. Barbara always closed the door, and he did too—it was a sound he didn't like and usually tried to avoid hearing, a sound so inert, so factual, that hearing it threatened to take away a layer of his good feeling. He was sorry to hear it now, sorry Joséphine didn't bother to close the door.

In an instant, however, she was out and down the hallway, picking up her briefcase while water sighed through the pipes. She gave Austin a peculiar, fugitive look across the room, as if she was surprised he was there and wasn't sure why he should be. It was, he felt, the look you gave an unimportant employee who's just said something inexplicable.

"So. I am going now," she said.

"I'll be right here," Austin said, looking at her and feeling suddenly helpless. "Hurry back, okay?"

"Yeah, sure. Okay," she said. "I hurry. I see you."

"Great," Austin said. She went out the door and quickly down the echoing steps toward the street.

FOR A WHILE Austin walked around the apartment, looking at things—things Joséphine Belliard liked or cherished
or had kept when her husband cleared out. There was an
entire wall of books across one side of the little sleeping al-
cove she'd constructed for her privacy, using fake Chinese
rice-paper dividers. The books were the sleek French soft-
covers, mostly on sociological subjects, though other books
seemed to be in German. Her modest bed was covered
with a clean, billowy white duvet and big fluffy white pil-
lows—no headboard, just the frame, but very neat. A copy
of her soon-to-be-ex-husband's scummy novel lay on the
bed table, with several pages roughly bent down. Folding a
page up, he read a sentence in which a character named
Solange was performing an uninspired act of fellatio on
someone named Albert. He recognized the charged words:
Fellation. Lugubre. Albert was talking about having his car
repaired the whole time it was happening to him. *Un
Amour Secret* was the book's insipid title. Bernard's scowl-
ing, condescending visage was nowhere in evidence.

He wondered what Bernard knew that he didn't know.
Plenty, of course, if the book was even half true. But
the unknown was interesting; you had to face it one way
or another, he thought. And the idea of fellatio with
Joséphine—nothing, up to this moment, he'd even considered—inflamed him, and he began to realize there was
something distinctly sexual about roaming around examining her private belongings and modest bedroom, a space
and a bed he could easily imagine occupying in the near
future. Before he moved away he laid the green paisley egg
on her bed table, beside the copy of her husband's smutty
book. It would create a contrast, he thought, a reminder
that she had choices in the world.

He looked out the bedroom window onto the park. It was the same view as the living room—the easeful formal garden with great leafy horse chestnut trees and tonsured green lawns with topiaries and yew shrubs and pale criss-crossing gravel paths, and the old École Supérieure des Mines looming along the far side and the Luxembourg Palace to the left. Some hippies were sitting cross-legged in a tight little circle on one of the grass swards, sharing a joint around. No one else was in view, though the light was cool and smooth and inviting, with birds soaring through it. A clock chimed somewhere nearby. The guitar music had ceased.

It would be pleasant to walk there with Joséphine, Austin thought, to breathe the sweet air of chestnut trees and to stare off. Life was very different here. This apartment was very different from his house in Oak Grove. *He* felt different here. Life seemed to have improved remarkably in a short period. All it took, he thought, was the courage to take control of things and to live with the consequences.

He assumed Léo to be asleep down the hall and that he could simply leave well enough alone there. But when he'd sat leafing through French *Vogue* for perhaps twenty minutes he heard a door open, and seconds later Léo appeared at the corner of the hall, looking confused and drugged in his BIG-TIME AMERICAN LUXURY shirt with the big red Cadillac barging off the front. He still had his little shoes on.

Léo rubbed his eyes and looked pitiful. Possibly Joséphine had given him something to knock him out—the sort of thing that wouldn't happen in the States. But in France, he thought, adults treated children differently. More intelligently.

"Bon soir," Austin said in a slightly ironic voice and smiled, setting the *Vogue* down.

Léo eyed him sullenly, still suspicious about hearing French spoken by this person who wasn't the least bit French. He scanned the room quickly for his mother's presence. Austin considered a plan of reintroducing the slightly discredited paisley egg but decided against it. He glanced at the clock on the bookcase: forty-five minutes would somehow need to be consumed before Joséphine returned. But how? How could the time be passed in a way to make Léo happy and possibly impress his mother? The Cubs idea wouldn't work—Léo was too young. Austin didn't know any games or tricks. He knew nothing about children, and, in fact, was sorry the boy was awake, sorry he was here at all.

But he thought of the park—the Jardin du Luxembourg—available just outside the window. A nice walk in the park could set them on the right course. He wasn't able to talk to the child, but he could watch him while he enjoyed himself.

"Voulez-vous aller au parc?" Austin smiled a big, sincere smile. *"Maintenant? Peut-être? Le parc? Oui?"* He pointed at the open window and the cool, still evening air where swallows soared and flittered.

Léo frowned at him and then at the window, still dazed. He fastened a firm grip on the front of his shorts—a signal Austin recognized—and did not answer.

"Whatta ya say? Let's go to the park," Austin said enthusiastically, loudly. He almost jumped up. Léo could understand it well enough. *Parc.* Park.

"Parc?" Léo said, and more cravenly squeezed his little weenie. *"Maman?"* He looked almost demented.

"Maman est dans le parc," Austin said, thinking that from inside the park they would certainly see Joséphine on

her way back from the lawyer's, and that it wouldn't turn out to be a complete lie—or if it did, Joséphine would eventually come back and take control of things before there was a problem. It was even possible, he thought, that he'd never see this kid after that, that Joséphine might come back and never want to see *him* again. Though a darker thought entered his mind: of Joséphine *never* coming back, deciding simply to disappear somewhere en route from the lawyer's. That happened. Babies were abandoned in Chicago all the time and no one knew what happened to their parents. He knew no one she knew. He knew no one to contact. It was a nightmarish thought.

Inside of five minutes he had Léo into the bathroom and out again. Happily, Léo attended to his own privacy while Austin stood outside the door and stared at the picture of Bernard's stuffed, bulbous face on the wall of the boy's room. He was surprised Joséphine would let it stay up. He'd suppressed an urge to tell her to stick it to Bernard, to get him in the shorts if she could, though later he'd felt queasy for conspiring against a man he didn't know.

As they were leaving the apartment, Austin realized he had no key, neither to the downstairs nor to the apartment itself, and that once the door closed he and Léo were on their own: a man, an American speaking little French, alone with a four-year-old French child he didn't know, in a country, in a city, in a park, where he was an absolute stranger. No one would think this was a good idea. Joséphine hadn't asked him to take Léo to the park—it was his own doing, and it was a risk. But everything felt like a risk at the moment, and all he needed to do was be careful.

They walked out onto rue Férou and around the corner, then down a few paces and across a wide street to a corner gate into the Luxembourg. Léo said nothing but insisted on holding Austin's hand and leading the way as if he were taking Austin to the park because he didn't know what else to do with him.

Once through the gold-topped gate, though, and onto the pale gravel paths that ran in mazes through the shrubberies and trees and planted beds where daffodils were already blooming, Léo went running straight in the direction of a wide concrete pond where ducks and swans were swimming and a group of older boys was sailing miniature sailboats. Austin looked back to see which building was Joséphine's, and from which window he'd stood looking down at this very park. But he couldn't distinguish the window, wasn't even sure if from Joséphine's window he could see this part of the park. For one thing, there hadn't been a pond, and here there were plenty of people walking in the cool, sustained evening light—lovers and married people both, by the looks of them, taking a nice stroll before going home for dinner. Probably it was part of the park's plan, he supposed, that new parts always seemed familiar, and vice versa.

Austin strolled down to the concrete border of the pond and sat on a bench a few yards away from Léo, who stood raptly watching the older boys tend their boats with long, thin sticks. There was no wind and only the boys' soft, studious voices to listen to in the air where swallows were still darting. The little boats floated stilly in the shallows with peanut shells and popcorn tufts. A number of ducks and swans glided just out of reach, eyeing the boats, waiting for the boys to leave.

Austin heard tennis balls being hit nearby, but couldn't see where. A clay court, he felt certain. He wished he could sit and watch people playing tennis instead of boys tending boats. Female voices were laughing and speaking French and laughing again, then a tennis ball was struck once more. A dense wall of what looked like rhododendrons stood beyond a small expanse of well-tended grass, and behind that, he thought, would be the courts.

Across the pond, seated on the opposite concrete wall, a man in a tan suit was having his photograph taken by another man. An expensive camera was being employed, and the second man kept moving around, finding new positions from which to see through his viewfinder. *"Su-perbe,"* Austin heard the photographer say. *"Très, très, très bon.* Don't move now. Don't move." A celebrity, Austin thought; an actor or a famous writer—somebody on top of the world. The man seemed unaffected, not even to acknowledge that his picture was being taken.

Léo unexpectedly turned and looked at Austin, as if he—Léo—wanted to say something extremely significant and exciting about the little boats. His face was vivid with importance. Though when he saw Austin seated on the bench, the calculation of who Austin was clouded his pale little features and he looked suddenly deviled and chastened and secretive, and turned quickly back, inching closer to the water's edge as if he intended to wade in.

He was just a kid, Austin thought calmly, a kid with divorced parents; not a little ogre or a tyrant. He could be won over with time and patience. Anyone could. He thought of his own father, a tall, patient, goodhearted man who worked in a sporting goods store in Peoria. He and Austin's mother had celebrated their fiftieth anniversary two years before, a big to-do under a tent in the city park, with Austin's brother in from Phoenix, and all the older cousins and friends from faraway states and decades past. A week later his father had had a stroke watching the news on TV and died in his chair.

His father had always had patience with his sons, Austin thought soberly. In his father's life there'd been no divorces or sudden midnight departures, yet his father had always tried to understand the goings-on of the later generation. Therefore, what would he think of all this, Austin wondered. France. A strange woman with a son. An abandoned house back home. Lies. Chaos. He'd certainly have made an attempt to understand, tried to find the good in it. Though ultimately his judgment would've been harsh and he'd have sided with Barbara, whose success in real estate he'd admired. He sought to imagine his father's very words, his verdict, delivered from his big lounger in front of the TV—the very spot where he'd breathed his last frantic breaths. But he couldn't. For some reason he couldn't re-create his father's voice, its cadences, the exact tenor of it. It was peculiar not to remember his father's voice, a voice he'd heard all his life. Possibly it had not had that much effect.

Austin was staring at the man in the tan suit across the lagoon, the man having his photograph taken. The man was up on the concrete ledge now, with his back turned, the shallow pond behind him, his legs wide apart, his hands on his hips, his tan jacket in the crook of his elbow. He looked ridiculous, unconvincing about whatever he was supposed to seem convincing about. Austin wondered if he himself would be visible in the background, a blurry, distant figure staring from across the stale lagoon. Maybe he would see himself someplace, in *Le Monde* or *Figaro,* newspapers he couldn't read. It would be a souvenir he could laugh about at some later date, when he was where? With who?

Not, in all probability, Joséphine Belliard. Something about her had bothered him this afternoon. Not her reluctance to kiss him. That was an attitude he could overcome, given time. He was good at overcoming reluctances in

others. He was a persuasive man, with the heart of a sales-
man, and knew it. From time to time, this fact even bothered him, since given the right circumstances he felt he
could persuade anybody of anything—no matter what. He
had no clear idea what this persuasive quality was, though
Barbara had occasionally remarked on it, often with the
unflattering implication that he didn't believe in very
much, or at least not in enough. It always made him uneasy that this might be true, or at least be thought of as
true.

He *had* believed that he and Joséphine could have a different kind of relationship. Sexual, but not sexual at its heart.
But rather, a new thing, founded on realities—the facts of
his character, and hers. With Barbara, he'd felt he was just
playing out the end of an old thing. Less real, somehow. Less
mature. He could never really *love* Joséphine; that he had to
concede, since in his deepest heart he loved only Barbara, for
whatever that was worth. Yet he'd for a moment felt compelled by Joséphine, found her appealing, considered even
the possibility of living with her for months or years. Anything was possible.

But seeing her in her apartment today, looking just as he
knew she would, being exactly the woman he expected her
to be, had made him feel unexpectedly bleak. And he was
savvy enough to know that if he felt bleak now, at the very
beginning, he would feel only bleaker later, and that in all
likelihood life would either slowly or quickly become a
version of hell for which he would bear all responsibility.

His thumb still vaguely ached. The women were laughing again on the tennis courts beyond the flowering rhododendrons. Austin could actually see a pair of woman's
calves and tennis shoes, jumping from side to side as
though their owner was striking a ball first forehand, then

backhand, the little white feet dancing over the red surface. "*Arrête!* Stop!" a woman yelled, and sighed a loud sigh.

Frenchwomen, Austin thought, all talked like children: in high-pitched, rapid-paced, displeasingly insistent voices, which most of the time said, "*Non, non, non, non, non,*" to something someone wanted, some likely as not innocent wish. He could hear Joséphine saying it, standing in the living room of her little apartment the only other time he'd visited there—a week ago—speaking on the phone to someone, spooling the white phone cord around her finger as she said into the receiver, "*Non, non, non, non, non, non. C'est incroyable. C'est in-croy-a-ble!*" It was terrifically annoying, though it amused him now to think of it—at a distance.

Barbara had absolutely no use for Frenchwomen and made no bones about it. "Typical Froggies," she'd remark after evenings with his French clients and their wives, and then act disgusted. That was probably what bothered him about Joséphine: that she seemed such a typical bourgeois little Frenchwoman, the kind Barbara would've disliked in a minute—intractable, preoccupied, entirely stuck in her French life, with no sense of the wider world, and possibly even ungenerous if you knew her very long (as her husband found out). Joséphine's problem, Austin thought, looking around for little Léo, was that she took everything inside her life too seriously. Her motherhood. Her husband's ludicrous book. Her boyfriend. Her bad luck. She looked at everything under a microscope, as if she were always waiting to find a mistake she could magnify big enough that she'd have no choice but to go on taking life too seriously. As if that's all adulthood was—seriousness, discipline. No fun. Life, Austin thought, had to be more lighthearted. Which was why he'd come here, why he'd cut himself loose—to enjoy life more. He admired himself for it. And because of that he didn't think he could become the savior in Joséphine's life. That would be a lifelong struggle, and a lifelong struggle wasn't what he wanted most in the world.

When he looked around again, Léo was not where he'd been, standing dreamily to the side of the older boys, watching their miniature cutters and galleons glide over the still pond surface. The older boys were there, their long tending sticks in their hands, whispering among themselves and smirking. But not Léo. It had become cooler. Light had faded from the crenellated roof line of the École Supérieure des Mines, and soon it would be dark. The man having his picture taken was walking away with the photographer. Austin had been engrossed in thought and had lost sight of little Léo, who was, he was certain, somewhere nearby.

He looked at his watch. It was six twenty-five, and Joséphine could now be home. He scanned back along the row of apartment blocks, hoping to find her window, thinking he might see her there watching him, waving at him happily, possibly with Léo at her side. But he couldn't tell which building was which. One window he could see was open and dark inside. But he couldn't be sure. In any case, Joséphine wasn't framed in it.

Austin looked all around, hoping to see the white flash of Léo's T-shirt, the careening red Cadillac. But he saw only a few couples walking along the chalky paths, and two of the older boys carrying their sailboats home to their parents' apartments. He still heard tennis balls being hit—*pockety pock*. And he felt cold and calm, which he knew to be the feeling of fear commencing, a feeling that could rapidly change to other feelings that could last a long, long time.

Léo was gone, and he wasn't sure where. "Leo," he called out, first in the American way, then "Lay-oo," in the way his mother said. *"Où êtes-vous?"* Passersby looked at him sternly, hearing the two languages together. The remaining sailboat boys glanced around and smiled. "Lay-oo!" he called out again, and knew his voice did not sound ordinary, that it might sound frightened. Everyone around him, everyone who could hear him, was French, and he couldn't precisely explain to any of them what was the matter here: that this was not his son; that the boy's mother was not here now but was probably close by; that he had let his attention stray a moment.

"Lay-oo," he called out again. *"Où êtes-vous?"* He saw nothing of the boy, not a fleck of shirt or a patch of his dark hair disappearing behind a bush. He felt cold all over again, a sudden new wave, and he shuddered because he knew he was alone. Léo—some tiny assurance opened in him to say—Léo, wherever he was, would be fine, was probably fine right now. He would be found and be happy. He would see his mother and immediately forget all about Martin Austin. Nothing bad had befallen him. But he, Martin Austin, was alone. He could not find this child, and for him only bad would come of it.

Across an expanse of grassy lawn he saw a park guardian in a dark-blue uniform emerge from the rhododendrons beyond which were the tennis courts, and Austin began running toward him. It surprised him that he was running, and halfway there quit and only half ran toward the man, who had stopped to permit himself to be approached.

"Do you speak English?" Austin said before he'd arrived. He knew his face had taken on an exaggerated appearance, because the guardian looked at him strangely, turned his head slightly, as though he preferred to see him at an angle, or as if he were hearing an odd tune and wanted to hear it better. At the corners of his mouth he seemed to smile.

"I'm sorry," Austin said, and took a breath. "You speak English, don't you?"

"A little bit, why not," the guardian said, and then he did smile. He was middle-aged and pleasant-looking, with a soft suntanned face and a small Hitler mustache. He wore a French policeman's uniform, a blue-and-gold kepi, a white shoulder braid and a white lanyard connected to his pistol. He was a man who liked parks.

"I've lost a little boy here someplace," Austin said calmly, though he remained out of breath. He put the palm of his right hand to his cheek as if his cheek were wet, and felt his skin to be cold. He turned and looked again at the concrete border of the pond, at the grass crossed by gravel paths, and then at a dense tangle of yew bushes farther on. He expected to see Léo there, precisely in the middle of this miniature landscape. Once he'd been frightened and time had gone by, and he'd sought help and strangers had regarded him with suspicion and wonder—once all these had taken place—Léo could appear and all would be returned to calm.

But there was no one. The open lawn was empty, and it was nearly dark. He could see weak interior lights from the apartment blocks beyond the park fence, see yellow automobile lights on rue Vaugirard. He remembered once hunting with his father in Illinois. He was a boy, and their dog had run away. He had known the advent of dark meant he would never see the dog again. They were far from home. The dog wouldn't find its way back. And that is what had happened.

The park guardian stood in front of Austin, smiling, staring at his face oddly, searchingly, as if he meant to adduce something—if Austin was crazy or on drugs or possibly playing a joke. The man, Austin realized, hadn't understood anything he'd said, and was simply waiting for something he would understand to begin.

But he had ruined everything now. Léo was gone. Kidnapped. Assaulted. Or merely lost in a hopelessly big city. And all his own newly won freedom, his clean slate, was in one moment squandered. He would go to jail, and he *should* go to jail. He was an awful man. A careless man. He brought mayhem and suffering to the lives of innocent, unsuspecting people who trusted him. No punishment could be too severe.

Austin looked again at the yew bushes, a long, green clump, several yards thick, the interior lost in tangled shadows. That was where Léo was, he thought with complete certainty. And he felt relief, barely controllable relief.

"I'm sorry to bother you," he said to the guardian. "*Je regrette.* I made a mistake." And he turned and ran toward the clump of yew bushes, across the open grass and the gravel promenade and careful beds in bright-yellow bloom, the excellent park. He plunged in under the low scrubby branches, where the ground was bare and raked and damp and attended to. With his head ducked he moved swiftly forward. He called Léo's name but did not see him, though he saw a movement, an indistinct fluttering of blue and gray, heard what might've been footfalls on the soft ground, and then he heard running, like a large creature hurrying in front of him among the tangled branches. He heard laughter beyond the edge of the thicket, where another grassy terrace opened—the sound of a man laughing and talking in French, out of breath and running at once. Laughing, then more talking and laughing again.

Austin moved toward where he'd seen the flutter of blue and gray—someone's clothing glimpsed in flight, he thought. There was a strong old smell of piss and human waste among the thick roots and shrubby trunks of the yew bushes. Paper and trash were strewn around in the foulness. From outside it had seemed cool and inviting here, a place to have a nap or make love.

And Léo was there. Exactly where Austin had seen the glimpse of clothing flicker through the undergrowth. He was naked, sitting on the damp dirt, his clothes strewn around him, turned inside out where they had been jerked off and thrown aside. He looked up at Austin, his eyes small and perceptive and dark, his small legs straight out before him, smudged and scratched, his chest and arms scratched. Dirt was on his cheeks. His hands were between his legs, not covering or protecting him but limp, as if they had no purpose. He was very white and very quiet. His hair was still neatly combed. Though when he saw Austin, and that it was Austin and not someone else coming bent at the waist, furious, breathing stertorously, stumbling, crashing arms-out through the rough branches and trunks and roots of that small place, he gave a shrill, hopeless cry, as though he could see what was next, and who it would be, and it terrified him even more. And his cry was all he could do to let the world know that he feared his fate.

8

In the days that followed there was to be a great deal of controversy. The police conducted a thorough and publicized search for the person or persons who had assaulted little Léo. There were no signs to conclude he had been molested, only that he'd been lured into the bushes by someone and roughed up there and frightened badly. A small story appeared in the back pages of *France-Dimanche* and said the same things, yet Austin noticed from the beginning that all the police used the word *"moleste"* when referring to the event, as though it were accurate.

The group of hippies he'd seen from Joséphine's window was generally thought to contain the offender. It was said that they lived in the park and slept in the clumps and groves of yews and ornamental boxwoods, and that some were Americans who had been in France for twenty years. But none of them, when the police brought them in to be identified, seemed to be the man who had scared Léo.

For a few hours following the incident there was suspicion among the police that Austin himself had molested Léo and had approached the guardian only as a diversion after he'd finished with the little boy—trusting that the child would never accuse him. Austin had patiently and intelligently explained that he had not molested Léo and would never do such a thing, but understood that he had to be considered until he could be exonerated—which was not before midnight, when Joséphine entered the police station and stated that Léo had told her Austin was not the man who had scared him and taken his clothes off, that it had been someone else, a man who spoke French, a man in blue and possibly gray clothing with long hair and a beard.

When she had told this story and Austin had been allowed to leave the stale, windowless police room where he'd been made to remain until matters could be determined with certainty, he'd walked beside Joséphine out into the narrow street, lit yellow through the tall wire-mesh windows of the *gendarmerie*. The street was guarded by a number of young policemen wearing flak jackets and carrying short machine pistols on shoulder slings. They calmly watched Austin and Joséphine as they stopped at the curb to say goodbye.

"I'm completely to blame for this," Austin said. "I can't tell you how sorry I am. There aren't any words good enough, I guess."

"You *are* to blame," Joséphine said and looked at him in the face, intently. After a moment she said, "It is not a game. You know? Maybe to you it is a game."

"No, it's really not," Austin said abjectly, standing in the cool night air in sight of all the policemen. "I guess I had a lot of plans."

"Plans to what?" Joséphine said. She had on the black crepe skirt she'd worn the day he'd met her, barely more than a week ago. She looked appealing again. "Not for me! You don't have plans for me. I don't want you. I don't want any man anymore." She shook her head and crossed her arms tightly and looked away, her dark eyes shining in the night. She was very, very angry. Possibly, he thought, she was even angry at herself. "You are a fool," she said, and she spat accidentally when she said it. "I hate you. You don't know anything. You don't know who you are." She looked at him bitterly. "Who are you?" she said. "Who do you think you are? You're nothing."

"I understand," Austin said. "I'm sorry. I'm sorry about all of this. I'll make sure you don't have to see me again."

Joséphine smiled at him, a cruel, confident smile. "I don't care," she said and raised her shoulder in the way Austin didn't like, the way Frenchwomen did when they wanted to certify as true something that might not be. "I don't care what happens to you. You are dead. I don't see you."

She turned and began walking away down the sidewalk along the side of the *gendarmerie* and in front of the young policemen, who looked at her indifferently. They looked back at Austin, standing in the light by himself, where he felt he should stay until she had gone out of sight. One of the policemen said something to his colleague beside him, and that man whistled a single long note into the night. Then they turned and faced the other way.

AUSTIN HAD a fear in the days to come, almost a defeating fear that deprived him of sleep in his small, risqué apartment above the rue Bonaparte. It was a fear that Barbara would die soon, followed then by a feeling that she *had* died, which was succeeded by a despair of something important in his life having been lost, exterminated by his own doing but also by fate. What *was* that something? he wondered, awake in the middle of the night. It wasn't Barbara herself. Barbara was alive and on the earth, and able to be reunited with if he wanted to try and if she did. And it wasn't his innocence. That had been dispensed with long before. But he *had* lost something, and whatever it was, Barbara seemed associated. And he felt if he could specify it, possibly he could begin to pull things together, see more clearly, even speak to her again, and, in a sense, repatriate himself.

Not to know what that something was, though, meant that he was out of control, perhaps meant something worse about him. So that he began to think of his life, in those succeeding days, almost entirely in terms of what was wrong with him, of his problem, his failure—in particular his failure as a husband, but also in terms of his unhappiness, his predicament, his ruin, which he wanted to repair.

He recognized again and even more plainly that his entire destination, everything he'd ever done or presumed or thought, had been directed toward Barbara, that everything good was there. And it was there he would need eventually to go.

Behind Joséphine, of course, was nothing—no fabric or mystery, no secrets, nothing he had curiosity for now. She had seemed to be a compelling woman; not a great object of sexuality, not a source of wit—but a force he'd been briefly moved by in expectation that he could move her nearer to him. He remembered kissing her in the car, her soft face and the great swelling moment of wondrous feeling, the great thrill. And her voice saying, *"Non, non, non, non, non,"* softly. That was what Bernard could never get over losing, the force that had driven him to hate her, even humiliate her.

For his part he admired her, and mostly for the way she'd dealt with him. Proportionately. Intelligently. She had felt a greater sense of responsibility than he had; a greater apprehension of life's importance, its weight and permanence. To him, it *had* all seemed less important, less permanent, and he could never even aspire to her sense of life—a European sense. As Barbara had said, he took himself for granted; though unlike what Joséphine had said, he knew himself quite well. In the end, Joséphine took herself for granted, too. They were, of course, very different and could never have been very happy together.

Though he wondered again in his dreamy moments after the fear of Barbara's dying had risen off and before he drifted to sleep, wondered what was ever possible between human beings. How could you regulate life, do little harm and still be attached to others? And in that context, he wondered if being *fixed* could be a misunderstanding, and, as Barbara had said when he'd seen her the last time and she had been so angry at him, if he had changed slightly, somehow altered the important linkages that guaranteed his happiness and become detached, unreachable. Could you *become* that? Was it something you controlled, or a matter of your character, or a change to which you were only a victim? He wasn't sure. He wasn't sure about that at all. It was a subject he knew he would have to sleep on many, many nights.

Jealous

IN THE LAST DAYS that I lived with my father in his house below the Teton River, he read to me. Seated at the kitchen table after work or on the cold mornings when I dressed in front of him by the stove, he read out loud to me from the Havre or the Conrad newspapers or from magazines— *Life*s or *Geographic*s—or from old schoolbooks that had been bound in twine and abandoned in the back rooms by some previous, unknown family who'd left behind the things they couldn't take.

We were alone there. These were the months following my mother's first departure, and we had lived out from Dutton since my school year began. My mother had left the summer before, at the end of a long period of troubles between them, and almost immediately after that my father quit his job in Great Falls and moved us up to Dutton, where he took a new job, working on farm machinery. He had always liked a drink, and so had my mother, and they had had friends who drank. But in Dutton he quit drinking altogether, quit having any whiskey around the house. He worked long days in town, and trained his bird dogs in the evening, and I went to high school. And that was what life was like.

It may have been, of course, that he was expecting some important event to take place, some piece of new news to suddenly reach him. Possibly he was waiting, as the saying goes, for lightning to strike, and what he wanted was to be in the right place and in the right frame of mind to make a decision when it happened. And it may have been that he read to me as a way of saying, "We don't know all there is to know. There's more order in life than seems to be. We have to pay attention." That is all another way of saying that he was at a loss. Though my father had never been a man who stood by and watched things get the better of him. He was a man who acted, a man who cared to do the right thing. And I know that even on the day these events took place he was aware that a moment to act may have come. None of it is anything I blame him for.

ON THE DAY before Thanksgiving, it rained an hour before daylight, when I was waking up, then rained through the afternoon, when the temperature fell and snow began and the front of the mountains disappeared into a bluish fog, so that it was no longer possible to see the grain elevators in Dutton, ten miles away.

My father and I were waiting for my mother's sister to arrive to take me to the train in Shelby. I was going to Seattle to visit my mother, and my aunt was going with me. I was seventeen years old then. It was 1975, and I had never ridden on a train before.

My father had come home early, taken a bath, dressed in a clean shirt and slacks, then sat down at the kitchen table with a stack of *Newsweeks* from the town library. I was already dressed. My bag was packed, and I was standing at the kitchen window watching for my aunt's car.

"Are you familiar with Patrice Lumumba?" my father said after reading to himself for a while. He was a tall, bony-chested man with thick black hair and thick hands and arms, and the table seemed small in front of him.

"Was she a singer?" I said.

"He," my father said, looking out the lower lenses of his glasses as if he were trying to read small print. "He was the African Negro Eisenhower wanted to poison in 1960. Only Ike missed his big chance. His other enemies blew him up first. We all thought it was mysterious back then, of course, but I guess it wasn't that mysterious." He took his glasses off and rubbed them on his shirt cuff. One of the setters barked out in the pen. I watched it come to the fence by the corner of the granary, sniff through the wires, then walk back in the misting snow to its house, where its sister was in the doorway. "The Republicans always have secrets," my father said, holding his glasses up and looking through them. "A great deal goes on before you wake up to life."

"I guess so," I said.

"But you can't change it," he said, "so don't let it eat at you."

Through the window I saw my aunt's big pink Cadillac appear suddenly up on the horizon road, rushing ahead of its snow cloud, still a mile out.

"What're you going to tell your mother about living out here out-of-sight-of-land all this fall?" my father said. "That there's an atmosphere of mystery on the open prairie?" He looked up and smiled at me. "That I've been neglecting your education?"

"I hadn't thought about it very much yet," I said.

"Well, think about it. You'll have time on the train if your aunt will leave you alone." He looked back at the *Newsweek* and laid his glasses on the table.

I had hoped to say something to my father before my aunt arrived, something about my mother, that I was happy I was going to get to see her. We had not talked about her very much.

"What do you think about Mother?" I said.

"With respect to what?"

"Do you think she'll come back out here after Thanksgiving?"

He drummed his fingers on the metal tabletop, then turned and looked at the clock on the stove. "Do you want to ask her about it?"

"No, sir," I said.

"Well. You can. Then you can tell me." He looked at the window as though he was checking the weather. One of the dogs barked again, and then the other one barked. Sometimes a coyote came into the yard out of the wheat fields and set them off. "Eventually the suspense falls out of the story," he said. He closed the magazine and folded his hands on top of it. "Who's your best friend now? I'm just curious."

"Just my ones in the Falls, still," I said.

"Who's your best one in Dutton?"

"I don't have one now," I said.

My father put his glasses back on. "That's too bad. It's your choice, of course."

"I know it," I said, because I had already considered that and decided I didn't have time to get to know anybody there.

I watched my aunt's car turn onto our road and the pale beams of her headlights burn through the snowy air.

A mile farther down the road, a blue mobile home sat out in the fields, unprotected from the wind. The farmer in town who owned our house owned it, too, and rented it to the civics teacher at the high school. Joyce Jensen was her name. She was in her twenties, and was a heavyset woman with strawberry-colored hair, and my father had slept some nights down there in the last month. "Yoyce Yensen," he called her, and always laughed. I could see a new car parked in front of her trailer, a red one beside her dark one.

"What do you see out there?" my father said. "Have you caught sight of your aunt Doris?"

"She's got her lights on," I said.

"Well," my father said, "then you're gone, you just haven't left yet." He reached in his shirt pocket and took out a little fold of bills with a rubber band around it. "When you get to Shelby, buy your mother a bijou," he said. "She won't expect it. It'll make her happy." He handed the money up to me, then stood to watch my aunt drive to the house. "There's a moment in the day when you miss having a drink," he said. He put his hand on my shoulder, and I could smell soap on his skin. "That's the old life. We're on to the new life now. The lucky few."

MY AUNT honked her horn as she came past the caragana row into the house lot. She drove an Eldorado Cadillac, a '69, faded pink with a white vinyl top. Her wipers were on, and the windows were fogged. She had parked that car in front of our house in Great Falls, and I had given it a good inspection then.

"Let me step out and tell your aunt Doris a joke," my father said. "You go lock the shutters on the pigeons. I'll forget about them tonight, and snow'll get in. I won't be but a minute." My aunt's window came down as my father started to the door. I could see her looking at our little farmhouse as if she thought it was abandoned.

My aunt Doris was a pretty woman and had a reputation for being wild, which my mother didn't have, or so my father had told me. She was my mother's younger sister, and was thirty-six and blond and thin, with soft, pale arms you could see her veins in. She wore glasses, and the one time I had seen her without them, a morning when I woke up and she was in the house, she looked like a girl to me, somebody younger than I was. I knew that my father liked her, and that they'd had something between them in Great Falls after my mother left, even though Doris was married to a Gros Ventre Indian man, who wasn't in the picture anymore. Twice she'd driven up and cooked dinner for us, and twice my father had gone down to the Falls to visit her, and there were a few times when they talked on the phone until late at night. But I thought it was finished between them, whatever it was. My father talked about Doris in a way that made it seem like some tragedy might've happened to her—he didn't know what—and I really thought he only liked her because she looked like my mother.

"There's something winning about Doris, you know," he said once, "something your mother could use." The day he said that, we were working dogs east of the house and had stopped to watch them cast into the wheat stubble. It was gold all the way down to the river, which was shining, and the sky above the mountains was as blue as I had ever seen blue.

"What's winning about her?" I said.

"Oh, she's sympathetic," he said. "One of these days that might seem important to you." And then we quit talking about it, though it was already important to me to be sympathetic, and I thought my mother was, and knew he thought so too.

My father walked out onto the gravel, still in his shirtsleeves. I saw Doris stick her arm out the window and wag her hand back and forth to the pace of my father's walking. I saw her smile and begin to say something, but I couldn't hear what it was.

I put on my wool jacket and took my bag and went out the back door into the yard toward the pigeon coop. It was four o'clock in the afternoon, and the sun—just a white light behind white clouds—was above the mountain peaks beyond Choteau, and it was already colder than it had been when I came out on the school bus at noon. The yard around the house had old farm implements sitting useless, except for the tank truck we hauled our water in, and snow was beginning to collect on their rusted surfaces and in the grass. I could see my father bent over, leaning on his elbows against the windowsill of Doris's Cadillac. She had her hand on his arm and was laughing at something. And I must've stopped, because Doris quit laughing and looked at me, halfway out to the pigeon house. She blinked the lights on the Cadillac, and I went on. It occurred to me that they might go inside.

The pigeon pen was an old chicken coop my father had boarded up the sides of to keep foxes and coyotes out. He kept pigeons to train his setters, and he had an idea he could make money training bird dogs if word got out he was good at it, which he was. There were plenty of birds in that part of Montana—pheasants and partridge and grouse—and he thought he'd have time for all that when the harvest was over. He and I would drive out into the cut fields in the evening with two dogs, and four pigeons stuck head-down in our coat pockets. My father would lead a dog out two hundred yards on a check cord, and I would tuck a pigeon's head under its wing and shake it and blow on it, then stash it in a wheat-straw tuft, where it would stay, confused, until the dog found it by its scent and pointed. Then my father or I would walk up and kick the bird flying, a red ribbon and a stick tied to its leg so it wouldn't fly far.

There was never any shooting involved. My father didn't like to shoot birds. There were not enough of them left, he said—what other people did was their business. But he liked to work dogs and see them point and for the birds to fly. He had grown up in western Minnesota—he and Mother both—and he liked to be out on the plains.

I heard the birds thumping inside their coop, cooing and fluttering. I peeped through the chicken wire and could see them, thirty or forty, gray and stubby and thick-chested, their smell thinner because of the cold. My father caught them in barns, using his landing net, standing in the middle of the barn floor with the door shut in the half-dark, swinging his net on a cord as the birds, excited by the motion, flew from rafter to rafter. He snared them one or two or three at a time and handed them out to me to put in a potato sack. I never knew about things like this before I lived alone with him. We had never done that. But he liked it, and I would stand outside in the daylight, peeking through the cracks in the boards, watching the pigeons, their wings flashing in the light that entered through the other walls, and my father making a humming noise in his throat—*hmmm, hmmm, hmmm,* a sound I've heard prizefighters make—as his net went around and the pigeons fluttered into the webbing.

I let the shutters down over the wire coops and latched them. Then I stood with my suitcase and watched my father. He was still leaning on Doris's car in the snow. She still had her hand on his wrist. As I watched, she put her cheek against his hand, and my father stood up straight and looked toward the road in front of the house beyond the caraganas. I thought he looked over Doris's car in the direction of Joyce Jensen's trailer. He said something into the window and pulled his hands back and stuck them in his pockets. Then he looked at me and waved his arm in a wide way for me to come on.

"THAT'LL CURL your hair, I'll tell you what," I heard Doris say when I got close to the car.

"Your aunt Doris is worried about getting stuck in the snow in her limo," my father said. He stood back a couple of feet from the car and was smiling. Snow was in his hair. "Get her to tell you her joke about Japanese cars. That'll amuse you."

Doris looked at my father as if he'd surprised her. "We'll wait a couple of years on that," she said. "I want your dad to ride up to Shelby with us tonight, Larry," she said through the window. "He claims he has other plans he doesn't care to discuss. I'm sure you'll explain it all to me."

"I'd have a hard time getting home tonight," my father said, still smiling. "I'd get in some kind of trouble."

It was now snowing harder. My father's arms looked cold, and I was cold myself and eager for Doris and me to get going. I went around and put my bag in the backseat and climbed in front, where the heater was on and it was warm and smelled sweet and the radio was turned on low. If my father had plans, he hadn't told me about them, though I thought he would probably go down to visit Joyce Jensen.

"You only get so many of these invitations, then people quit asking," Doris said. She was smiling, too, but I knew she wanted him to come with us. She patted me on the knee. "How're you, honey bunch?" she said. "Did you take a little happy pill today? I hope so."

"I just took one," I said. I could smell her perfume. She had on bright-red earrings and a brown wool coat, under which I could see the hem of a red wool dress. She always wore a lot of red. My father took a few steps farther back from the car.

"You ought to put a sign on your mailbox, Donny," Doris said out her window. " 'N.H.Y.'—Nothing's Happened Yet. That'd be the truth."

"We're moving cautiously," my father said. He leaned down without touching the car and looked in at me. "Explain to your aunt about the atmosphere of mystery out here on the Great Plains." He was smiling. "She'll get a kick out of that." Doris pulled the car down into gear. "Say Happy Thanksgiving to my old friends in Seattle," my father said, looking in at me then, and he had an odd expression, standing in the snow by himself, as if he thought what he'd just said was silly but he hadn't meant it to be.

Doris started the window up as she turned the wheel. "You think you can't make life better, Donny, but you can," she said. "You two've been out here too many nights alone. It's making you squirrelly."

"We're working on that, too," my father said, and he shouted it for some reason. I didn't know what he meant, but what I wished then was that we could get the hell out of there and get on the road to where we were going.

DORIS DECIDED to have a drink before we got to the interstate. She had a little bottle of schnapps under the windshield visor and told me to pour some into a Styrofoam cup from a stack on the backseat floor. On the wet floor with the cups was a cardboard FOR SALE sign, a drinking glass, a padded snow glove, a hairbrush, a bunch of postcards—one showing a bear dancing on a beach ball—and some snapshots of Doris sitting at a desk in an office, wearing a short skirt and smiling up at the camera. They'd been taken at the police department in Great Falls, where Doris worked. Part of a man's sleeve with sergeant's stripes on it was visible in the corner of one of the pictures.

"Those are my glamorous mug shots," Doris said, holding her schnapps bottle in the hand she held the steering wheel with, "in case I forget who I am—or was—or in case somebody ever found me dead and wondered. I wrote my name on the backs."

I turned over one of the photographs, and Doris's name was written in ink that had faded. There were other things on the floor—a copy of a magazine called *World Conflict,* and two or three paperback books with their covers torn off. I took a cup from the stack and gave it to her. "Who do you think'll find you?" I said.

We were going up onto the interstate, and I was pouring schnapps in her cup. The little town of Dutton, where I had been in school since September, sat just on the other side of the highway. Ten streets of houses, two bars, a Sons of Norway, three churches, a grocery, a library, three elevators, and a VFW with an old Sabre jet from Korea mounted as if it were taking off into the snowy sky. All around everywhere else was plow ground being covered in snow.

"Never can tell who'll find you," Doris said, watching her rearview mirror as we got out onto the highway. "I don't really like Montana," she said, "and I particularly hate the roads. There's only one way to get anywhere. It's better seen from an airplane." She straightened her arms toward the steering wheel as if she were taking off in a jet herself. We picked up speed and shot slush behind us. A bead of water entered the windshield through a crack at the top, then froze before it could drip in. "So. What's it about this atmosphere of mystery?"

"He was just reading to me out of a magazine," I said. "He made it up."

"I see." She had a sip of schnapps. "And do you think you understand what the trouble is between your mom and your dad?"

"They don't get along enough right now," I said. "My mother decided to go to school." That had been what my mother told me when she left. She was in school in Seattle, learning how to make out income tax forms. She'd be finished by Christmas.

"They know too much about each other," Doris said. "They have to figure out what the hell difference that makes. Sometimes it's good, but not always."

"Isn't that supposed to happen?" I said.

"Certainly is," Doris said and looked up in the mirror again. There were no other cars on the highway, only big tractor-trailers going north, running to get someplace by Thanksgiving. "When I was living with Benny as man and wife, he had many, many things I never understood inside *his* head. Indian things. Spirits. He believed they came to our house. He believed you had to give your valuables away—or gamble them away, in his particular case. He told me once that he wanted to be buried on a wood platform on a high hill. He believed in all that Indian medicine—which was fine, and I mean it. It was." Doris rubbed her nose with the heel of her hand, then just stared at the highway, where white mist was collecting like fog.

"What did you say about it?" I said, and looked at her.

"About the wood platform?" she said. "I said, 'Fine, a wood platform's all right with me. But don't expect me to build it or get you up there, because I'm a Seventh-Day Adventist and we don't believe in platforms.' "

"What did Benny say?" I had only met Benny once, and remembered him as a big, quiet man with black-rimmed glasses who smelled like cigarettes.

"He laughed. He was a Lutheran, of course. Converted by missionaries in Canada or North Dakota someplace. I forget. It might've all been a joke. But he was a tribal member. He was that. Spoke the Indian tongue."

"Where is he?" I said.

"That's the sixty-four-dollar question." Doris reached forward and turned down the heater. "Shaunavon, Saskatchewan, is my guess, where Thanksgiving comes later or earlier, one or the other. I still wear a wedding ring." She held up her ring finger. "But I was on about Don and Jan knowing each other so well. I never had that problem with Benny, and we're still married. In a sense we are, anyway."

"In what sense?" I said, and I smiled at her because something in that seemed funny. I could remember her and my father talking in the living room until late, and then everything getting quiet and finally the sound of lamps being clicked off.

"In a distant sense, Mr. Genius," Doris said, "and in the sense that if he comes back we'd start back right where we left off. Or try to. Though if he's intending to stay gone, I wish we could get divorced so I could begin to pick up the pieces." She laughed. "That wouldn't take a lifetime."

"What do you think'll happen?" I asked, referring to my father and mother. I'd never asked anybody but my father about that before, and when I'd asked him the first time, he said my mother was going to come back—this was before we left Great Falls. Though one time in the car, on the ride home from a baseball game, he'd suddenly said, "Love's just what two people decide to do, Larry. It's not a religion." He must've been thinking about it.

"What do *I* think's going to happen?" Doris said. She adjusted her glasses upwards on her nose and took a deep breath, as though this was not an easy question. "It depends on timing and the situation of third parties," she said very seriously. "If your mom, for instance, has a young pretty boyfriend out in Seattle, or if your dad has a girl-friend back there where Jesus left his ankle shoes, then that's a problem. But if they can hold out long enough to get lonely, then they'll probably do fine—though they don't want to hold out *too* long. This is my opinion, of course, based on nothing." Doris looked over at me and reached and adjusted the collar of my coat, which was turned up. "How old are you?" she said. "I should proba-bly know that kind of thing."

"Seventeen," I said, thinking about my mother's hav-ing a pretty boyfriend in Seattle. I'd thought about it some in the months she'd been gone and decided she didn't have one.

"Then you've got your whole life in front of you for worrying," Doris said. "Don't start now. They ought to teach that in school instead of history. Worry management. Would you, by the way, like to know something about yourself?"

"What?" I said.

She didn't look at me, just kept driving. "You smell like wheat!" Doris said and laughed. "Ever since you got in this car it's smelled like a silo in here. Won't Don let you sleep in the house with him?"

And I was shocked to hear that, because I didn't like living out on the farm or in that house and I knew already I might smell that way, because I could smell it in all the rooms and in my father's clothes. And I felt angry, angry at *him,* though I didn't want to let Doris know. "They stored grain in our house before we moved in," I said, and didn't want to say anything else.

"You're a real hick," she said. "You better check your shoes." She laughed again.

"We're just out there for this year," I said. And I felt even angrier about the whole subject. Out the clouded window, the first dark rows of tilled winter wheat began just beyond the road verge and the fence line—snow crusting between the new rows. What I wanted to do, I thought then, was stay in Seattle with my mother and start in at a new school after Christmas even if it meant beginning the year over. I wanted to get out of Montana, where we didn't have a TV and had to haul our water and where the coyotes woke you up howling and my father and I had nobody to talk to but each other. I was missing something, I thought, an important opportunity. And later, when I would try to explain to someone how it was, that I had not been a farm boy but had just led life like that for a while, nobody'd believe me. And after that it would always be impossible to explain how things really were.

"I was depressed, myself, for a long time after Benny left," Doris said. "Do you know what that means—to be depressed?"

"No," I said gloomily.

She reached up and put her finger on the hole in the windshield where water had come in and frozen. She looked at the tip of her finger, then looked at me and smiled. "You're way too young for turmoil," she said, "because I'm too young for it myself." She licked her finger. "Tell me about your dad. Has he got a girlfriend out there in Siberia? I'll bet he has. Some little diamond in the rough."

"He does," I said, and I didn't care if she told my mother. "There's a teacher down the road from us."

"Well, good for him," Doris said, though she didn't smile about it. "What's her name?"

"Joyce."

"That's a cute name. I guess your mother doesn't know about this."

"I don't know if she does."

"I'm sure she doesn't, not that it matters," Doris said. I wondered if my father was down at Joyce Jensen's trailer right then. I remembered the red car sitting in front.

Doris took her bottle of schnapps and handed it and her cup to me. "I'd have another, please."

I thought maybe she was going to get drunk because I'd told her my dad had a girlfriend. It was nearly dark and snow was building up and it was colder, and even though we were close to Shelby it was still three hours until the train. And I had a fear that we'd miss it, that Doris would get drunk and go to sleep someplace where I couldn't wake her up and I'd end up back at home that night, going in the front door after midnight and finding no one there.

I poured less than I'd poured before. The schnapps was gluey on my fingers and tasted like root beer. I had been in bars with my father and seen that schnapps before, but I hadn't actually seen someone drink it.

"You know," Doris said, and she sounded indignant about something, "you certainly understand you don't *belong* to your dad, don't you? Nobody belongs to anybody. Some people think they do, but that's ridiculous."

"I know that," I said. "I'll be on my own when the school year's over."

"You're on your own right now. School doesn't determine that," Doris said. "And I'm not your mother. You know that, too, don't you? I'm your aunt. A technicality. It doesn't matter to me what you do. You can move right back to Great Falls tomorrow if you want to. You can live with me. That'd be an innovation." Doris cut her eyes at me, still indignant. I thought she might invite me to have a drink of schnapps, but I didn't want it. I remembered a little tattoo she had on her shoulder, a blue-and-red butterfly I'd seen the summer before, when she was around the house and spending time with my father. "You're like a bird in a glass cage, aren't you?"

"I won't stay there much longer," I said.

"We'll see about that," Doris said, staring out into the snowflakes. "Did you buy your mother a nice present?"

"I'm going to," I said.

"Did your dad give you a lot of money, now that he's collecting a big check?"

"I had some already," I lied, thinking that nice stores would probably be closed in Shelby. I pictured the main street, where I'd only been once, with my father, when my mother had taken the train back from the Cities, and all I could remember was a row of bar and motel signs with

Route 2 running through the town toward Havre. "I worked at the elevator in the harvest," I said.

"Is Don still off the drink?"

"Yes, he is," I said.

"And you two get along just great?"

"Yes," I said, "we do."

"Well, that's wonderful," she said. Out in the snow and fog haze I could see faint yellow lights all in a string at the bottom of a hill. It was Shelby. "I used to think your father'd married the wrong sister, since we all met at the same time. You know? I thought he was too good for Jan. But I don't think so now. She and I have gotten a lot closer than we used to be since she's been out in Seattle. We talk on the phone about things." Doris let her window down and poured out the schnapps she had left. It hit the back window and froze. "She's pretty wonderful, did you know that? Did you know your mother was wonderful?"

"I knew that," I said. "What do you think about Dad?"

"He's fine," Doris said. "That's how I feel about him. I don't particularly trust him. He's not equipped to care for things very much—he's like a cat in that way. But he's fine. You can't go back on your important decisions."

"Are you sorry you didn't marry him?" I said. I thought she was wrong about my father, of course. He cared about things as much as anybody did, and more than Doris did, I felt sure.

"Put it like this," Doris said, and she smiled at me in a sweet way, a way that could make you like her. "If I had married him, then we wouldn't have you here, would we? Everything'd be different." She tapped me on the knee. "So there's good to everything. That's a belief Seventh-Day Adventists hold." She scratched her fingernails on my knee and smiled at me again, and we drove on into town, where it was snowing still, and almost dark except for lights down the main street.

CHRISTMAS DECORATIONS were already up in Shelby, strings of red and green and white lights hung across the three intersections, and little Christmas trees on top of the traffic lights. Plenty of cars and trucks were on the streets in the snow, and all the stores looked open. We drove past a big lighted Albertson's, where the parking lot was full of vehicles and people carrying packages. I saw a drugstore and a card shop and a western-wear on the main street, all with their lights on and customers moving around the aisles inside.

"Something's physically odd about Shelby, don't you think?" Doris said, driving slowly along and looking out at the business signs and Thanksgiving cutouts in the store windows. "It has a foreignness. It just seems pointless somehow up here. Maybe it's being so close to Canada. I don't know."

"Maybe I can get out and go buy something now," I said. I'd seen a Redwing store and thought about buying my mother a pair of shoes, though I didn't know her size. I remembered some green high heels I'd seen her wear, and it surprised me that I didn't remember more than that.

"You want to eat Chinese food in town, or dine in the dining car?" Doris said.

"I'd rather eat on the train," I said, because I wanted to get out of the car.

"I want you to enjoy yourself when you're under my protection."

"I'm enjoying myself," I said. We were stopped at a light, and I turned and looked back. I wanted to get back to the card store before it got too far away.

"Can you find the train station by yourself?" Doris glanced at the traffic in the rearview mirror.

"I'll ask somebody," I said, and opened the door and slid out onto the snowy pavement.

"Don't ask an Indian," Doris said loudly. "They lie like snakes. Ask a Swede. They don't know what a lie is. That's why they make the good husbands."

"I will," I said, and closed the car door while she was talking.

People were on the sidewalk and going in and out of stores. There were plenty of cars and noises for a small town, although the snow had softened everything. It was like a Saturday night in Great Falls, and I walked in a hurry down the block in the direction we'd just come from. For some reason, I didn't see the card shop where I thought it would be and didn't see the western-wear shop, though there was a Chinese restaurant and a bar, and then the drugstore, where I went in to look.

The air was warm and smelled like Halloween candy inside. A lot of customers were in the store, and I walked down the three aisles, looking for something my mother might like to receive from me and trying to think of what I knew she liked. There was a section that had pink and blue boxes of candy, and a wall that had perfume, and a long row of cards with Thanksgiving messages. I went around the center section twice, then looked at the back of the store, where the pharmacist was and where there were footbaths and sickroom articles. I thought about something for her hair—shampoo or hair spray, but I knew she bought those for herself. Then I saw there was a glass dis-

play of watches with mirrored shelves you rotated by pushing a silver button at the bottom. The watches were all
around thirty dollars, and what my father had given me
was fifty, and I thought a watch would be better than perfume because my mother wouldn't use it up, and I liked
the way the watches looked revolving behind the glass, and
I was relieved to have almost decided so fast. My mother
had a watch, I remembered, but it had been broken since
sometime in the spring.

I walked around the store one more time to look at anything I'd missed or to find something else I wanted, but I
didn't see anything but magazines and books. Some boys
my age, wearing their maroon-and-gold Shelby jackets,
were standing looking at magazines and talking to two
girls. They all looked at me when I went by but didn't say
anything, though I knew I wouldn't have played football
against them in Great Falls, because Shelby was too small.
My own football jacket was at home in a back room in a
box, and wouldn't have been warm enough for that night.
The girls said something when I had gone by, though none
of them seemed to register seeing me.

I passed a section with ladies' bedroom slippers in clear
plastic cases. Pink and yellow and red. They were ten dollars, and one size fit all. But they looked cheap to me. They
looked like something Doris would put on. And I went
back down to the watch case and pressed the button until I
saw one come by that was gold and thin and fine-appearing,
with a small face and Roman numerals, which I thought
my mother would like. I bought it from a saleslady and had
her wrap it in white tissue paper. I paid for it from the bills
my father had given me, and put it in my coat pocket and
felt that I'd done the right thing in buying a watch. My
father would've approved of it, would've thought I had

good instinct and had bought a watch for a good price. Then I walked back outside onto the cold sidewalk to begin looking for the train depot.

I remembered from the time I'd been in Shelby with my parents that the train station was behind the main street, in an older part of town, where there were bars they'd visited. I wasn't sure where this was, but I crossed Main and went between two stores, down an alley away from the Christmas lights and traffic and motel signs, and walked out into a gravel back street, beyond which was the little switchyard and the depot itself on the far side, its windows lit yellow. Down the rails to the right I could see a row of grain gondolas and a moving engine light and, farther on, a car crossing the double tracks. The yard was dark, and it was colder and still snowing. I could hear the switch engine shunting cars, and as I stepped on the ties I looked both ways, east and west, and could see the rails shining out away from me toward where yellow caution lights and, farther on, red lights burned.

The station waiting room was warmer than the drugstore, and there were only a couple of people sitting in the rows of wood benches, though several suitcases were against the wall, and two people were waiting to buy tickets. Doris wasn't in sight. I thought she might be in the bathroom, at the back by the telephone, and I stood by the bags and waited, though I didn't see my suitcase or hers. So that after the other people had finished buying tickets, I decided she wasn't there and walked to the ticket window and asked the lady about her.

"Doris is looking for you, hon," the lady said, and smiled from behind the metal window. "She bought your tickets and told me to tell you she was in the Oil City.

That's across the street back that way." She pointed toward the rear door of the building. She was an older woman with short, blond hair. She had on a red jacket and a gold name tag that said *Betty.* "Is Doris your mom?" she asked, and began counting out dollar bills in a pile.

"No," I said. "She's my aunt. I live in Dutton." And then I said, "Is the train going to be on time?"

"Yes, indeed," she said, still counting out bills. "The train's always on time. Your aunt'll get you on it, don't worry." She smiled at me again. "Dutton rhymes with Nuttin'. I been there before."

Outside on the concrete platform, I saw Doris's Cadillac in the little gravel lot and, across the street, a dark row of small older buildings that looked like they'd been stores once but were empty now except for three that were bars. They were bars my mother and father had gone into the time I'd been here. At the end of the block a street began, with regular-looking houses on it, and I could see where lights were on in homes and cars were in the driveways, the snow accumulating in the yards. Beyond the corner, a fenced tennis court was barely visible in the dark.

The bars looked closed, though all three had small glass windows with lighted red bar signs and a couple of cars parked outside. When I came across the street I saw that the Oil City was the last one before the empty stores. A cab was stopped in front with its motor running, its driver sitting in the dim light reading a newspaper.

I hadn't been in too many bars, mostly just in Great Falls, when my father was drinking. But I didn't mind going in this one, because I thought I'd been in it once before. My father said a bar wasn't a place anybody ever wanted to go but was just a place you ended up. Though there was something about them I liked, a sense of something expected that stayed alive inside them even if nothing ever happened there at all.

INSIDE THE OIL CITY it was mostly dark and music was playing and the air smelled sweet and thick. Doris was sitting at the bar, talking to a man beside her, a small man wearing a white plastic hard hat and a canvas work suit and with a ponytail partway down his back. Drinks were in front of them, and the man's work gloves and some dollar bills were on the bar. He and Doris were talking and looking at each other straight in the eyes. I thought the man looked like an Indian, because of his hair and because there were two or three other Indians in the bar, which was a long, dark, almost empty room with two poker machines, a booth, and a dimly lit jukebox by itself against the wall. Chairs were scattered around, and it was cold, as if there wasn't any heat working.

Doris looked in my direction but didn't see me, because she turned back to the Indian in the hard hat and picked up her drink and took a sip. "That's entirely different," she said loudly. "Caring and minding are entirely different concepts to me. I can care and not mind, and also mind and not care. So fuck you, they're not the same." She looked toward me again, and she did see me. She was drunk, I knew that. I'd seen her drunk before. "You could be a private dick the way you come sneaking up," she said, and glanced at the man beside her. "You just missed the Shelby police on a sweep through here. They said they were looking for you." Doris smiled a big smile, then reached out, took my hand, and pulled me close to her. "The two of us were just discussing absolute values. This is

Mr. Barney Bordeaux. We've only been informally intro-duced. He's in the wine-tasting business. And he's just told me a terrible story about his wife being robbed at gunpoint right here in Shelby, sad to say, and all her money and rings stolen. So he favors honesty as an absolute value under the circumstances."

Barney frowned at her as if what she'd just said was stu-pid. He had narrow, dark eyes and a puffy dark Indian face under his white hard hat, which had a green Burlington Northern insignia on the front. "What's this cluck want?" he said, and squinted at me. One of his teeth in front was gone, and he looked like he'd been drinking a long time. He was small and thin and sickly, and had a little mustache at the corners of his mouth that made him look Chinese. Though he also looked like he could've been handsome at one time but had had something bad happen to him.

"This is my sister's child—Lawrence," Doris said, let-ting go of my hand and putting hers on Barney's arm as if she wanted him to stay there. "We're going to Seattle on the train tonight."

"You forgot to mention that," Barney said in an un-friendly way.

Doris looked at me and smiled. "Barney just got out of Fort Harrison. So he's celebrating. He hasn't said what he was ill with yet."

"I'm not ill with anything," Barney said. He turned straight and looked at himself in the mirror behind the back bar. "I can't see where this is taking me," I heard him say to himself.

"It's not taking you anywhere," Doris said. Fort Harri-son was the government hospital in Montana. My father had told me crazy Indians and veterans went there and saw doctors free of charge. "I had just said," Doris went on, "that loyalty was more important than honesty, if honesty meant always having to tell only the strict truth, since there're always different kinds of truth." She had taken her car coat off and piled it on the stool beside her. Her red wool dress was up above her knees. Her purse was on the bar beside her keys and the dollar bills.

Barney suddenly turned and put his hand right on Doris's knee where her legs were crossed. He smiled and he looked right at me. "You're in trouble when people younger than you are seem smart," he said, and his smile widened so his missing tooth was evident. I could smell sweat on him, and wine. He laughed out loud then and turned back to the bar.

"Barney's starring in his own movie," Doris said.

"Where's my suitcase?" I asked, because all at once I thought about it and couldn't see it anywhere. I wanted to put my mother's watch in it.

"Oh, let's see," Doris said, giving Barney a look to make sure he was paying attention. "I gave that away. A poor penniless colored man came through who'd lost his suitcase and I gave him yours." She picked up her car keys off the bar and dangled them without even looking at me. Then she reached in her purse, brought out my ticket, which was just a little white card, and handed it to me. "Hold your own," she said. "That way, you're responsible for yourself." She took a sip of her drink. She had switched from schnapps to something else. "What about *your* absolute values?" she said to me. "What do *you* think? I'm not sure loyalty's a good one to stay with. I may have to choose something else. Barney thinks honesty. Now you choose one."

I didn't want to choose one. I didn't know what an absolute value was or why I needed one. Doris was just playing a game, and I didn't want to play it. Though when I thought about it, all I could think of was *cold*. It was cold in the Oil City, and I thought the temperature was still going down outside, and cold was on my mind.

"I don't know one," I said and thought about leaving.

"Well," Doris said, "then I'll start for you. You could say 'love,' okay? Or you could say 'beautiful,' or 'beauty.' Or you could probably even say the color 'red,' which would be strange." Doris looked at her lap, at her red dress, then at me standing beside her. " *'Thought,'* " she said. "You could say that, even though you probably don't do much of it. You just can't say nothing. And you can't say 'marriage' or 'adultery' or 'sex.' They're not absolute enough." She glanced at Barney and laughed a nasty little laugh.

The poker machine clicked and dinged back in the dark. A man was talking on the pay phone by the bathroom, and I heard him say, "That's in Lethbridge. That's an hour and a half away." The bar felt empty to me, and I realized I was wrong about ever being in it before. I turned around and looked at the one window. Beyond the neon sign, snow was coming harder, and I saw headlights of cars going by slowly. I wondered if the snow could make our train late. I heard two car doors close outside and looked at the door, expecting it to open, but it didn't.

Barney motioned to the bartender, who was a very small, thin girl who looked like she might be a Chinese too. She poured Barney a glass of red wine out of a bottle on the back bar, then picked a dollar out of the pile in front of him.

"Oh, choose one, God damn it, Lawrence," Doris said suddenly and glared at me. "I'm tired of fucking around with you. I wish I'd left you at home."

"Cold," I said.

"Cold?" Doris looked stunned. "Is that what you said? Cold?"

"Yes," I said.

"Did you hear that, Benny?" Doris said to Barney.

Barney looked up at me from his glass of wine and said, "Don't let her confuse you. I been there before."

"Cold isn't one," Doris said in an aggravated way. "Try to be smart."

"Brave, then," I said. "I mean, bravery."

"All right, then." Doris picked up her glass without drinking. Only ice was left in it. She sat for a few seconds without saying anything, as if she was thinking about something else. "What have you been so brave about?" she said, and turned the glass up to her nose.

Barney leaned over and whispered something in her ear, which Doris ignored.

"Nothing," I said.

"It's an abstraction to you, then," she said. "Is that it?"

"Mutts fuck mutts," Barney said, and he said it seriously and to me. He suddenly grabbed my arm tight and high above the muscle. "When I get back, Lawrence, I'll show you what I mean." He pulled himself off the stool, using my arm, and started toward the dark end of the room, where the rest-room hallway was and where the man was still talking on the pay phone. He didn't walk steadily at all, and when he got to the entrance of the hallway he held the corner of the wall and turned and looked at us. "Don't confuse love with pain, you two," he said, and he stood for a moment, staring in our direction. I noticed his silver belt buckle was pushed off to the side in a way I'd seen some men do. Then he just disappeared down the little hall.

"Don't confuse me with your wife," Doris said loudly, then motioned for another drink. "All boats seek a place to

sink is what I believe." And I stood closer to the bar, wanting to think of a way to get her to leave and wondering what
Barney was going to show me when he came back. "I told
him Esther was my given name," Doris said in a whisper.
"It's my least favorite name. But it's biblical, and Indians are
all so religious, he likes it. He's pathetic, but he's a hoot."

Doris was staring at a door behind the bar. There was a
little circular glass window in the door, like a kitchen door
in a restaurant. A man's large white face was in the window,
looking all around inside the bar from the back room. The
man had on a big hat you could see part of the brim of.
"Look at that," Doris said. She was staring right at the window, and the man's face was staring right at her. "What
party is he looking for, do you suppose?"

The face was there another moment, then went away.
But slowly the door opened and the man we'd just seen,
with another one right behind him in the dark, looked out
into the bar. He had on a sheriff's uniform. He looked one
way and then the other. He was holding a big silver pistol
with a long barrel out in front of him, and was wearing a
heavy coat with a badge, and heavy rubber boots with his
pants tucked in the tops. The man behind him was a sheriff too, though he was younger and didn't look much older
than I was. He had a short-barrel shotgun he was holding
with two hands and high in front of him, with the barrel
pointed up.

Neither one of the men said anything. They just stepped
slowly into the room, looking around as if they expected to
be surprised by something. The little bartender saw them
and went completely still, staring at them. And so did
Doris and I. I heard one of the two or three Indians in the
other part of the room say, "This machine loves me." Then
I heard the front door of the bar push open and felt cold air

flood in. There were three more deputies outside, all wearing hats and heavy coats, all carrying short-barrel shotguns.
None of the men looked at me or at Doris. They looked at
all the Indians, then around the room at each other, and
suddenly they seemed nervous, as if they didn't know what
was about to happen.

One of the men—I didn't know which—said, "I don't
see him, Neal, do you?"

The man with the pistol said, "Look in the bathroom."

And then Doris, for no reason at all, said, "Barney's in
the bathroom." She pointed at where Barney had gone a
few moments before.

And immediately, as if that had been their signal, two of
the deputies at the front door moved across the room on
their tiptoes to the head of the little dark hallway where
the pay phone and the rest-room door were. One deputy
grabbed the man who had been talking on the phone but
had stopped talking and was just standing, holding the receiver at his side, and pushed him out of the way. Both
deputies got on either side of the hallway entrance and
pointed their shotguns down toward where I guessed the
rest-room door was. And then the two other deputies started
whispering to us and motioning with their shotguns. "Get
down on the floor, get down on the floor *now!*" they said.

And we all did, all of us. I got on my belly and put my
cheek on the wet floorboards and held my breath. Doris got
down beside me. I could hear her breathing through her
nose. She made a grunting noise, and she grabbed my hand.
Her glasses had come off and were lying on the floor, but she
didn't say anything. Her eyes were shut, and I pulled myself
close to her and put my arm over her, though I didn't see
how I could protect her if something bad happened.

Then someone, and it must've been the man with the pistol, shouted in the loudest voice I'd ever heard, "Barney. God damn it. Come out of the bathroom. It's Neal Reiskamp. It's the sheriff. I've got people out here with guns. So just come on out. You can't get away from me."

The deputy who was closest to me moved quickly, almost jumped, over to where he could get behind the two in the doorway, and he pointed his shotgun into the hallway too.

"Give me some light," the man who was the sheriff shouted. "I can't see anything down there."

Another deputy ran out the front door. It had been standing open, with cold and snow blowing in. I heard his boots on the snow, then the sound of a car door opening. I didn't want to look up, but I could hear feet shifting and scuffling on the floor. The wood was hard against my cheek, and I tightened my arm around Doris until she made another little grunting noise, but didn't open her eyes. The rotating beer sign over the jukebox flashed little stars across the floor.

There were no sounds from Barney in the bathroom. And I wondered if he was even in there, or if he'd gone out a window or out another door, or even—and this felt like a dream I was dreaming—if he might've gone up through a trapdoor in the ceiling and into the attic and was on the floor above us all, in some deserted room in the dark, pacing around, trying to decide what to do, how to escape, how to come out of this in good shape. I even thought about his wife, about her being robbed of her money and her rings. Then I heard a noise like more feet scuffling, and the sound of something or somebody beating on something, a wall maybe. The deputy who'd gone outside ran back in with a long black flashlight.

"Shine the son of a bitch down there," the sheriff said. "No. Up. Up more, God damn it." The pounding kept going on somewhere. Bang, bang. First it sounded like metal, and then I heard glass break. Then more banging. "Barney!" the sheriff yelled very loud. "Barney!" The banging kept on. The little bartender, who must've been on the floor behind the bar, began to make a high-pitched sound—*eeee, eeee,* like that. I thought the banging had made her afraid, because it was making me afraid. I could feel my jaw closed tight, and both my fists were clenched. There was more of it—bang, bang, bang—and then I looked up and saw that the two deputies were still pointing their shotguns down the hallway at what I still couldn't see. Their legs were spread way apart, and the man with the flashlight was squatting behind them, shining his light between one man's legs.

Doris said, "I'm all wet, Lawrence." She opened her eyes and stared at me, and wrinkled her nose up in a strange way. Then, from the hallway where the deputies were looking and pointing their shotguns, there was a very loud crashing, breaking sound, as if a door had been broken in or out. There was more noise I couldn't identify, and I couldn't even say now what it was, though for some reason I thought Barney was kicking something, even though it was like a noise made by metal. But whatever it was, the deputy holding the flashlight suddenly jumped back out of the way, his light going crazy across the ceiling, the long black barrel hitting the floor. And then two of the men who were holding shotguns shot almost at the same instant, right down into the little hallway, into the dark. And the noise of those two guns going off inside the barroom was an awful noise. My ears went deaf and there was pressure on my brain, and my eyeballs felt like air was pushing on them. The shots made a yellow flash and dust was all in the air and falling out of the ceiling, and there was the thick, sour smell of burned gunpowder. When the guns went off I felt Doris jump, and she squeezed my hand until her wedding ring cut down into my knuckle, and I couldn't get it free.

"Okay," I heard Barney say to the policemen in a loud, odd voice. "I'm all shot up now. You shot me up. You shot me. I don't feel good now."

Two other deputies, ones who hadn't shot, ran into the little hallway, right in front of Doris and me, though a third one knelt beside the man who'd held the flashlight. "I'm all right," that man said. "I'm not shot." His white hat was on the floor. I heard the bartender say, "Oh, my heavens," though I couldn't see her.

Then Barney—it must've been him—said, "How are you?" almost in a casual voice, then he yelled, "Ohhhhhh," and then he said, "Stop that! Stop that!" And then he was quiet.

The two men who had shot Barney stayed where they were, pointing their guns into the hallway. They had each ejected a shell, both of which were on the floor.

The sheriff, who was standing behind everybody, said even louder, as if he was even more afraid now, "Careful. Be careful. He's not dead. He's just hit. He's just hit." One more deputy, who had been across the room, suddenly moved into the hallway in front of the men holding guns. "Barney, you son of a bitch," I heard him say, "stay down there." But Barney didn't make a noise. I heard footsteps behind me, and when I looked, the Indians and the man who'd been talking on the phone were going out the front door. I saw headlights outside, and from a distance I heard a siren, then the noise of a two-way radio and a woman's voice saying, "It probably is. But I can't be sure. You better check that out. Ten-four."

I looked at Doris, and her eyes were wide open, her cheek flat against the wet wood. Her mouth was drawn tight across, as if she thought something else might happen, but she had begun to loosen her grip on my hand. Her ring came off my knuckle, and she breathed very deeply and she said, "They killed that man. They shot him all to pieces." I didn't answer, because my jaw was still clenched and my ears hollow, but I thought that what she said was probably true. I was close to what had happened, yet I wasn't a real part of it. Everything had happened to Barney and the policemen who shot him, and I was better off, or so I felt, to stay as far away from it as I could and not even discuss it.

IN A FEW MINUTES one of the sheriff's deputies came and helped us to stand up and go sit in the booth against the wall. There were a lot of police in the room all of a sudden. The front door stayed open, and two Montana highway patrolmen and more sheriff's deputies and two Indian policemen all came in and out. I could hear the voices of other people outside. More cars drove up with two-way radios going, and an ambulance arrived. Two men in orange jumpsuits came inside and went down the little hall carrying equipment in black boxes. I heard someone say, *"No problema aquí."* And then the sheriff said, "Go ahead, I'll just sign all that now." Barney never said anything else that I heard. After a couple of minutes, the men from the ambulance left. One of them was smiling about something, but I didn't think it had to do with what had happened. It had to have been something else.

"I'm freezing," Doris said across the little table. "Aren't you freezing?" She had found her glasses and put them back on, and she was shivering. Almost immediately after she'd said it the same deputy came in and brought her a blanket and one for me too, though I wasn't so cold, or didn't know I was. My nose was running, that was all, and the front of me was wet from the floor.

For some reason, two deputies took the bartender away with them. I could hear them put her in a car, and heard it drive away. And then the ceiling lights in the bar were turned on, and a man came in with a camera and took pictures in the hallway, using a flash. He came out afterwards and took pictures of the room itself, one of which Doris and I were in, wrapped in our blankets.

In about ten minutes, while we sat waiting, two more ambulance men came in the door with a folding stretcher on wheels. They pushed it into the hall, and I guess they picked Barney up and put him on, because when they pushed it out through the bar he was on it, covered up by a sheet with blood soaking through. One of the men was holding Barney's white Burlington Northern hard hat, and I could actually see part of Barney's ponytail out under the edge of the sheet. I had to turn to see all that. But Doris didn't look. She sat with her blanket around her and stared down at the cup of coffee the deputy had brought. When the cart had gone by she said, "Was that him?"

"Yes," I said.

"I thought so," she said.

After a few more minutes, a big man wearing a light-gray suit and western boots and a western hat came in and looked around the room. He appeared very clean and neat and had pale white skin and thin hair and a bad complexion, and at first he only glanced at us before he looked behind the bar and into the back room, where the sheriff had come from. He stepped down the hall where Barney had been and into the bathroom—though I couldn't see him do that. When he came out he said something to the sheriff, who had put his hat on again, then he brought a chair over to the booth and sat down at the end of the table in front of us.

He took out a little spiral pad and wrote something in it with a ballpoint pen. Then he said, still writing, "I'm Walter Peterson, I'm the lawyer for Toole County. I'd like to find out some things from you people."

"We don't know anything," Doris said. "We don't live here. We're on our way to Seattle. We just stopped in." She had her blanket clutched up to her neck, and her fists were holding the edges together.

"Did you know the deceased man?" the lawyer said without answering Doris. I realized that was what they were calling Barney now. The lawyer had a tiny pin on his lapel—a pair of silver handcuffs—and when he sat down I saw he was wearing a leather holster under his coat. He didn't take off his hat when he was talking to us.

"No," Doris said, "we didn't."

"Did *you* know him?" he said to me.

"No, sir," I said.

"Did either of you talk to him?" the lawyer said, writing something in his little notebook.

"I *tried* to talk to him," Doris said. "Just practically by accident. But he didn't care to say much." She looked at me and then looked all around the barroom, which seemed larger and even dirtier with the ceiling lights on. "Was he carrying a gun of some kind?" she said. "I had the feeling he was."

"He didn't say anything about his wife?" the lawyer said, still not answering her.

"He said she'd been robbed at some point. He admitted that."

The lawyer stopped writing and looked at Doris as if he expected her to talk some more. Then he said, "Did he say anything else about that?" He began writing again, and I saw that he wrote with his left hand and in the regular way, not turned backward.

"No, sir," Doris said. "He didn't. Lawrence, of course, wasn't here then. He came in just toward the end."

"The end of what?" the man said. He had short thick hands with a big gold-and-red ring on one finger.

"At the end of the time we were sitting at the bar beside each other. Before he went to the bathroom."

"What's your name?" the lawyer said to me, and I told him. He asked Doris her name and wrote it down along with our addresses. He asked us what relation we were to each other, and Doris said she was my aunt and my mother was her sister. He looked at me as if he wanted to ask me something, then he ran the blunt end of his pen across his cheek, where his complexion was bad, and, I guess, changed his mind.

"Did the deceased say anything to either of you after he went to the bathroom?"

"He didn't have time after that," Doris said. "They shot him."

"I see," the lawyer said, though I remembered Barney had said he intended to show me something when he got back. But I didn't mention that. The lawyer wrote something else down and closed his notebook. He nodded and stuck his pen inside his coat. "If we have to call you, we'll

call you," he said. He started to smile at Doris, then didn't.
"Okay?" he said. He took two business cards out of his
pocket and laid them on the tabletop. "I want you to keep
my card and call me if you think of anything you want to
add to your statements."

"What was the matter with him?" Doris asked. "He said
he'd been in Fort Harrison, but I didn't know whether to
believe that or not."

The lawyer stood up and put his notepad in his back
pocket. "Him and his wife got in a set-to. That's all I've
heard about it. She's missing at the moment."

"I'm sorry that all happened," Doris said.

"Are you both going to Seattle?" he said, and he didn't
smile, though he said it to me.

"Yes," Doris said. "His mother lives there."

"It'll be warmer over there. You'll like that," he said. He
looked around at one of the deputies, who had been waiting for him to finish with us, then he just walked away, just
walked toward that man and began talking beside the bar.
Once, he looked over as if he was saying something about
us, but in a minute he went outside. I could hear his voice,
then I heard a car start up and drive away.

DORIS AND I sat in the booth for ten more minutes while
the deputies and a highway patrolman stood at the bar and
talked. I thought I might go look at the place where Barney
had gotten shot, but I didn't want to get up by myself and
I didn't want to ask Doris to go with me. Though after we'd
sat there for a while longer Doris said, "I guess we're free to
go." She stood up and folded her blanket and laid it on the
table, and I stood up and folded mine the same way. She
went to the bar and gathered up her money and her coat

and her purse and keys. Barney's work gloves and wine were still on the bar, and I noticed a pint bottle of whiskey on the floor under the stool Barney had been sitting on. One of the deputies was picking up the empty shotgun shells, and he said something to Doris and laughed, and Doris said, "I just stopped in for a drink, that's all," and laughed herself. I walked quickly over to where the men with shotguns had aimed down the hallway. And what I saw was the bathroom door knocked off of its top hinge and hanging on the bottom one, and bright light shining out of the bathroom. But nothing else. No holes in the wall or any marks anywhere. There wasn't even any blood I could see, though I was sure there must've been blood someplace, since I'd seen it on the sheet when Barney had been taken out. It was just empty there, almost as if nothing had happened.

Doris walked over to me, putting things in her purse. "Let's break out of this place," she said and pulled my arm, and then the two of us walked out of the Oil City without saying anything to anybody else, and right out into the cold night, where there was new snow and more still sifting down.

Outside, all the sounds were softened and I could hear better. Across the railroad yard were the dark backs of stores on the main street of Shelby, and through the alleys I could see hanging Christmas lights and a big yellow motel sign and the lights of cars cruising. I could hear car horns blowing and a switch-engine bell ringing in the dark. Two police cars sat parked in front of the bar with their motors running and their lights off, and two women stood in the snow across the street, watching the door to see what would happen next. One of the boys I'd passed in the drugstore when I'd bought my mother's watch was talking to the women, his hands stuck in his jacket pockets. Maybe they thought there would be some more excitement. But what I thought was that someone would come and close the bar soon and that would be all. I thought it might not ever open again.

Doris stopped on the sidewalk then and didn't say anything. She crossed her arms and put her hands under them to get warm. Her chin was down, her red patent-leather shoes were covered with snow. She seemed to be considering something that hadn't occurred to her until she was outside. We were facing the depot, farther down the street, its windows lit. The taxi that had been in front of the Oil City was parked there now, its green roof light shining. Other cars had arrived, so I couldn't see Doris's car. My own feet were starting to be cold, and I wanted to go on to the depot and wait inside for the train. There was only an hour left until it would come.

"That was *such* a goddamn unlucky thing it just makes me sick," Doris said, and bunched her shoulders and pulled her elbows in. "Of course it's not what happens, it's what you do with what happens." She looked around at the two other bars on the block, which looked exactly like the Oil City—dark wood fronts with red bar signs in the windows. "I've got snakes in my boots right now," she said, "which is what the Irishman says." And she spit. She spit right in the street in the snow. I had never seen a woman do that. "Did you ever hear your dad say he had snakes in his boots when he was drinking?"

"No," I said.

"It means you need another drink. But I don't think I can approach another bar tonight. I need to go sit in my car and regain my composition." In the Oil City the jukebox started up, loud music bursting into the street.

"Can you stand to sit with me? You can go wait in the depot if you want to." She smiled at me, a smile that made me feel sorry for her. I thought she must've felt bad about Barney, and must've thought she was responsible for what happened.

On the platform beside the depot two men in heavy coats were standing talking, shifting from foot to foot. A switch engine moved slowly past them. I wanted to go inside there and get warm. But I said, "No, I'll come with you."

"We don't have to stay very long," Doris said. "I just don't want to see anybody for a while. I'll calm down in a minute or two. Okay?" She started walking up the middle of the street. "Everyday acts of heroism are appreciated," she said as she walked, and she smiled at me again.

Doris's pink car was covered with snow and was down among the other cars that had arrived behind the depot. She started the motor right away and turned the heater up, but didn't wipe the windshield, so that we sat in the cold while the heater blew cold air on our feet, and couldn't see out, could only see the blurred lights of the depot as if they were painted on the frosted window.

Doris put her hands in her lap and shivered and stamped her feet and put her chin down and blew ice smoke. I just sat. I put my hands in my pockets and tried to be still until I could feel the air start to blow warm. The front of my coat was still wet.

"Double shivers," Doris said, pushing her chin farther down into her coat. She looked pale, as if she'd been sick, and her face seemed small and her eyes tired. "You know when you watch TV on New Year's Day and all the soap-opera characters stop in the middle of their programs and turn to the camera and wish you Happy New Year's? Did you ever see that?"

"No," I said, because I had never watched soap operas.

"Well, they do it. Take my word for it. But it's my favorite moment of the whole year for the soaps. They just step out for a second, then they step right back in and go on. It's wonderful. I watch it religiously."

"We watch football that day—when we have a TV," I said, and clenched my toes down, because I was cold and couldn't help wondering if exhaust fumes were getting inside. I tried to feel if I was getting sleepy, but I wasn't. My jaw was still stiff, and I could feel my heart beating hard in my chest as if I'd been running, and my legs were tingling above my knees.

"Is that what you care about—football?" Doris said after a while.

"No," I said. "Not anymore."

"You're just ready to start life now, I guess."

"I already started it," I said.

"You certainly did tonight." Doris reached for the schnapps bottle, where she'd left it on the floor, and unscrewed the cap and took a drink. "I've got a sour taste," she said. "You want to drink a toast to poor old Barney?" She handed the bottle to me, and I could smell it.

"No, thanks," I said, and didn't take it.

"Honor the poor dead and our absent friends," she said, then took another drink. The heater was blowing warmer now.

"Why did you say to the police that he was in the bathroom?" I said.

Doris held the bottle up to the depot lights. "I didn't mean that to happen. If they'd spoken to him in the Indian tongue, none of it would've ever taken place. They just didn't speak it. It was a matter of mutual distrust." She said something then in what must've been the Indian tongue—

something that sounded like reading words backward, not like something you heard wrong or mistook the meaning of. "Do you know what that means?"

"No," I said.

"It means: 'Come out with your hands up and I won't kill you,' in the Gros Ventre language. Or it means something like that. They don't really have a word for 'hands up.' Barney could've understood that if he'd been a Gros Ventre."

"Why'd you tell them that, though?" I said, because I thought Barney might've survived if he hadn't gotten trapped in there and maybe gotten scared. He could be in jail now, asleep, instead of dead.

"I didn't mean him to get shot." Doris looked at me as if she was surprised. "Do you think I'm rotten because I did that?"

"No," I said, though that wasn't exactly the truth.

"He murdered his wife. I'm sure about that. They'll find her someplace over in Browning tonight, beat to death or stabbed or burned up in a ditch. That's what happens. She probably had a boyfriend. The police were already looking for him, I knew that the instant he sat down beside me. People get a smell on them." She blew more ice breath in the air. "I don't think the heater's working." She turned the knob around and back. "Feel my hands." She put her small hands together and shoved them toward me, and they were cold and hard-feeling. "They're my prettiest feature, I believe," Doris said, looking at her own hands. She looked at my hands then, and touched the place where her wedding ring had worked into my knuckle. "Your skin's *your* nicest feature," she said, and looked at my face. "You look like your mother, and you have your father's skin. You'll probably look like him eventually." She pushed closer to me. "I'm so cold, baby," she said, holding her two hands still clasped together against my chest and putting her face against my cheek. The skin on her face was cold and stiff and not very soft, and the frames of her glasses were cold too. There was a smell of sweat in her hair. "I feel numb, and you're so warm. Your face is warm." She kept her cheek against my cheek, so I could feel that mine was warm. "You need to warm me up," she whispered. "Are you brave enough to do that? Or are you a coward on that subject?" She put her hands around my neck and below my collar, and I didn't know what to do with my hands, though I put them around her and began to pull her close to me and felt her weight come against my weight and her legs press on my cold legs. I felt her ribs and her back—hard, the way they'd felt when we'd been on the floor in the bar. I felt her breathing under her coat, could smell on her breath what she'd just been drinking. I closed my eyes, and she said to me, almost as if she was sorry about something, "Oh, my. You've just got everything, don't you? You've just got everything."

"What?" I said. "What is it?"

And she said, "No, no. Oh, no, no." That was all she said. And then she didn't talk to me anymore.

On the train, I sat facing Doris as the empty, dark world went by outside our compartment in a snowy stream. She had washed her face and cleaned her glasses and put on perfume, and her face had color in it. She looked nice, though the front of her red dress had stains from where we'd had to lie down on the bar floor in the wet. We sat and looked out the window for a while, not talking, and I saw that she had taken off her stockings and her earrings, and that her hands *were* pretty. Her fingers were long and thin, and there was no polish on her finger-nails. They looked natural.

In the depot I had called my father. I thought I should tell him about Barney and what had happened and say that I was all right, though I knew I could explain it wrong and he could decide to come and get me, and I wouldn't get to Seattle, or ever get to see my mother.

The phone rang a long time, and when my father answered it he seemed out of breath, as if he'd been running or had come in from outside. "It's snowing in Montana, bud," he said, catching his wind. I heard him stamp his feet on the floor. "It feels like you've been gone a long time already."

"We're still in Shelby," I said. "It's snowing here too." Doris was at the ticket desk, talking to the woman I had talked to—Betty. I knew they were talking about Barney. There were other people in the waiting room now, with suitcases and paper packages, and it was noisy. "We saw a man get shot up in a bar tonight," I said to my father, just like that.

"What is it?" my father said, as though he hadn't heard me right. "What's it you said?"

"The police did it."

"Where's Doris?" my father said. "Put her on." And I knew that what I'd said had shocked him. "Where are you?" he said, and his voice sounded scared.

"In Shelby," I said. "In the depot. I was on the floor with Doris. Nothing happened to us."

"Where's she now, son?" my father said and suddenly seemed very calm. "Let me speak to her now."

"She's talking to somebody," I said. "She can't come to the phone."

"Are the police there?" my father said, and I knew he was thinking right then about coming up and getting me and taking me back. But it was snowing too hard, and the train would get there before he could.

"We were in the Oil City bar," I said, and I said it calmly. "It wasn't somebody we knew. It was an Indian."

"What in the world's going on now?" my father said, and he said this loudly, so that I wondered if he'd had a drink. "Was she with somebody?"

"No," I said, "she wasn't. It's all right now. It's finished."

And then there was a long time on the line during which my father didn't say anything but I could hear his feet moving on the floor and hear him breathing hard, and I knew he was trying to think of what he should do at that moment.

"I can't save you from very much, can I?" he said softly, as if he didn't care if I heard it or maybe didn't even want me to. So I didn't answer, and waited for him to say something he wanted me to hear. I tried thinking of something to ask, but I didn't want to know anything. Telling him what had happened had made anything else not important.

And then he said, and he said it more loudly, as if he had a new idea, "Are you all right?"

"Yes, sir," I said.

He waited for a moment. "Your mother called up here tonight."

"What did she say?"

"She wanted to know if you'd gotten away all right and how you felt. She asked me if I wished I was coming with you, and I told her she'd need to ask me earlier if she wanted that to happen. I said I had other plans."

"Is Jensen there?" And I called her by her last name. I don't know why.

My father laughed. "Yoyce? No, Miss Yensen's got different visitors tonight. It's just us hounds in the house. I let them both in. They're searching around for you right now."

"You don't have to worry about me," I said.

"All right, then, I'll quit." And he paused again. "Your mother said she might try to keep you out there. So don't be surprised."

"What did you say to her about it?"

"I said it was up to you. Not me."

"What did she say then?"

"Nothing," he said. "Not about that." And I decided then that he hadn't had a drink. "Before you called I was just sitting thinking about when I was your age. My parents had several big dustups—yelling and everything. Fighting. My dad once got my mother up against a wall in the house and threatened to hit her because he'd invited over some friends of his from Moorhead, and she didn't like them and told them to get out. I had a good seat for that. Nobody moved away, though. That was better than all this foolishness. I don't know what *you're* supposed to do about it, of course."

Doris looked at me across the waiting room and smiled and waved. She pointed her finger at herself, but I didn't want her to talk to my father. "Do you remember when you said Doris was sympathetic?" I said, watching her. "You were talking about her one day. I wondered what you meant by that."

"Oh," my father said, and I heard one of the dogs bark, and he shouted out, "Hey now! Dogs!" Then he said, "I must've meant she was generous with her affections. With me she was. That's all. Why'd you think about that? Is she nice to you?"

"Yes," I said, "she is." Then I said, "Do you think it'd be better if I stay out with Mother?"

"Well, only if you want to," my father said. "I wouldn't blame you. Seattle's a nice place. But I'm happy to have you come back here. We should talk about that when you've been there. You'll know more about it."

"Okay," I said.

I heard a dog's collar jingling, and I thought he was probably petting one of them. "Are you sure you're all right?" my father said.

"I'm fine," I said. "I am."

"I love you, Larry. I forgot to tell you that before you left. That's important."

"I love you," I said.

"That's good news," he said. "Thank you."

And then we hung up.

AFTER AN HOUR of watching the night go by—the town of Cut Bank, Montana, some bright headlights behind a flashing, snowy barricade and a road sign toward Santa Rita and the Canada border, then a long, dark time while the train ran beside the highway and there were no cars, only a farm light or two in the distance and a missile site off in the dark and a few trucks racing to get home by Thanksgiving—after an hour of that, Doris began talking to me, just saying whatever was in her mind, as if she thought I might be interested. Her voice sounded different in the compartment. It had lost a thickness it'd had, and was just a plain voice that only meant one thing.

She remarked again that the town of Shelby had felt very foreign to her, and that it reminded her of Las Vegas, Nevada, where she and Benny had gotten married. She said both were remote from anyplace important and both were unpredictable—unlike Great Falls, which she said was too predictable. She said she knew the sheriff had not intended to shoot Barney, that they would've done anything to avoid it but that they didn't know enough. Then she said again that she was the wrong person for my father, and that there were important things she'd always wanted to say to my mother, things she thought about her—some good, some not—but that she could never express them, because my mother had locked on her as a rival years before. Then she talked about how it would feel to be divorced, that the worst part of that would be your thinking, not being able to control what went through your mind, and that the next day, Thanksgiving Day, she was going to tell my mother to come home right then, or else run the risk of being on her own forever. "Your life'll eat you." Those were the words she used. And then she leaned back in her seat and looked at me.

"I was involved with another woman for a while. Quite a while, in fact. It was very fulfilling," she said. "Though I'm not now. Not anymore. Does that shock you? I'm sure it does."

"No," I said, although it did. It shocked me very much.

"It shocked me," Doris said. "But *you* couldn't admit that. It's not how you're made. You don't really know how to trust people with the truth. You're like your father." She took her glasses off and smoothed under her eyes with the tips of her fingers.

"I can tell the truth," I said, and I wanted to be able to. I didn't want to be a person who couldn't tell the truth, though I didn't want to tell Doris I was shocked by what she'd said.

"It doesn't matter," she said, and smiled at me in a way she had earlier that day, as though she liked me and I could trust her. She put her glasses back on very carefully. "Did you buy a nice present for your mom? I bet you have good taste."

"I bought her a watch," I said.

"You did?" Doris leaned forward. "Let me see it." She seemed pleased.

I reached in the pocket of my coat, which was beside me on the seat and also had the lawyer's card in it, and took out the little clear-plastic box wrapped in white tissue, and unfolded it so Doris could look. She took the box and opened it and picked up the watch with its tiny moving hand ticking seconds by—I could almost hear it—and she looked at it very closely, then put it up to her ear. "Okay," she said, and smiled at me. "It works." She put it back in my hand. "Jan'll love that," she said as I folded it away. "It's the perfect gift. I wish somebody would give me a watch. You're such a sweet boy." She took my cheeks between her warm hands and squeezed me, and I thought she was going to kiss me, but she didn't. "Too bad there aren't sweet boys like you everywhere," she said. She sat back on her seat and put her hands in her lap and closed her eyes, and I believe she might've gone to sleep for a minute. Though after a while she said, with her eyes still closed and the snowy night flashing by outside, "I wish there were Thanksgiving carols so we could sing a song now." And then she did go to sleep, because her breath slowed and evened, and her head sank over her chest, and her hands were still and limp.

And for a long time after that I sat very still and felt as though I was entirely out of the world, cast off without a starting or a stopping point, just shooting through space like a boy in a rocket. Though after a while I must have begun to hold my breath, because my heart began to beat harder, and I had that feeling, the scary feeling you have that you're suffocating and your life is running out—fast, fast, second by second—and you have to do something to save yourself, but you can't. Only then you remember it's you who's causing it, and you who has to stop it. And then it did stop, and I could breathe again. I looked out the window at the night, where the clouds had risen and dispersed and the snow was finished, and the sky above the vast white ground was soft as softest velvet. And I felt calm. Maybe for the first time in my life, I felt calm. So that for a while I, too, closed my eyes and slept.

Occidentals

CHARLEY MATTHEWS and Helen Carmichael had come to Paris the week before Christmas. When they'd made eager plans for their trip, back in Ohio, they'd expected to stay only two days—enough time for Charley (who'd published his first novel) to have lunch with his French editor, for the two of them to take in a museum, eat a couple of incomparable meals, possibly attend the ballet, then strike off for England, where Matthews hoped to visit Oxford, the school where he'd almost been admitted fifteen years earlier. (At the last minute, he'd been turned down and instead taken his PhD at Purdue, a school he'd always felt ashamed of.)

Things in Paris, however, had not turned out as they'd hoped.

In the first place, the late-autumn weather, which the newspaper in Ohio had predicted would be crisp and dry, with plenty of mild afternoon sunshine—perfect for long walks through the Bois de Boulogne or boat rides on the Seine—had almost overnight turned cold and miserably wet, with a dense, oily fog and rain that made it impossible to see anything and made walking outside a hardship. Matthews noticed in the Fodor's, during the taxi ride from the airport, that Paris was much farther north than he'd imagined—he'd had it nearer the middle. But it lay, he saw, on the same parallel as Gander, Newfoundland, which made what the book said seem logical: that it rained more in Paris than in Seattle and that winter usually started in November. "No wonder it's cold," he said, watching the unknown, rain-darkened streets drift past. "It's only a half day's drive to Copenhagen."

The second piece of unexpected news was that François Blumberg, Matthews' French editor, had called up their first afternoon to see how they were but also to say that his own plans had changed. He was, he said, flying that very afternoon with his wife and four children to somewhere in the Indian Ocean, and so wouldn't be able to invite Matthews to lunch or to visit the publishing house— Éditions des Châtaigniers—which he was closing for the Christmas holidays. The suddenness and rudeness of the cancellation seemed to cause Blumberg satisfaction, though it was Blumberg who'd proposed the whole trip ("We will become good friends then") and Blumberg who'd made promises to act as Matthews' guide to Paris, "to special parts tourists would never be lucky enough to see"—secret Oriental gardens in Montparnasse, personal holdings of Blumberg's rich, titled friends, private dining rooms in five-star restaurants, special closed galleries in the Louvre, full of Rembrandts and da Vincis.

"Oh well, of course, certainly, when you come *next* to Paris we shall have a long, long visit," Blumberg said on the phone. "No one knows you in France now. But this will all change. After your book is published, everything will change. You'll see. You'll be famous." Blumberg made a little gasping sound then, the quick, shallow intake of breath that suggested he'd said something which surprised even him. All French people must make this noise, Matthews believed. The one Frenchwoman who taught at Wilmot College, where he'd once taught, made it all the time. He had no idea what it meant.

"I guess so," Matthews said. He was in bed, dressed in only his pajama top. Blumberg had awakened him from his arrival nap. Helen had gone out into the weather to find lunch, something their hotel, the Nouvelle Métropole, was too impoverished to provide. Outside, on cold, rainy rue Froidevaux, a cadre of motorbikes was revving up and popping, and angry male voices were shouting in French as if a fight was breaking out. Somewhere, a blaring police horn was coming nearer. Matthews wondered if it was heading for their hotel.

"I would personally consider it a favor, though," Blumberg continued, "if you could stay and meet your translator. Madame de Grenelle. She is very, very famous and also very difficult to persuade on the subject of American novels. But she has found your book fascinating and wishes to see you. Unfortunately, she is also away and will not be in Paris until four days."

"We weren't planning to stay that long," Matthews said irritably.

"Well, of course, exactly as you please," Blumberg said. "Only it would help matters. Translation is not a matter merely of converting your book into French; it is a matter of *inventing* your book into the French mind. So it is necessary to have the translation absolutely perfect, for people to know it correctly. We don't want you or your book to be misunderstood. We want you to be famous. People spend too much time misunderstanding each other."

"Apparently," Matthews said.

Blumberg then gave Matthews Madame de Grenelle's phone number and address and said again that she would be hoping he'd call. From their correspondence, Matthews had always pictured François Blumberg as an old man, a kindly keeper of an ancient flame, overseer of a rich and storied culture that only a few were permitted to share: somebody he would instinctively like. But now he pictured Blumberg as younger—possibly even his own age, thirty-seven—small, pale, balding, pimply, possibly a second-rate academic making ends meet by working in publishing, someone in a shiny black suit and cheap shoes. Matthews thought of Blumberg struggling up a set of rain-swept metal steps toward a smoky, overbooked charter flight, a skinny wife and four kids trailing behind, laden with suitcases and plastic sacks, all shouting at the top of their lungs.

"So," Blumberg said, as though pressed for time. "Now is, of course, a perfect time to be in Paris. We all go away where it's warm. You have it all to yourselves, you and your friends the Germans. We'll take it back when you're finished." Blumberg laughed. Then he said, "I hope we can meet each other next time."

"Right," Matthews said. "Me, too." He intended to say something more to Blumberg, to register the upset this change of plans was certain to cause. But Blumberg blurted some indecipherable phrase in French, laughed again, made another quick gasping sound and hung up.

This was, of course, an insult, Matthews understood. No doubt a peculiarly slighting French insult (though he didn't know what a French insult was). But the proper response was to pack their bags, call a taxi, abandon the hotel and take the first conveyance out. He wasn't sure where. Only the rest of the trip would be cast in shadow then, a shadow of disappointment before it ever had a chance to be fun.

Matthews crawled out of bed and went to the window in his bare feet and pajama top. Outside the cold panes, the air was dirty and thick. It didn't feel anything like Christmas. It didn't feel like Paris, for that matter. Directly across rue Froidevaux, a great cemetery spread out into the fog and trees to beyond where he could see, and off to the right in the mist was a huge stone statue of a lion, in the middle of a busy roundabout. Beyond that were ranks of buildings and cars beating up and down a wide avenue, their yellow lights lit in the afternoon gloom. This was Paris.

A police car had stopped in the street below, its blue light flashing, two uniformed officers in luminous white helmets gesticulating to three men on motorcycles. In the past, when he'd imagined Paris, he imagined jazz, Dom Pérignon corks flying into the bright, crisp night air, wide shining streets, laughter. Fun. Now he couldn't even guess which direction he was looking. East? Which direction was the Eiffel Tower? This was the Fourteenth Arrondissement. The Left Bank. Many famous American writers had lived near here, though for the moment he couldn't remember who or where, only that the French had made them feel at home in a way their own countrymen hadn't. He had never particularly wanted to come to Paris. The problem had always seemed to him how to convert anything that happened here into anything that mattered back home. He thought of all the bores who came back and droned on stupefyingly about Paris, trying to make their experience of it matter. It didn't happen *naturally*. Therefore, to come to Paris with a serious intent meant you'd need to stay. Except you couldn't go to a place you'd never been, expecting to stay. That wasn't travel.

That was escape. And he had nothing to escape from. Penny, his estranged wife, had always wanted him to take her "abroad," but he'd resisted—which had possibly been a mistake.

But outside the window now, Paris seemed baffling. It might as well have been East Berlin. Even leaving would be difficult. Plus he'd come so far. Paid for both of them. To leave would be a total loss.

In Matthews' novel—*The Predicament*—the main character's wife, Greta (a thin, unflattering disguise for Penny), had suddenly walked out of her snug but airless academic marriage in a small college town in "Maine," collected her lover in the family car (her lover being a blond and athletic Catholic priest, just then abandoning his clerical collar after having been seduced by Greta immediately upon converting her), driven to Boston, then flown to Paris, where they both came to separate but equally bad ends (a much altered version of the truth: Penny was in California).

Matthews, however, having never been to Paris, had simply chosen it on a whim, the way he thought of picking a place now to leave Paris for. Just choose a word. Prague. Cairo. Gdansk. For his novel, he'd researched everything out of library books, tourist guides and subway maps, and made important events take place near famous sites like the Eiffel Tower, the Bastille and the Luxembourg Gardens, or else in places he'd made up, using French words he liked the sounds of. Rue Homard. Place de Rebouteux. Eventually the Paris section had been scaled back to emphasize the narrator's emotional plight of being left alone, and to contain less of "Greta"'s fate of being struck by a car on the rue de Rivoli— the pretty street running beside the long, beautiful arcade he'd happened to notice out the taxi window this morning. It had made him happy to see the rue de Rivoli street signs.

Paris, for just that brief moment, had seemed knowable. Unlike now, when he couldn't figure out which way north was.

In the cemetery, just beyond the wall separating it from rue Froidevaux, some people were lined up beside an open grave. They were all wearing yarmulkes and using a tiny spade, which they passed back down the line to drop bits of dirt into the hole. As the mourners turned away, they quickly opened umbrellas and disappeared into the mist and clutter of gravestones. He'd read that Jews had their own sections in French cemeteries, unlike in America, where they had their own cemeteries.

"Joyeux Noël! Parles-toi anglais ici?" Helen said, letting herself into the cold little room. She was carrying a paper sack with lunch, her raincoat and hair dripping. "Did you see the cemetery full of dead Frenchmen across the street? One side of the wall has life, oblivious and ignorant. One side has death, complete and inescapable. They don't communicate. I like that. Maybe it'd be good to be buried here." She stuck her tongue out and made cross-eyes at him. Helen was in good spirits.

"Blumberg called," Matthews said gloomily. "He can't see me now. He's going to the Indian Ocean."

"That's too bad," Helen said.

"But he wants me to stay and meet my translator." He realized he was presenting this as though it was Helen's problem to solve.

"Well," Helen said, setting the damp sack on the bed table. "Is there some reason why you can't stay?"

"She's not in Paris now," Matthews said. "She won't be back for four days."

"What else do we have to do?" Helen said brightly, taking off her wet raincoat. "We'll find something to do in Paree. It's not like Cleveland."

"I wanted to go on to Oxford," Matthews said.

"You still won't get into Oxford," she said. "But you *did* get into Paris. And aren't translators important? I like your outfit, incidentally." Matthews was standing at the window with no pajama bottoms on. He was in a fourth-floor room, in a foreign country where no one knew him. He hadn't been thinking about that. Helen pooched out her lips provocatively. Helen had become increasingly voracious about sex, more voracious than she needed to be, Matthews thought. She would necessarily see this as an incitement.

"I'll have to figure out how we can keep the room," he said, stepping away from the window and looking for his pajama bottoms.

"I don't think there'll be much demand for this place." Helen looked around at the tiny room. Arabs owned the hotel and Indians ran it. A few Arab-looking pictures were on the walls as decoration: an oasis with one scrawny camel standing in the shade; some men wearing burnooses, sitting in a circle beside another camel in the desert.

"It's desolate here," Matthews said, hating the sound of his own complaining voice. It was jet lag. "I was thinking we ought to call a cab and get out. Take a train somewhere."

"Take a train where?" Helen said.

"The Riviera maybe. I thought Paris was closer to the Riviera, anyway."

"I don't want to go to the Riviera," she said. "I like it here. I've wanted to come here all my life. Just let the unexpected happen. It'll be romantic. It's Christmas in Paris, Charley. Isn't there some song about that?"

Matthews knew no song about Christmas in Paris. "I never heard of one."

"Well, then we'll have to make it up," Helen said. "I'll make up the music, and you can make up the words. You're the novelist. It's not like you need Proust to make up a song about Christmas in Paris."

"Probably not," Matthews said.

"See, I told you." Helen was smiling. "You're already happier. I've translated you into being happy. We'll have you singing in no time."

MATTHEWS HAD KNOWN Helen Carmichael nearly two years. She had been a student in the adult course he taught in the African-American Novel—his specialty at Wilmot College (though he was not of African descent). He and Helen had liked each other at once, met regularly for coffee after class, then started sleeping together when the course ended, a time roughly coinciding with the dark grainy period after Penny had taken their daughter, Lelia, and left for California, the period when Matthews figured out he hated teaching and everything about it, determined he should seek a less governed life and began writing a novel as a way of occupying himself until the school year was over and he could resign.

Helen was eight years older than he was, a tall, indelicately bony ash-blond woman with a big-breasted, chorus-girl figure, a wide, sensuous mouth and big benevolent blue eyes behind tortoiseshell glasses. Matthews liked looking into her eyes and found solace there. All men, he noticed, stared at Helen. There was a bigger-than-life quality to her, though not necessarily bigger and better. Helen enjoyed believing men had "a hard time handling" her and that most men were afraid of her because she was "hard to keep up with," which meant she thought she was savvy and ironic. Helen came from a small West Virginia coal-mining town and had already been married three times, but was unmarried now and had no wish to try again. She worked for an advertising company across the Ohio River in Parkersburg, not far from where she grew up, and had told Matthews she believed this was as far as life had taken her and where it would probably leave her—and that at forty-five she had made her pact with destiny and was able to be a realist about it. He liked her for her independence.

She and Matthews had begun enjoying a casual and altogether satisfactory sexual intimacy, spending afternoons in bed in his house, taking weekend trips up to nearby Pittsburgh and occasionally as far away as D.C., but mostly just enjoying a twilight drive and dinner in one of the cozy inns or restored cider mills that dotted the Ohio River banks, often ending up in some rickety old four-poster in a hot little third-floor garret room, attempting but usually failing to make as little noise as possible while still getting the most from the evening and each other.

As a general matter, they shared a view of themselves as random voyagers who'd faced life's stern blows (Helen had had cancer of the something a year before and was still officially in recovery and on medication; Matthews had, of course, been abandoned). Only they'd emerged stronger, more resolute and no less hopeful of providence and life's abundance. Matthews realized it wasn't typical to fall for an older woman after your wife leaves you. Except he hadn't really fallen for Helen; he simply liked her and liked her way of treating him seriously yet also ironically; whereas Penny had treated him with nothing but the greatest sincerity, sweetness and seemingly loving patience until the day she walked out. He wasn't at all sure what he offered Helen—he couldn't see much—though she seemed happy. The only promise she seemed to want and want to give in return was never to expect anything from the other unless the other was physically present to fulfill it. Marriage, Helen felt, should append this proviso to its solemn vows. Matthews felt the same.

Matthews' defeated marriage, however, was his great source of disappointment and woe. He had begun *The Predicament* intending it as a plain yet accurate portrayal of his marriage to Penny, a marriage in which meaningful language had been exhausted by routine, in which life's formalities, grievances and even shouts of pain had become so similar-sounding as to mean little but still seem beyond remedy, and in which the narrator (himself, of course) and his wife were depicted as people who'd logged faults, neglect and misprisions aplenty over twelve years but who still retained sufficient affection to allow them to recognize what they could and couldn't do, and to live in the warmth of that shared understanding. In that way, he felt, it was a typical academic marriage. Other people forged these same accommodations without ever knowing it. His parents, for instance. It was possible they hated each other, yet hating each other was worth more than trying to love somebody else, somebody you'd never know in a hundred years and probably wouldn't like if you did. Better, they'd found, to focus on whatever good was left, set aside all issues they would never agree on, and call it marriage, even love. How to do this was, of course, the predicament. (At one point, he'd come close to calling his book a memoir and not a novel at all.) But having the book published, Matthews had hoped, would be a dramatic and direct public profession of new faith to Penny, who had left town with an undergraduate (not a priest) and taken Lelia to live in the Bay Area. The student had eventually come back to school.

None of this, however, had worked. Penny hadn't read *The Predicament*, had declined delivery of an early proof

Matthews had couriered to her with an inscription, and had almost completely stopped communicating with him. So that at the last minute he revised the Greta part in such a way that instead of coming home to Maine, eager to reconcile, Greta died in a traffic accident.

In the year and half since Matthews had left teaching, he had finished his novel, seen unwanted divorce proceedings begun against him, sold the white-clapboard, blue-shuttered faculty colonial he'd occupied with Penny, set aside some money and moved miles from campus, into a smaller, brick-and-clay-tile, rough-hewn bungalow in a country setting, where he'd begun getting used to what had departed (conceivably his younger and callower self), what had arrived (not very much), and what the consequences for the future were. The idea of himself as a novelist seemed to be one appealing arrival: a silent artist living obscurely alone in small-town Ohio. Once, he'd been a teacher, but retired early. His wife had left him because he was too eccentric. There had been a child. Occasionally he made a brief appearance in New York, but was mostly content to go on writing small, underappreciated masterpieces that were more popular in Europe than in his own country.

Matthews' parents still owned a large and successful retail furniture company up in Cleveland—a company that had been in the Matthews name since before the Depression—and there was room for him, if he wanted, to fit right into the management scheme and before long be running things. His father had expressed this hope even after Matthews got tenure, as if teaching literature was widely accepted as an ideal preparation for the furniture business. Matthews' mother and sister were involved in a profitable interior-design venture connected to the furniture company, and they had made noises about his coming home and taking over the accounts end while they concentrated on the creative decision-making.

But Matthews had told them that he couldn't entertain either of these offers at the moment, that he had more important things on his mind: his divorce, his daughter, his life as a thirty-seven-year-old former professor who knew a great deal about African-American literature and furniture, a man who'd made big mistakes and wanted to make fewer if possible.

His parents had willingly conceded it was a good idea, given the difficult transitions in his life, that he take some time off to "sort things out." They even acknowledged that writing a novel was sound as a form of therapy before getting down to real life. They seemed to understand about Matthews' divorce and why it was regrettably necessary, and had made their own private overtures to Penny and Lelia. They had *not* been especially happy about Helen's unexpected and seemingly impermanent presence in his life, or about her age. But they'd refrained from passing judgment on human adaptations they didn't comprehend but which their only son considered necessary and good. (He frequently brought Helen along on his visits, where she good-naturedly tried to fit herself in, take part and act at ease, though the two of them always stayed downtown in a hotel.)

Nine months after Matthews finished his novel, it had been published by a small, aggressive imprint of a large, prestigious New York house, and once published had gone immediately and completely out of sight. There were a few respectful if insignificant reviews, a few copies were sold. But he quickly lost touch with his editor, and there was never any mention of another contract or of a book he might want to write at a future date. Privately (though he told Helen) he wasn't surprised. He was a novice—a

college professor who'd jumped out into the wider world—
plus he hadn't believed his novel was really good enough
in the way it depicted ordinary, middle-class people caught
in the grip of small, internal dilemmas of their own messy
concoction. That was not usually a popular subject, he
understood, unless the people were lesbians with sexually
abusive fathers, or else homicide detectives or someone suffering from a fatal disease—none of which was the case in
The Predicament, which was too much about his own life.
Still, he was satisfied to have written it, happy to have done
it on his own and to have used it to break with teaching.
He might, he felt, start thinking of something else to
write—something more far-reaching.

Though one gray afternoon in November, just at dusk,
he'd received a call from a woman at the publishers in New
York (he was on the back porch, reglazing loose panes in
his storms before crawling up onto the stepladder). The
woman told him that to everyone's pleasure, a French
publisher—a Monsieur Blumberg—had called to make
an offer on Matthews' book and wanted to publish it in
France if Matthews would agree to a small price.

"I can't think why anybody'd read my book in France,"
Matthews said to the publishing woman, Miss Pitkin or
Miss Pittman. "Nobody wanted to read it over here." He
was, though, happy that one of his imaginings was coming
true.

"You can never tell with the French," the woman said.
"They get things we don't. Maybe it'll turn out better in
French." She laughed a small laugh.

Matthews thought of what it meant for his book to
"turn out" better in a language other than the one it was
written in. It didn't seem very good. Though possibly it
meant he was a genius.

"It's hard to think Dante could be better than in French, isn't it?" Miss Pitkin/Pittman said.

"I don't believe Dante was written in French," Matthews said. He wondered what she looked like. He was staring out toward the line of thin woods behind which was another house and the big autumnal sun descending prettily.

"Well. Go to France and live it up." She chuckled. She was typing something on a computer. *"Honi soit qui mal y pense."*

"I don't know what that means," Matthews said. He knew very little French.

"It's something about Prince Charles. Something he said, supposedly. It probably means 'Live it up.' "

"Maybe so," Matthews said. "Maybe I'll live it up." And then they said goodbye.

THAT NIGHT, because of the cold and rain, and because Helen felt she might be coming down with something, they ate dinner in a dreary, nearly empty Japanese restaurant only a few doors down rue Boulard from the hotel. Matthews didn't like Japanese food, but Helen said she needed the important iron contained in raw fish to combat jet lag and to strengthen her in case she was catching a bug.

Over maguro and awabi, and Matthews' sea bass tempura, Helen told him how interesting she thought it'd be to meet your translator, someone—so it seemed to her—who would have to know your book better than you did and who would give up so much time just for your (Matthews') words. In advertising—her line of work—the trick was to get people to read things *without* knowing they were reading and to slip messages into their heads like spies behind enemy lines.

"It's their profession," Matthews said, giving up in frustration on his chopsticks and opting for a fork. "People dedicate their lives to translating. It's not a sacrifice to them."

"It's like a marriage," Helen said. "At least it's like one of my marriages. Spend years trying to read the tea leaves about what somebody else might've meant. And I never did find out." Helen was eating a big chunk of red tuna and dredging parts of it in soy sauce, using her chopsticks. Some kind of Japanese violin music was playing in the background.

"I don't think it's like that," Matthews said.

"What *do* you think?" Helen said, chewing.

"I think it's inventing," Matthews said. "I think it's using one book to invent another one. It's not just putting my book into a different language, like moving your clothes from one suitcase to another one. It's creative. And there's a lot of satisfaction accompanying it, is what I think."

"Oh," Helen said. "But you're pretty excited, aren't you?" She had lost interest. He had bored her. He was aware he bored her all the time. Helen had a good, practical, earthy, goodhearted take on the world, and he frequently bored it into silence.

"I'm excited. I am." He smiled at her.

Helen, however, wanted to plot out an itinerary for the next day's events. She had her Fodor's book and studied it on her side of the table while Matthews got through his broccoli and fish and sherbet. All the Japanese waiters and busboys seemed to be French, which felt peculiar. It was France, though. Everyone was French.

Helen wanted to visit Napoleon's tomb tomorrow, then she wanted to go up the Eiffel Tower and, afterwards, walk down the Champs Élysées. She wanted them to see the Louvre, though not necessarily go in (it was crowded with Japanese, she whispered, especially at Christmas). Then she wanted to take a ride in a glass-sided boat and finish the day at the Place de la Concorde, where people had had their heads cut off, including the king and the queen and Robespierre. She didn't know who Robespierre was, she admitted. At night they'd have their first incomparable meal someplace; "then," she said, "we'll take *your* tour the next day." Helen looked pleased. Though she also looked pale, Matthews thought. Travel took a greater toll on women. They registered everything. She had forgotten about the ballet.

"I don't have a tour," Matthews said dolefully.

"What about all the places where Negro musicians played and famous Negro writers lived in terrible poverty and slept with white women? The stuff you used to teach."

Matthews had talked about these matters as side issues in the course he'd taught, and Helen still remembered. But he had really known nothing about any of it. He'd only read about it in other books. He knew nothing about the Negro Experience, period. Just before he'd finished his PhD, his adviser at Purdue had called him in one day to say that a colleague at Wilmot College had telephoned the previous night to say a black woman professor had suddenly quit to take another job, leaving her classes without a teacher, and did he have anyone who could step into the breach? Matthews' professor said if Matthews could get down to Wilmot in two days and be ready to give a lecture on sexual imagery in Langston Hughes' late poems, some provision might be made for him to stay on longer. He simply had to be flexible. Matthews knew nothing about Langston Hughes. His own work had been in the English

Romantics, who'd begun to bore him to death. But he arrived in Wilmot the next morning, spent the following two days reading, then gave a lecture to a group of surprised black students, who seemed not to mind as long as *somebody* arrived at nine o'clock and talked about something while they mostly slept or smirked at each other. Eventually the chairman decided he could stay on and even work for tenure if he promised to go on teaching African-American studies, so that the college could keep from hiring another black woman, who everybody felt would inevitably turn out to be a lot of trouble. Matthews thought it was a good idea and didn't particularly care what he taught. Anybody could teach anything, was his view. Helen thought the whole story was a riot, though she said she'd never known many black people personally. There weren't that many in West Virginia.

"I don't really know where any of those places are," Matthews said. "I just read about them. They aren't real to me. They never were."

"So much for the African-American Experience," Helen said, refolding her map.

"I've said goodbye to teaching, okay?" Matthews said irritably. "I'm not a teacher anymore. I'm interested in a new life."

"You're hoping to translate *yourself* now, I guess," she said. Helen was nearsighted and would sometimes blink her big blue eyes behind her glasses and open them very wide, as if she could get more sight in that way. It made her seem to be looking at something over your head and being surprised by what she saw there. It was unnerving instead of consoling.

"Maybe," Matthews said. "Maybe that's exactly right. I'm hoping to be translated into something better than I was."

"What about your daughter?" Helen said, very pointedly. Helen knew nothing about Lelia, had never laid eyes on her, but periodically liked to mount an aggressive, parental-style sensitivity when she wanted to make points with him or get under his skin. It always caught him unawares, and he in fact disliked her for it. Helen had no children after her three unsuccessful marriages, and Matthews felt this was her way of expressing disappointment about that misfortune and sharing it around with others.

"We don't have to talk about Lelia," Matthews said, and felt disheartened, looking around now for the Japanese/French waiter to bring their check.

"I guess not. She isn't in on the big changes," Helen said.

"She lives in California. With Penny," he said. "She's fine. She's a normal six-year-old, if you can be normal in California. She has parents who love her."

"Would that include you?" Helen wrinkled her mouth as if she was disgusted by him.

"It would. It really would," Matthews said. Finally spotting the waiter where he lurked in the shadows near the kitchen, he flagged a hand in the air.

"Just checking." Helen wiped her mouth with her napkin and began looking all around herself. The restaurant contained only two more diners, seated by the dark other wall. Outside the front window, narrow rue Boulard was empty except for parked cars. It was still raining, and streetlights shone on the dappled pavement.

"I'm just feeling jet-lagged tonight," Helen said. "I'm sorry, baby doll." She smiled across the plates and small soiled dishes, then sniffed once, as though she might be crying. "You've brought me to Paris. I don't want to pick on you."

"Then *don't*," Matthews said. "I'm doing the best I know how." He felt that was exactly what he was doing, but was getting precious little credit for it. Lelia was his daughter and his problem, and he was taking care of it.

"I know you are, sweetheart," Helen said. "A lot goes on in that head of yours."

"I wouldn't say that," Matthews said. He wished they'd left town ten minutes after Blumberg called. They could be happier someplace else.

"I'm guilty of that too," Helen said to no one in particular. He didn't know what she was talking about. Possibly she hadn't heard him correctly. She was looking out the window, staring wistfully at the Parisian rainfall. "I am," she said. "We're all guilty of that sin."

BACK IN THE cold room, Helen quickly undressed in the dark, which was not usual. She had always been proud of her taut chorus-girl figure and preferred the light. But when she got under the covers in the small, chilly bed, she demanded that Matthews get in bed immediately and fuck the very breath out of her, which he did to the best of his abilities, two hands buckled onto the flimsy headboard, one bare foot wedged into a nubbly corner of the wall, the other actually on the tile floor and getting fouled up with his shoes and socks as he whaled away in the still, heatless air, and Helen grew strangely delirious and almost seemed to chant, "Patiently, patiently, patiently," until they were both complete and lay huddled for warmth, as the rain swept against the windows and the wind hissed through the streets and out through the cemetery's bare treetops.

Sometime later—he'd thought he heard a clock chime somewhere close by, four bells—Matthews awoke and went to the window, the bedspread wrapped around him, his wool socks on. To his surprise, the wind and rain had stopped, and much of the afternoon mist had been sucked away, leaving the cemetery sharply illuminated by moonlight, the ranks of six-story apartment buildings beyond it vivid under the unexpected stars. Though even more surprisingly, the specter of the great Montparnasse Tower blocked the sky in what Matthews now felt must be the west. Farther on, if the night were clearer, he would see the Eiffel Tower itself (this he knew from maps he'd studied when writing his novel).

In the first moments when he'd lain awake beside Helen in the warm bed, listening for the wind, he knew unquestionably that he should never have come here, or *should've* left after Blumberg's call, and that the whole event was already somehow spoiled, splattered onto everything. The feeling that he "would've" loved Paris overcame him, "would've" but for something he'd already done wrong— some novice's error—but didn't know about. Not that you ever knew about most of the mistakes you were making, or ever much caught yourself. Events, reliances, just began not to work out right for seemingly no reason, then life began to descend into disastrous straits. Helen seemed that way, seemed to be diminishing in a way he couldn't describe but only feel. He liked Helen. He admired her. But he shouldn't have come to Paris with her. That was his mistake. Bringing her was his hopeless attempt to take an experience with him, and afterwards bring it home again, converted to something better. Only if he'd brought Penny with him could that have worked—worked in the sense that the two of them had once been so close as to be two parts of one person. That was years ago. Whatever he'd liked then, she'd liked. Though that was over now.

But at the cold window, with Helen snoring in bed and the thin pink counterpane around his shoulders, Matthews began to feel different, as if the new moonlight and crinkled stars had configured the world newly, and Paris, even in the frosted glowing night, seemed to lie forth more the way he would've wanted had he ever let himself want it. A metropolis of bounteous issue; a surface to penetrate; a depth in which to immerse oneself, even reside in. Coming to Paris now, at his age, with a serious, mature intent, might mean exactly what he'd thought, a wish to stay. Only he wasn't here to convert anything to a commodity he could take back but to suit himself to the unexpected, to what was already here. Helen had been exactly right about that.

Still, he wondered about the translator. Madame de Grenelle. What had "fascinated" her about his not very good book? Some terrible flaw in it? A small, cruel and embarrassing ignorance? Some vast and subtle opportunity missed or misconstrued, which all the French would immediately see but that she meant to correct for him? This, though, was how a novelist thought: things were infinitely mutable and improvable, revisable, renewable—each surface only one side of a great volume to be revealed.

Matthews thought fitfully of Lelia. What time was it in California? He would mount a proper accounting of himself if the moment finally arrived—some California court where he would achieve joint custody. A sensible visiting arrangement. Summers. School vacations. Christmas. Still, he didn't feel like the father of a six-year-old daughter, unseen for nearly two years owing to her mother's intransigence. Occasionally he confused Greta in his book with Penny and imagined Penny dead. He'd made her up and in time would stow her away.

But was it *that* odd not to see your daughter, given conditions of relative hostility? A settled, more predictable life seemed better, even in California, though Penny seemed increasingly if mysteriously disapproving the longer they were apart. As if he was missing some opportunity he didn't even know about. Eventually it would resolve itself.

Across rue Froidevaux, at the far corner of rue Boulard, in an apartment building that must've been the exact nineteenth-century vintage as the Nouvelle Métropole, only one window was left lighted. But in it was a Christmas tree, its red and green and orange bulbs blinking in the windless night. No person was visible. The tree simply stood alone, high up and unnoticeable from the street: a beacon of a sort for no one. Possibly, Matthews thought, Americans lived there and couldn't do without a tree far from home. The French, of course, would never be bothered. *"Joyeux Noël"* was enough for them. For a long moment, his feet beginning to ache, the cold slicing in between the folds of his coverlet, he tried to stare across at the tree's shimmery lights and focus on them, to receive the tree's tiny fancy festiveness as his own. Matthews stared and stared, and in a time which wasn't so long he felt he'd succeeded in at least that small wish.

In the morning they slept late, almost until noon. Though in his sleep bells had been ringing and ringing, and twice he thought he felt Helen get out of bed, heard her throwing up behind the closed bathroom door, followed by her climbing back in bed, cold and apparently dampened. It was colder in the room now. That he was certain of.

When he opened his eyes, Helen was sitting in the green, plastic-covered armchair, wrapped in the pink percale bedspread he'd covered himself with hours before. That was why he felt cold.

"How do you feel?" he said from beneath his thin blanket.

"I'm fine," Helen said noncommittally. She had on his red wool socks and was smoking a cigarette. He'd never seen her smoke before, though he knew that years ago she had. The room smelled smoky and also sweaty. It was this smell that had waked him, that and being cold. "I guess I caught a bug when I went out in the rain. Who knows? I could've eaten something too."

"Did you throw up?" Matthews said.

"Mmmm," Helen said, big white smoke jets exiting her nostrils. Helen had her glasses on, and her blond hair was bedraggled, as if she'd been sweating or feverish. She looked pale and tired and thin. Helen always seemed big and healthy. "A big, pushy blond" was what she called herself. Now she looked worn out.

A nice light was coming in the window, a gray steely light with some yellow-stippled sun in it. No more rain, though the wind was up again, blowing on the Boulevard Raspail, past the big lion. He pictured wind riffling the glassy puddles in the street. He did not particularly want to be there.

"I was just thinking about having a translator," Helen said. "What an experience that is. I don't know why I was thinking about it. It's just an experience I'll never have." She blew smoke at the windowpanes and watched it cling to the glass, grow thin and disappear.

"*I'm* not going to be translated," Matthews said from under the covers. "My book is. Or maybe not."

"That's right," Helen said, and cleared her throat.

"Do you feel like the Paris tour today?"

"Of course." Helen pulled her head back and gave him a stern schoolmarm's frown. "I'm not about to sit here with it right outside my window. No way, René."

"I thought you might not feel good enough." With the return of Helen's bedspread, he felt he could just as easily forgo Paris, in spite of what he'd decided in the middle of the night. He was *in* Paris. Whatever he did was the right thing. Staying in bed, for instance, and later finding dinner. That would be as much Paris as Napoleon's tomb.

"What would you do if I died over here?" Helen said.

"Jesus!" Matthews said. "Why would you bring that up?" The thought shocked him. This was jet lag. He'd read it was a kind of small-scale clinical depression. All chemical. No doubt Helen's medication made it worse. "Let's think about something more pleasant."

"Would you have me buried?" she said. "Do you have to live someplace to be buried there? Here, I mean."

"I have no idea," Matthews said. He thought about inviting Helen back into the bed to warm him up. But he knew what would happen. Even feeling like shit, Helen would be up to that.

"I'm serious," she said, still smoking avidly but giving him a disapproving eye for not being serious.

"I'd have you buried on the spot," Matthews said. "Right where you fell, if that's what you wanted."

"I *would* want that," Helen said. "If I died in this room, for instance, I'd want to be buried in the Montparnasse

Cemetery. With Baudelaire. Or at least near where he is. I was reading about it."

"I'd personally see to it."

"Not that I've ever read Baudelaire."

"Fleurs du Mal," he said from bed.

"Fine," Helen said. She looked speculatively out the window at what Matthews knew to be the wide expansive winterscape of the cemetery, beautiful and bleak. They would've covered over the Jewish grave by now. Helen didn't need to see an open grave, in her present state of mind.

"What do you long for, Charley?" Helen said. "Not that I long for death." Helen smudged out her cigarette on the metal lip of the window casement and stared at the smoldering white butt.

"I don't know what you're talking about," he said.

"Just answer, okay?" Helen said. "For God's sake, the little professor. Just answer one question. Last night you said you wanted to remake yourself into something better. Okay. What's that? I'm in the dark here. We're having a serious conversation."

"I'd like for things not to center so much on me, I guess," Matthews said, feeling cold, as if she had the window open.

Helen turned and frowned at him again, her eyelids hooding her large, pale-blue irises. She bit a tiny corner of her lower lip. "So, is that your answer?"

"Yes," he said. But it was true. He simply hadn't known it was true until now. He longed to be less the center of things. He realized this was what a foreign country—any foreign country—could offer you and what you could never get at home. The idea of home, in fact, was the antithesis of that feeling. At home *everything* was about you and what you owned and what you liked and what everybody thought of you. He'd had enough of that. He couldn't, of course, expect Helen to appreciate this idea, given the mood she was in. But he didn't know what else to say. So he just nodded in what he knew to be an unconvincing gesture of seriousness, performed ridiculously from the bed.

"That's how cancer makes you feel too," Helen said quietly, raising her chin and resting it on her fist, almost touching the glass. Matthews could see only the white sky outside, suddenly cluttered with soaring swifts. Days were as short as they got now. "You feel like everything's about *you* all the time."

"I can imagine," Matthews said, and felt he *could* imagine it. He could imagine it pretty easily.

"That's probably why I like you, Charley."

"Why's that?" Matthews said.

"When I'm with you I don't think about myself very much. Really almost never."

"What do you think about?" Matthews said.

"Well," Helen said, "nothing much. Not the same things at least. I just think about what we do, where we go for our drives. Nothing important. It's perfect for me, really. I'm thinking just about Paris now. When you think about Paris, you don't have to think about yourself and what might be wrong with you."

"I was thinking the same thing."

"Well, good," Helen said. "Then we're probably suited for each other, aren't we?" She smiled at him and pulled her pink bedspread more closely around her chin.

"I guess we are," Matthews said.

"Brrr, I'm cold now," Helen said. "It's time to go see Paris." She extended one bare leg out of her coverlet and touched her toes to the cold floor. "We don't have all the

time in the world now. We have to make our happy moments last."

"Yes, we do. We certainly do," Matthews said, and he
believed that was absolutely true.

OUT IN THE STREETS it was much too blustery and cold
to walk far. Helen had wanted to walk all the way to where
Napoleon's tomb was housed in the Invalides, then to the
Eiffel Tower (which she said was close by), and from there
use the metro to the Champs Élysées, then walk to the
Place de la Concorde. A day of walking and seeing Paris up
close.

But on the first block of the Avenue du Maine, Matthews
realized their cloth coats weren't thick enough to hold off the
batting wind and street grit, and Helen announced that she
now felt "too stiff" to walk a long way. So they stood shivering in a cab queue outside the Montparnasse station and
took a taxi straight to the Invalides.

Helen, upon arrival, seemed to know a lot about absolutely everything having to do with Napoleon, Louis XIV,
the Domed Church and all the buildings. Napoleon had
been her father's lifelong fascination back in West Virginia,
she said. There had been books and battle plans and postcards and portraits and busts and memorabilia all over their
family home. It had been her father's greatest wish, Helen
said as they inched about quietly and reverently beneath the
echoing dome, to someday stand at the railing above the actual tomb itself, just as they were doing, and exactly as the
terrible Hitler had done back in 1940, and offer a better
honor than the Führer's to the great man of France. Helen
pointed out the portraits of the four evangelists and of St.

Louis offering Christ the sword with which he would defeat the infidels. She knew exactly who was buried with Napoleon (his brothers and his son, the Eaglet) and that the emperor's remains were divided into six coffins like a pharaoh's, each one made of a different precious material. And she could identify the twelve statues encircling the big red porphyry tombstone as being Winged Victory, who represented the French people reunited finally by their great leader's death.

Outside again, in the afternoon chill, Helen stared up at the great gold dome. She had her glasses off, her hand sheltering her eyes, as if from a sun, though one wasn't visible. Avenue de Breteuil lay behind her, cars and buses honking and letting off new crowds of tourists. "My single regret is my father isn't here with me. Or instead of me," she said, gazing up. "He'd appreciate this so much."

Matthews at that moment was thinking about his novel, his hands thrust in his trench-coat pockets. He was wondering whether he shouldn't just have called it a memoir and been done with it. He should, he felt. He didn't hear what Helen said, but sensed it was about being in the army in France and visiting this very spot not long after Hitler had been here.

"I know it meant a lot to him," he said, looking all around. Again he had no idea what part of Paris he was in. Which arrondissement.

"You know what people want when they come to Paris?" Helen said, still staring up at the glowing dome, with the white sky in the background.

"I don't," Matthews said. "I have no idea."

"To be French." Helen sniffed. "The French are more serious than we are. They care more. They have a perspective on importance and unimportance. You can't become them. You just have to be happy being yourself."

Looking away, Matthews suddenly noticed the great colossus of the Eiffel Tower almost springing into the sky, more huge and grave but also so much prettier than he'd imagined it could be. None of the miniatures ever showed you how pretty and graceful it was. It was the most wonderful thing he had ever seen. Better than Niagara Falls. Only the Pyramids, he felt, were probably more wonderful. He was shocked by how happy he was to see it.

"That's right," Matthews said, and he took Helen's cold, stiff hand, the one that held her glasses. He thought she'd been crying, and he wanted her to stop and be happy. "There's the Eiffel Tower," he said brightly. "It was hidden, but now there it is."

"Well, oh my," Helen said, seeing it. "It sure is. There it is. I'm so happy to see it. I wondered if I would."

"Me, too," Matthews said. "I wasn't sure we would."

"Aren't we lucky," Helen said. "It's the miracle of the Occident."

"I guess it is," Matthews said. "I guess we are."

And then they walked on.

THEIR WALK to the Eiffel Tower turned out to be longer than Helen had thought. This, she said—referring to the Fodor's—was because of a broad turn in the river Seine. "It's like New Orleans that way." New Orleans, she said, was her favorite American city.

She announced that she was feeling better, due to the crisp air, and thought the day could go on the way she'd hoped—her "first day in Paris": the stroll down the Champs

Élysées, the visit to the famous execution site, the Louvre, the romantic boat ride, then the search for an incomparable meal.

Helen spoke much better French than Matthews expected and, because she felt better, went in several shops along the Avenue de la Bourdonnais and talked animatedly to the clerks, and to flower vendors and newsagents on the side streets leading toward the Champ-de-Mars. In all of this Matthews felt Helen became a kind of spectacle—the tall, pale, buxom blond American woman with thick glasses spouting out French to small aproned Frenchmen who looked up at her in annoyance, often before simply turning around and ignoring her. It was rude, but he didn't think he could blame them. They'd all seen Helens before, and nothing in life had changed.

Avenue de la Bourdonnais was a rich area, Matthews could see, with tall, elegant apartment buildings, big Jaguars and BMW wagons lining the wide, tree-lined boulevard, and many people talking on cell phones, standing in the middle of the sidewalk. Possibly this was the diplomatic sector, he thought. Possibly the American embassy itself was nearby, since there were a lot of Americans on the street, trying to act as if they spoke the language—his grad school French was too poor to even try. Though the French, he thought, seemed like *they* were acting too. They were like amateur actors playing French people but trying too hard. There was nothing natural to the whole enterprise.

Yet he found there was another, good side to it: since, when he would listen in on some conversation Helen was having with a clerk or a flower vendor and would try to figure out from this word or that what either one of them was saying, he got almost everything wrong. Listening this way, he made up whole parts and sometimes the entirety of conversations based on an erroneous interpretation of a hand gesture or a facial expression or some act of seemingly familiar body language coupled with a word he thought he knew but was usually also wrong about. It could get to be addictive, he believed, not understanding what people were saying. Time spent in another country would proba- bly always be spent misunderstanding a great deal, which might in the end turn out to be a blessing and the only way you could ever feel normal.

In a tiny, unheated religious curio shop on rue Mari- noni, Helen went rooting through bins of plastic crucifixes in several sizes and materials, then through framed color depictions of Christ in various aspects of dolor and be- seechment, and finally through a stack of colored tea tow- els with religious mottoes stamped on them in several languages, like sweatshirts. Eventually she held one up, a pink one, that had THE GLORY OF GOD IS TO KEEP THINGS HIDDEN printed on it in white block letters.

"What's that mean?" Matthews said. "Is it a joke?"

"I'll give it to somebody back home for Christmas, somebody who lies to her husband." She was staring down at her palm, trying to identify the right money to pay with. She seemed exhausted again. The young female Chinese clerk frowned at her. "It's a proverb," Helen said, fingering through her coins. "It'll mean something different to any- body you give it to." She smiled at him. "Do you love Paris now?" she said. "Do you feel like you're not the center of everything? Because you're certainly not."

"I don't feel much like it's Christmas."

"That's because you're not religious. Plus you're spoiled," Helen said. "For spoiled people the real thing's never enough. Don't you know that?"

"I don't think I'm spoiled," Matthews said.

"And spoiled people never do. But you are, though." She said this sweetly, not to accuse him, just to acknowledge the truth everyone knew and needn't talk about. "Not to want to be the center of things, that's what spoiled people *think* they want," she said. "I'm the same way. I'm just not as bad as you are. But it's all right. You can't help it. It's gotten you this far." She smiled at him again and looked around the little shop, where a thousand colored likenesses of Christ gazed down on them in attitudes of compassion and acquiescence.

ON THE FIRST LEVEL of the Eiffel Tower, at 187 feet, Helen's stomach went immediately queasy and her knees unsteady, and she told Matthews she could feel the whole construction swaying and weaving in the "winds aloft" and that she'd never make it to level two, the 377-foot platform, much less to the top, where it was 899 and the view extended forty-two miles and Paris could be seen as it really was.

She ventured, however, over to the big banked window that looked north and, according to the colored map provided below the glass panorama, toward the Arc de Triomphe, the Champs Élysées and, farther on, though invisible beneath the low sky, toward the Sacré-Coeur church and Montmartre.

"Montmartre's where all the painters painted, including Picasso," said Helen, focusing out over the great dun-colored grid of the city in winter. "I, of course, thought I'd never get to see it. And I don't feel like I can actually take it all in now. I can't, I guess."

Most of the other viewers on level one were Germans, the ones Blumberg had said could hold the city in joint custody with the Americans until the French came back from where it was warm. Matthews understood no German, but admired them for looking so well-off and for feeling happy to come back to the city they'd once invaded. He wondered how Helen's father would absorb that.

He seemed to remember a book he'd read or even taught in which two men took a taxi to the red-light district near Montmartre, and an orchestra was playing in a club and a lot of GIs were dancing with French girls. Teaching was finally good for this and only this, he thought—intruding on and devaluing life as lived into an indecipherable muddle of lost days and squandered experiences. He wondered how much life he'd already lost to it and for a moment tried to calculate how many days he'd lived on earth, and how many more he might hold on, and how many he'd thrown in the garbage. He got to how many days he'd lived—13,605—then felt too irritated to go on.

"Richard Wright," he said.

"Hmmm?" Helen said. She had been silent for what seemed like a long time, taking it all in through the observation window. More Germans were circulating around them, shouldering in, pointing to places on the map and then to the same places in the real city spread in all directions in front of them. Matthews heard the words *die Bedienung.* He imagined it meant something admiring: the recognition of a paradise lost for the fatherland. Whatever it was, it made the Germans laugh. *"Die Bedienung,"* he mouthed to himself, and made the little gasping sound Blumberg had made.

"What did you say?" Helen said.

"I just remembered I once read a book where an important scene takes place in Montmartre," Matthews said. "Richard Wright wrote it, I think."

Helen looked at him as if she had no idea what that might mean to him. She blinked behind her glasses and looked troubled.

"Die Bedienung," Matthews said, but did not gasp.

"Who?"

"It's all right," he said. "It doesn't matter."

"The professor," Helen said, and looked back intently at the gray-brown matte of Paris, as if it were hers to command.

WHEN HELEN CAME BACK from her trip to the Eiffel Tower ladies' room, she was not alone. She was with a man and a woman, and all three of them were having a loud joke.

"Look who's got nothing else to do but climb the Eiffel Tower," Helen said, even more loudly. She mimicked being thrown off balance by the sway of the tower in the wind. "Whoa," she said, and laughed again. Helen seemed no longer sick but happy. Matthews was sorry to see these people. You could ruin your whole experience, he thought, by running into someone you knew. You could lose the feeling of being set adrift in a strange sea, which he was beginning to enjoy.

"This is Rex and Cuddles," Helen said.

"Cuddles, my butt," Cuddles said, rolling her eyes and winking at Matthews.

"Cuddles too much," Helen said.

The Germans were staring at them. Matthews felt sorry to find these people.

"This is Charley," Helen went on. "Charley's my *amour impropre.* My *amour temporaire,* anyway."

He shook hands with Rex, who volunteered that he and this woman were friends of Helen's from "the old days in Pittsburgh."

"We're American," Cuddles said, brimming.

"Can't you guess." Helen gave Cuddles, whose actual name turned out to be Beatrice, a fishy look. "Bea-*at*-rice the actress," Helen said. "They're taking us to our incomparable meal tonight."

"It's been decided coming out of the *Mesdames*," Beatrice said. She was a much too slender woman, with tanned skin that was too tanned, and tight black pedal pushers that she wore with white ankle socks and ballet slippers. She had on a large black motorcycle jacket and looked like somebody out of the fifties, Matthews thought. Somebody who'd lived in coffeehouses for years, smoked a lot of marijuana, read too much awful poetry and probably written plenty herself. These people were always bores and had strong, idiotic opinions about everything. He looked around him. Germans and Japanese—Axis-power tourists—were eddying noisily this way and that on the viewing platform. His gaze fell out onto the city, the City of Light, a place where no one knew him, a provocative place until this moment. He felt slightly dizzy.

"Bea and Rex come to the Eiffel Tower once a year," Helen said. "Isn't that romantic?"

"It is," Matthews said.

"Otherwise you could forget you're in Paris," Rex said solemnly.

"You might think you're in Tokyo up here, though," Helen said, eyeing the clusters of Japanese pressing toward the observation windows, jabbering and adjusting their cameras for good snaps.

Rex was watching the Japanese without smiling. He was a big, mealy-skinned, full-bellied man who wore cowboy boots and what Matthews remembered his father calling a car coat. He'd had one when he was ten, and his had matched his father's. Rex had endured a hair transplant that'd left a neat row of stalky-thin hair follicles straight across his dome. It was recent, or possibly it hadn't worked out perfectly. But Rex seemed happy to meet Helen up here, where he was happy to be, anyway. Rex, he thought, was undoubtedly Helen's age and was what men Helen's age looked like if everything hadn't gone right. Rex must've weighed two fifty. Bea, on the other hand, might've made a hundred.

"You're a writer?" Rex said in a jokey voice.

"Not exactly," Matthews said. A man in the milling crowd, plainly an American, looked right in his face after hearing Rex say he was a writer. The man was clearly wondering if Matthews was somebody famous, and if so, who.

"Bea writes poetry," Rex said.

"That's wonderful," Matthews said. Helen and Bea were sharing a private word. Bea was shaking her head as though expressing surprise, then her eyes flickered at Matthews and away again. Some accusation, he assumed, Helen had lodged that would never have been made if they hadn't bumped into Cuddles and Rex. All at once a choir of voices, from somewhere on the platform, began singing a Christmas carol in German. *"O, Tannenbaum . . ."* It turned the whole place, 187 feet aloft, calamitous and chaotic.

"It must be a burden to have a compulsion to write," Rex practically shouted.

"It's not, no," Matthews said, trying to be heard.

"I never had it," Rex said. "I wasn't compelled."

Suddenly the caroling stopped, as if somebody in authority had decided it was much too loud.

"That's all right," Matthews said more normally. "I'm not compelled either."

"Hell, yes, it's all right," Rex said, sternly for some reason. "What any person chooses to do is all right."

Rex's big sad brown eyes were set wide apart and separated by a wide barge of a nose that had probably been broken many times. Rex seemed as stupid as a bullock, and Matthews did not want to have dinner with him. More than likely, Helen would not be up to it anyway.

"I guess so," Matthews said, and smiled, but Rex was looking around for the carolers.

Helen and Bea rejoined them, with a plan worked out.

"Clancy's. We're dining at Clancy's," Helen said eagerly.

"I know, it doesn't sound French," Bea said. "But how much French food can you eat? You'll like it."

"Matthews just wants it to be incomparable," Helen said. "But he eats what I tell him to."

"That's good," Bea said, and patted Matthews on the arm.

Matthews didn't like being called Matthews. Sometimes Helen did it when she was in her cups, then would often keep doing it for hours. It was also Helen's choice of words that they have an "incomparable" meal. It was her Paris fantasy. It was a word he wouldn't use.

"So, look, we're off, you kids," Bea said, grabbing Rex's big arm and pulling herself close to him. Matthews realized he was gazing at Rex's hair re-seeding, though he was sure Rex was used to people staring at it. "See you at eight. Don't be *en retard,*" Bea said, and then away they went into the crowds.

"Bea's a firecracker," Helen said.

"I see," Matthews said. Bea and Rex stood waiting for the elevator. Bea waved back through the wandering tourists. He wanted to stay until they disappeared, after which he would conceivably never see them again.

"Are you taking mental notes for your next novel?" Helen said. "I hope so."

"Who said I was writing another novel?"

"I don't know," Helen said. "What else are you going to do? Sell sofas? Seems to me it's all you know how to do anymore. That and not like things."

"What don't I like?" Matthews said uncomfortably. "I like you."

"Yeah, right. And pigs have ears."

"Pigs do have ears," he said. "Two of them. Apiece."

"Wings. Okay, pigs have wings. You get the point."

He didn't get the point at all. But Helen had started for the elevator. Bea and Rex were no longer in sight. There was no chance to talk about what he did and didn't like. Not now. He simply came after and followed her to the elevator and out.

ON THE CROWDED Quai Branly, at the foot of the tower, Helen stopped in the gusty wind and gazed again straight up at the swirling misty sky, in which the spire had become obscured.

"We couldn't have seen anything way up on top, anyway," she said. "Do you think? We got the best view there was."

"I'm sure," Matthews said.

Across the busy boulevard was the Pont d'Iéna, and the river, which they could barely see. They'd passed over it in the cab from the airport, but now that he was closer to the water, brown and churning and slightly rancid-smelling in winter flood, Matthews felt it gave the whole city a menacing aspect, which he suspected wasn't accurate but only seemed so at this moment. Yet that Paris could seem menacing was a new sensation: a city with such a river shares in all its aspects. He thought about telling this to Helen but presumed she wouldn't be interested.

When they had walked ten minutes along the quai, as far as the Pont de l'Alma, where the Fodor's required them to cross the river in order to seek the Champs Élysées and the Arc de Triomphe and to satisfy Helen's desire for an epic stroll, she sat down on a iron bench, put her head back and took an enormous breath, then exhaled it.

This, he believed, was Helen's way of "taking it all in."

He stood and looked across the charged river at the Trocadéro and the Palais de Chaillot—names he'd seen in the Fodor's and could now place, though without a clue to what went on there or made them important. They looked like something put up for a world's fair, which the city had then had to find uses for—like Shea Stadium in New York. Basically a mistake. All around Paris's skyline you could see profiles of construction derricks. In the cab, he'd counted seventeen in one small bombed-out piece of ground.

He felt, however, like *he* was with *Helen* now, that she was the person in charge; whereas before, even yesterday, it had been his trip and she'd only been along for it. Now, though—at least this afternoon—she'd appropriated events to her wishes, so that what he felt was surprisingly, uncomfortably *young,* much younger than the eight years that separated them. Yet she was more vitally involved than he was. How, he wondered, could that be?

"I'm done for," Helen said. "I can't go another step. I've had too much fun." She had her glasses off and was sticking a pill in her mouth.

"We can take a taxi to the Place de la Concorde," Matthews said. "It'd still be nice to see where people had their heads chopped off."

"I can skip it," Helen said. "I'm stiff and I feel dizzy. I got dizzy in the Eiffel Tower. I'm still glad I went, though." She swallowed her pill down hard. "I think I have to go home now."

"Home all the way to West Virginia?"

"Just to the hotel right now," she said. "I have to lie down for a while. I'm weak." Cars and motorcycles and buses were surging by in front of them along the quai. "I'm sorry I got pissy," she said, her head back again, staring up at the white sky.

"You weren't very pissy," Matthews said. "You just said I didn't much like you. But I do. I like you quite a lot. It's not very easy being here now."

"I know. It's just supposed to be," Helen said. With her fingertip she lightly touched the tiny dent her glasses had pressed on her nose. "It's supposed to be the time of your life. You're supposed to die and go to heaven, all in the same day."

"We ought to be used to what's *supposed* to happen," Matthews said.

"Spoken like a man who's unhappily separated from his first wife," Helen said, and grinned, still staring up. "That's just hind-spite. You should take the brighter side of things."

"Which one is that?"

"Oh, let me see," Helen said almost dreamily. "What does my little motto say, my little proverb?"

" 'The glory of God is to keep things hidden.' "

"There you go," Helen said. "Doesn't that just mean: Take two pills and call me in the morning, sayeth the Lord?"

"I guess it could," Matthews said. "It could mean why don't you shut up, too."

"There you go. So why don't you shut up?" Helen smiled sweetly at him where he stood alone on the cold sidewalk, hands in his coat pockets, head bare to the wind. "No offense."

"No, none taken," Matthews said, and he began to wave for a taxi out on the crowded avenue along the river.

IN THE HOTEL, they both fell into bed and into dense sleeps, from which he did not awaken until after dark, so that when his eyes found only darkness, he had no idea where he was or what day it was or, for an instant, who Helen Carmichael might be, breathing beside him. The air all around was steamy, and he was sweating and could feel warm sweat on Helen's bare back. He lay, then, for a long time as though a great burden of sleep and fatigue was resting on his chest, and finally he let the weight sink him back into darkness as if the darkness of sleep was better than the darkness of the unknown.

In his second sleep he dreamed vividly. There, he was both sitting at what seemed to be a typical Parisian sidewalk café (something he had never done) but also watching himself do the very same thing. Wearing a heavy black overcoat and a red scarf and a disreputable-looking black beret, he was talking to someone at an extremely high rate of speed. He couldn't, in the dream, see who he was talking to, but the thought that it was Penny seemed foregone. He was still wearing a wedding ring.

And he was speaking French! French words (all unfathomable) were flooding out of his mouth just the way they flooded out of every Frenchman's mouth, a mile a minute. No one—whoever he was talking to—offered anything in reply. So that it was only he, Charley Matthews, rattling on and on and on in perfect French he could miraculously speak, yet, as his own observer, in no way understand.

This dream, in its own dream time, seemed to go on until, when he suddenly awoke with the feeling he'd rescued himself from some endless, winnerless race, he was exhausted and his heart was pounding, his legs aching, and even his shoulders were stiff, as though his sleep was truly a burden he'd been forced to carry for days.

The stingy fluorescent ceiling light had been turned on in the room, and for a long time Matthews lay naked and stared at the pale tube as if it was a source of assurance, though still without completely comprehending where he was or why.

"Don't sleep forever," he heard Helen say.

"Why not?"

"It'll ruin your sleep. You have to wake up now so you can sleep later."

Matthews raised only his head and looked down the length of his body. Helen was standing in the bathroom door, a towel wrapped around her breasts and waist. With another towel she was drying her hair in the stronger light of the bathroom. She looked large and important in the doorway. "Junoesque" was the word she liked. It was this particular attitude and incarnation that allowed Helen to think most people couldn't handle her and that she was too much for most men. Matthews stared at her in the lighted doorway, thinking that the soapy flower smell from the shower had now overpowered the sweaty smell from earlier. "We haven't eaten all day," Helen said. "Did you realize that? Not that I'm hungry."

The thought of Beatrice and Rex floated unhappily back into his mind. "Did we cancel dinner with your friends, or did I dream that?"

"You dreamed it." Helen tilted her head sideways so her long, pale hair fell to the side and she could dry the parts that were underneath.

"We should have," Matthews said. "I'd rather die here now than eat dinner at—where was it?"

"Clancy's," Helen said, then took a deep breath and sighed. "Clon-cee. You don't have to go with me."

"I have to if you do," Matthews said. "How do you feel?"

"I feel absolutely wonderful," she said. "I've decided I'm going to read your book next."

"My book?" Matthews said.

"Yes," Helen said. *"Ton livre."*

"You won't like it," Matthews said. "Nobody but the French like it."

As a first perfectly clear thought, this was not welcome news. Helen had always acted as though his book and the fact that he'd written it were merely amusing if not actually embarrassing and ridiculous anomalies, in no way worth taking time to investigate. A kind of engrossing but value-less hobby. Her standard line—offered even to Matthews' parents and sister in Cleveland—had been that she didn't intend to read *The Predicament* because she was afraid she'd either like it so much Matthews would then hopelessly in-timidate her, or else hate it so much she'd never be able to take him seriously again and their relationship would be over. (Privately, she'd told him only explanation two was the real one.)

This had suited Matthews fine, inasmuch as in the last months of writing *The Predicament,* and not long after he'd begun his affair with Helen, he'd inserted a character who was—even he knew—somewhat modeled on her: a tall, ash-blond, Buick-bumper, Rockette type he'd exaggerated into a garish woman who wore mules, slit-up-the-sides dresses, and talked in a loud voice about coarse subjects, but whom the protagonist clings to after his wife abandons him, even though they have little in common but sex. In Matthews' mind, this was not Helen Carmichael; only one or two superficial details were appropriated. And it was in no way meant to size Helen up or be her portrait.

Except try to tell Helen that. Helen maintained strong certainties about her own substance and integrity, but also spent considerable time scanning the no-man's-land around her like a razor-beam searchlight, on the lookout for possible adversaries and nonbelievers. Plus she wasn't stupid—though her personal reading tastes were always for best-sellers and ghoulish police mysteries. She would certainly see the character of Carlette as a not especially flattering image of herself and would be mad as hell about it. It was not a prospect Matthews felt eager to confront in the midst of an expensive and already half-wrecked trip to Europe.

And not that he'd blame her—assuming she got to the Carlette part. Probably people never had kind thoughts about seeing themselves in someone else's made-up book. It was a matter, he understood, of power and authority: one person's being usurped or stolen outright by another, for at very best indifferent purposes. And that was definitely how Helen would view it. So, if he could, he would like to keep her from feeling any of these bad ways by discouraging her from reading *The Predicament* anytime soon.

"I'm sure I won't like it," Helen said, having disappeared back into the tiny bathroom, where Matthews could hear her unscrewing the top of some kind of jar, then popping the cap on a container of pills. "I just thought it might tell me something interesting about you."

"I'm not very interesting." Matthews stared unhappily up at the fluorescent tube, which produced its thin, mint-colored and quaverous light. He pulled the blanket over his lower half, though the room still felt steamy.

"I'm sure you're not," Helen said. She opened the medicine cabinet and closed it. "I just want to uncover the *real* Charley Matthews. The man behind the whatever. Whatever the French think is so thrilling. Maybe you're deep and I don't know it." Helen stuck her head around the doorjamb and smiled at him meanly. "You know? Deeeeep," Helen said. "You're deeeeep."

"I'm not deep at all," Matthews said, feeling trapped.

"No, I know that," she said, disappearing once more.

Though in a moment she emerged wearing a slip, her hair almost dry. She stepped across the tiny cluttered room to where her blue plastic suitcase was open on the floor and squatted beside it to unpack clean clothes.

Turning sideways, prepared to say something about the utter inanity of his own novel, Matthews noticed surprisingly that Helen had an enormous purple and black and even brown bruise halfway up her left thigh. And another one, he saw now, was on her other thigh, close to her underpants, just where her buttocks began to bloom outward in the way he liked.

"Jesus, what in the hell are those big bruises!" he said, and leaned up on one elbow as if to get closer. "They look like you fell off a damn truck."

"Thanks," Helen said, still going through her packed clothes.

"What caused them?"

"I don't know." Helen stopped her hands for a moment in their busy delving and looked up at the window, a perfect blank curtain of night that seemed to block any light from escaping. She took a breath and let it out. "Maybe it's my medicine," she said, and shook her head. Then she knelt on one knee and went back to her clothes. "You should get dressed if you're coming with me."

"Did they just show up?" Matthews said. He was transfixed by these bruises, which looked like big gloomy expressionist paintings or else thunderclouds.

"Did what show up?"

"Those bruises."

"Yep. They did." She seemed to want to look at her hip where her slip's hem was above the bruise, but didn't look.

"Have you had them before?" he said, still in his bed. "I've never seen them."

"Look. What difference does it make?" Helen said, supremely annoyed. "I have a goddamn bruise. Okay? I can't help it."

"Do they hurt?"

"No. They don't hurt. If you hadn't pointed them out like I was a goddamn sideshow, I wouldn't have thought about them. So leave it alone."

"Do you want to see a doctor?" He understood mysterious bruises of that sort were serious. You didn't get bruises like these—and maybe there were others too—from bumping into bedposts and armchairs. These were possibly related to Helen's cancer. She could be sick again, and how she felt this morning—stiff and weak—and then dizzy this afternoon could be interpreted as symptoms of cancer coming back. She probably knew it herself but didn't want it to interfere with the trip.

"I'll go to my doctor when I get home," she said. She was pulling one of her signature short skirts, this one peach-colored, over her hips, so that her two bruises went out of sight.

Helen knew what he'd been thinking, that was clear, and he realized he shouldn't say anything more now, since she'd said she didn't want to find a doctor. Though where would you find a doctor on rue Froidevaux at seven o'clock the week before Christmas? He remembered shiny brass plaques set into the sides of the rich brownstones on the Avenue de la Bourdonnais. "Dr. So-and-so, Chirurgien." You couldn't get one of these guys at seven p.m. They were all away, were just at that very moment sitting down to a jolly dinner beside a warm ocean beach where dry palms were gently clattering. To see a doctor, you'd need to call an ambulance and get carted out through the lobby on a stretcher. If you were lucky.

"Are you sure you feel up to going to dinner?" he said.

"I feel absolutely wonderful." She was pulling a matching peach-colored sweater over her thick hair. Helen liked matching colors—down to her shoes, the tint of her stockings, sometimes her lipstick and eye shadow. It made her feel good to match. He began climbing out of bed, stiff from his dream but happier to worry about Helen's health than about whether she'd read his novel. Helen's health was important, and that was what he intended to concentrate on.

"Do you think I look nice enough for Paris?" Helen said. She was standing in the middle of the crummy room, up on her peachy high heels, her glasses catching a glimmer from the gauzy light.

"You look terrific," Matthews said, holding his blanket up to cover himself. He smiled at her too animatedly. "I'd happily take you anywhere in the world." Except Clancy's, he thought.

"Would you really?" He heard a rare, faint trace of West Virginia accent in Helen's voice. Her eyes were wide, as if his declaration surprised her.

"Absolutely," he said. He thought about putting his arms around her, but she was all dressed and ready, and he was, in essence, naked.

"I wish I had some champagne right now," she said.

"We'll get you champagne." He began moving toward his suitcase. "We'll have champagne at Clancy's."

"I just meant right then. It's already gone. I just had a moment when to be holding a glass of champagne would've been very nice."

"I bet you'll have a glass before you know it," Matthews said.

"Oh. I bet I will too." Helen smiled at him, then turned to gaze out the dark window, while Matthews got himself ready to go.

CLANCY'S WAS a big, noisy, brassily lit room off the rue St.-Antoine, near the Bastille, in what, Rex gloated, was "the Frenchiest part of Paris." He and Beatrice had already downed one bottle of champagne by the time Matthews and Helen arrived, and were awaiting the arrival of another one.

"They mix up the best martinis in the world here," Rex said loudly, standing up and giving Matthews' hand a big engulfing pump. "But I hate to drink gin on an empty stomach. Don't you, Bill?"

"We didn't think you kids would mind if we got a head start," Beatrice said, grinning and clearly drunk.

"That's exactly how I feel," Helen said, getting seated and into the spirit of things. "The race goes to the drunkest. Sit down, Bill," she said. "This is where we're going. In case you didn't know it."

Rex began explaining that two American Pan Am pilots, "a couple of guys named Joe from Kansas City," got tired of not finding steaks in Paris up to their high standards and decided to retire early and open a place for people like themselves, who were stranded here with similar needs and tastes. They found this place, put in the good lighting, got the ambience established with a lot of vintage black-and-white photographs—Babe Ruth hitting a homer, Rocky Marciano KO'ing some black guy. And the rest was history. Both the pilots had unfortunately died of AIDS, Rex said soberly, but the business had been kept going by loyal family members, including one pilot's former wife. It was the best-kept secret in town, and generally considered the unofficial headquarters for the overseas community, a place where you could relax, be yourself and get shit-faced in peace, just like back home. Regrettably, it was beginning to get crowded, and even some French people were showing up, though they were always given the worst tables.

Matthews had realized, on the cab ride over, that he'd set a scene in *The Predicament* exactly where rue St.-Antoine entered the Place de la Bastille, directly across from a big opera house they passed, and that the crowded, brightly lit roundabout they'd driven through looked precisely the way he'd imagined it, though he'd made it possible to walk down to the Seine in less than five minutes, which was clearly impossible.

Rex Mountjoy, it turned out, was in the machine parts business, specializing in farm implements. American manufacturers had a hammerlock on the big farm-machinery market, Rex said, but their Achilles' heel was that their parts-and-service was way too expensive and they were essentially shooting themselves in the foot. Rex's big, heavy-jowled, heavy-lidded face grew even more solemn in the discussion of his own affairs. From thousands of miles across the ocean, in the corporate parts department of a big-market-share company headquarters, Rex had spied an opening where a smart gunslinger type could pick up refurbished parts in the States, sell them direct into the infant retail implement market here in France, and come away with a bundle. He hadn't thought his business would stay profitable for longer than two, maybe three years, until the competition in the EU got wise to him and some bureaucrat up in Brussels tailor-made a regulation to embargo exactly what he was doing. "But we're still here," Rex said, putting his giant farm-implement mitts around a big martini glass and sniffing the simple pleasures of his success. "The French all hate to work. It's that simple," Rex said prodigiously. "They're fighting a rearguard action against the success ethic. If you had a good idea, you'd definitely want to bring it over here and sell it on the street."

"That's good advice," Matthews said. He had ordered a glass of Pouilly-Fuissé, which Beatrice had immediately begun calling "foolish pussy." Both Beatrice and Helen, who were again locked in an intensely private conversation, occasionally looked up to refer to Matthews' "foolish pussy"—Helen with an blazing smile that seemed to him feverish and hot.

"Have some more foolish pussy, Bill," Helen practically shouted, then laughed noisily, her mouth open so Matthews could see her tongue, wide and flat and café-au-lait-colored—a color he knew doctors associated with illness. The tongue, his mother had always said, the tongue tells the story of your health. Helen's tongue wasn't telling a good story.

Rex, it became clear, had ordered everything for everybody—which included more martinis, big iceberg salads with beefsteak tomatoes and onion slabs drenched in white vinegar, continent-sized sirloins with two accompanying Idahos on platters all by themselves. A boat full of butter, sour cream, chives, bacon crumbles, steak sauces, horseradish, mustard and ketchup was set in the middle of the table on a lazy Susan with three previously aired bottles of Côtes du Rhône. Rex announced that if anyone wanted anything else, they only had to ask for it, "just as long as it isn't *poulet* and *haricots verts.*"

"Really. If I don't eat two of these a week, I get goddamn anemic," Beatrice said, sawing straight into her red meat, holding her fork like a shoehorn. Beatrice was dressed in the same black bohemian outfit she'd had on in the Eiffel Tower; and because she was drunk now and seemed irritable, she looked, Matthews thought, like the picture of an anemic person.

Rex, on the other hand, seemed to have grown jollier and much more companionable as the day and now the night wore on. He was dressed like somebody headed for a college football game, a big red crewneck sweater over a green plaid sport shirt and a pair of brown corduroys— clothes Matthews hadn't noticed earlier because of the car coat. He'd refashioned his hair transplant so it didn't make him look as absurd—though his big-browed forehead still appeared tender and slightly angry in spots.

"It must be a real burden to have the compulsion to write," Rex said confidentially, his mouth full.

"No, it really isn't," Matthews said, trying to eat his own steak and keep eye contact with Rex. The noise in Clancy's rose and fell like a tide. New people constantly came through the door, people the other diners knew, and a clamor would crescendo and then fall off. Everybody seemed to be shouting in English, though he and Rex were able to talk under the roar by getting closer. Rex, he noticed, had on some loud minty aftershave that seemed familiar—also something his father wore.

"I guess all your family are writers too," Rex said.

"No, they're in the furniture business in Cleveland," Matthews said. "I've only written one book, and I don't think it's very good. So you couldn't really call me a writer. Not yet, anyway."

"I see," Rex said. "I guess it's all just personal expression."

"Rex traces his family directly back to Adam and Eve," Beatrice said. She'd been talking to Helen but listening to them. Parentage was obviously an issue she liked to bring up at Rex's expense.

"She's jealous because my parents had last names," Rex said, and pushed his big lips out and made a juicy, insolent kiss at Beatrice.

"Right. Like Zigolowsky and Prdozilewcza—the ones you don't need many vowels for. Mountjoy's his stage name. I hardly need say that, though, I guess."

The din in Clancy's rose and fell again, and somewhere, apparently in the room with them, a dog started barking.

Several people seated near Clancy's big, white-flocked Christmas tree started laughing. "Gordon," someone said. "Here, Gordon." There was another brisk bark, then a squeal of sudden intense pain.

"French people," Rex said, straining his big neck around to find the offenders. "Yep, yep, there they are," he said. "I see 'em. Four of 'em with their fuckin' pooch."

"Gordon. Great." Beatrice looked disgusted. In the bright restaurant light, Matthews could see that Beatrice's skin was more leathery and tough-looking than he'd thought. He wondered how old she really was. Once again he felt ridiculously young, though he was thirty-seven and already had an ex-wife, an ex-profession and a daughter he never saw. Rex and Beatrice and even to some extent Helen seemed like his parents' age and, much like his parents, almost completely unreachable.

"The UN's a loada crap. I know that," Rex was saying in answer to some remark of Helen's about differing nationalities needing to get along better. Helen was a strong believer in the UN.

"Oh, let's don't get him started on the UN," Beatrice said, and rolled her eyes. She decided to have another big gulp of her martini. "*Or* the EU. Another of his big all-time faves."

"Yeah. Don't get me started on that," Rex said, inserting lettuce into his big mouth and breathing a heavy breath at the same time.

"Charley knows all about Negroes. The ones who came to Paris, anyway," Helen said. "He was once a prof. He can tell you who wrote what and where they lived and why, all that kind of thing. He doesn't *look* black, does he?"

"You can't always tell," Beatrice said. "They're not like the French—visible for miles in every direction."

"I thought you said you were a novelist," Rex said, head down, negotiating a slice of meat onto a square chunk of potato with the intention of eating them as one.

"I didn't say that," Matthews said, shaking his head.

"Who said it, then?" Rex said, lifting the loaded fork to his mouth.

"And who cares?" Beatrice said.

"Charley's a novel-*least*," Helen said, her eyes hot. "I haven't read his *ro-man* yet. But I'm going to. I want to see if I'm in it. Part of it's set in Paris."

"You're not in it," Matthews said, feeling in a hurry to eat, though with no idea what to do when he was finished. Helen had to be in pain, he thought. That was why she was acting agitated—solicitous one second, ready to turn on him the next. She was also drunk and undoubtedly taking painkillers.

"Is Josephine Baker in it?" Beatrice said, going on eating.

"That's who I was thinking of too," Helen said.

"No," Matthews said. "It's all made up. No real people are in it." Everything he said sounded asinine. He wished he could shut up, finish his meal and take Helen home.

"I thought they only let black people teach that stuff," Beatrice said. "Of course, I've been over here so long I've forgotten what happens at home."

"It was pretty unusual," Matthews said.

"No kidding," Rex said.

"We're putting Charley on the spot here," Helen said.

"That's all right," Rex said. "I'll be next."

Gordon suddenly gave three sharp reports from near the Christmas tree. Several diners shouted, then laughed. Then everyone heard a fierce, yowling cat hiss. There was then a scramble of scratching claws and growling, and something hurtled past Matthews' legs under the table, with something else hurtling after it. The French people—all small men and women in pastel sweaters and nice jackets—seemed vaguely dismayed. One of the men got up and made his way through the tables in the direction Gordon seemed to have escaped. He didn't seem the least bit surprised, only annoyed.

Rex glared at him as he sidled past. "Monkeys'll be next," he said menacingly. "Then talking birds. This place is going to hell."

"Everyone's going to Prague now, anyway," Beatrice said. "Paris is finished. I wish I'd learned Czech instead of French."

"Or Budapest," Rex said, pronouncing it *Budapesht,* like Matthews' colleagues at Wilmot College. "Now, *there's* a place you can really make some money. You oughta try to publish your books in Hungarian. What's the title?"

"It's the Paris of the east," Beatrice said.

"What is?" Rex was pushing his empty plate away.

"Prague," she said.

"Right. I've been there. Once was enough, though."

"Behold, the alpha male," Beatrice said, with reference to Rex.

"I'm a man only one woman has to marry, though," Rex said.

Matthews pretended he hadn't heard Rex ask about the title of his book. He didn't want to hear himself say the words, if only for fear of what Helen might say. In truth, he didn't want to hear himself say anything. Half of his steak was uneaten. Helen had touched none of hers. Beatrice and Rex had cleaned their plates. He wondered if he and Helen could apologize and leave. Plead jet lag.

The Frenchman in the pink sweater and the ascot came back through the restaurant, carrying a small tan poodle cradled in his arms. The poodle was panting as though it was exhausted, its little tongue lolled to the side. The Frenchman was smiling as if everyone in Clancy's was happy to finally see the dog. Outside the big clean front window, it was starting to snow.

"Did you know Helen was a wonderful dancer?" Rex said, running his wide hand over his skull, through the new hair seedlings. "She was on her way to Radio City."

"June Taylor, anyway," Helen said. "They were on TV when I was a little girl." She smiled and shook her head as though the idea was funny. "That was in Pittsburgh."

"Except what happened?" Beatrice said.

"Helen would dance till she dropped," Rex said, setting his hands on the table in front of him, lacing his fingers and staring down at them. He was paying no attention to Beatrice.

"We all did then," Helen said, and looked like she might break into tears. "I'm tired. I'm jet-lagged, that's all. I'm sorry."

"These two were a marquee item once upon a blue moon," Beatrice said to Matthews by way of explanation. "In case you were wondering."

"While it lasted," Helen said, her eyes glistening behind her glasses.

"While *we* lasted," Rex said.

"And they always do this," Beatrice said. "They get drunk, and then they get overcome with everything. I usually just leave."

"Don't leave now," Helen said, and smiled sweetly.

"Turkwoz," Matthews heard someone say at a nearby table. "It was Egyptian turkwoz—that's the very best. Better than that American garbage."

Rex turned to look at who'd said this. He had phased out of the conversation for a moment, thinking about dancing with Helen in faraway Pittsburgh.

"That was a different era," Beatrice said solemnly. "It was long before I came on the scene."

"I don't believe in eras," Helen said. "I believe it's all continuous. Now and then. Women and men."

"Well, good for you," Beatrice said, and she stood up to attend whatever was going on in the ladies' room, leaving the three of them alone.

"Matthews isn't divorced yet," Helen said. "He also has a daughter he almost never sees. I don't think he wants to be divorced, if the truth were known, which it always is eventually. But I think he needs to be divorced. You need to be divorced, Charley."

"Helen always has plenty of opinions," Rex said. Waiters were clearing away plates.

"I'm aware of that," Matthews said.

"Don't you have to be pretty obsessive to be a writer?" Rex asked again.

"No. I don't think so," Matthews said. "I don't think I am."

"You're not?" Rex said. "That's funny. I'd have thought you needed to be. Shows you what I know anymore. About anything."

ON THE TAXI RIDE back up the Boulevards St. Marcel and Arago it was snowing, the large heavy flakes seeming not to fall but to stay suspended in the yellow streetlight halos, backed by red taillights and darkness.

They had said good night to Rex and Beatrice on the snowy side street outside the restaurant. Dessert had ultimately been decided against. Helen said she wasn't holding up well, that it was only their second day, that her stomach was involved. Rich food. Drinking too much. Matthews' translator was invoked. A need to sleep.

Beatrice and Rex both seemed to regard Helen with amazement that she could be whatever she still was, while they had "gone on" to be whatever they so clearly were: a nothing businessman and a bad-tempered counterculture failure, in Matthews' view. Helen, he thought, was much better at being Helen than they were at being Rex and Cuddles.

Helen had stood in the snowy street in her pumps and peach outfit, and waved at them as their taxi disappeared toward the lights of the Bastille and wherever they lived in the suburbs behind Montreuil. Inside Clancy's the party wore on.

"I used to love Rex," she said, putting a pill in her mouth, one she'd dug with some difficulty out of her handbag. "God, memory's a terrible thing. Whoever invented it—I'd like to get my hands on him."

As their taxi passed the lion statue in the middle of Place Denfert-Rochereau, Helen gazed out at the rich old apartment buildings down Boulevard Raspail. Suddenly she said, "Do you have a belief in any spirituality of any kind, Charley?"

"Like what?" Matthews said. "Like church? We were Protestants. We gave at the office."

"Not like church," Helen said languidly. "I went to church. That's not the same as spiritual. I mean a convic-

tion about something good that you can't see. That kind of
thing."

Matthews thought about Lelia. She came to mind, surprisingly. He hadn't seen her in more than a year and a half,
and wasn't sure exactly when he would again. Her future,
he felt, was something he believed in, although he wasn't
currently acting on it. But he didn't want to say that to
Helen. She'd turn it on him, as she already had.

"I do. Yes," he said.

"And what would that be?" Helen said. She inscribed a
little rainbow with her finger on the sweated window, fastened her gaze outside on the sky full of snowflakes.

"What would that be?" Matthews said. "Well. I have
a conviction about the idea of change. I believe things
change for the better. If they can. Sometimes we think they
can't, so that's where the faith part comes in." He didn't know
why he'd said that and in that particular way—as though he
were explaining it to a student. Only it didn't sound lame,
and now that he'd said it he was satisfied it was true. He
wished Penny could've heard it. It would've fixed her good.

"Yes, well," Helen said as the blue neon sign of the Nouvelle Métropole materialized out of the night. "That wasn't
what I wanted, but it's what you said. So I accept it. It's
vague. But *you're* a little vague."

"Maybe I am," Matthews said. "I could be."

"And what of it, right?" She looked at him and smiled a
not very friendly smile.

"Right," he said in the dark taxi seat. "What of it, is
right."

IN THEIR ROOM, the air was dank-smelling and cold
again. It was past the hour when heat came in the pipes.

Bed was the only place to find warmth. Possibly Paris was not always this cold now, Matthews thought.

Helen went in the bathroom and closed the door and locked it. He heard her running bathwater, heard the toilet flush several times, heard what might've been vomiting but could've been only coughing. Helen hadn't eaten, but she was ingesting medicine of some kind, and that could make you nauseated. She was in pain, he felt sure. She acted as if pain was her companion. Cancer *meant* pain, and those bruises on her legs were from the cancer she'd had but didn't, reasonably enough, care to discuss.

He did not, in truth, know what to do with himself in the tiny, cold room. Some fearful tension had been alerted in him, and Helen's importance (what else could he call it?) in the overall scheme of things had overshadowed his own. He sat down on the bed and tried to envision his upcoming visit to his translator, but none of that was interesting enough to be distracting. He tried to think about Penny and Lelia, in the middle of their happy day. Christmastime—what was it like in the Bay Area? That didn't hold, either. Helen was possibly in some dire way, and that seemed what everything was about. Best to give into it, yet quietly hope he was wrong.

He got up and tried to move his suitcase in such a way that Helen could walk out of the bathroom and straight to the bed without stepping over part of it. To do that he had to close it; but even closed it had to lie on top of hers, which made the room neater but rendered the suitcases inaccessible. They needed to be opened and on the floor to be available, only then the TV or the bathroom couldn't be reached. He decided to leave them stacked, for convenience' sake.

He did not, however, want to get into bed. Helen would not be up for sexual shenanigans, but to be in bed when she appeared could indicate that he was, which could cause problems of an unpredictable character. Helen had recently made some nasty cracks about how full-throatedly eager he was for the kind of sex she specialized in—"grown-up sex," she called it; or, other times, "sex without hand-holding." Possibly he *had* been less than full-throated about that. For some reason, women all seemed sexually insatiable now. A woman at the college, a professor of economics he'd had an encounter with in the first bewildering week after Penny's departure, had needed to be fucked all the time, which he hadn't much liked. It had made him hesitant. There was no *meeting,* nor was one even wished for. To deny her anything had been deemed a vicious insult. Women had always been able to say "No," or "Let's go slow at first," or "I'm not ready"—whatever they wanted. And men had been required to think it was fine. Now men couldn't say those same things without pissing everybody off. So, if he got in bed, Helen would in all likelihood taunt him for wanting sex when it was obvious she wasn't interested, even if he wasn't interested either. Of course, it was also possible she *might* be interested—bruises, pain, jet lag, nausea, cancer— who cares. She might think of it as analgesic. It was another reason to stay out of bed, though he was tired and ready for sleep.

He walked to the cold window and peered out again. He could feel both the cold from outside and the last vestiges of heat in the boxed radiator below the sill. Outside, however, the air was all snow and blackness. He could see the Montparnasse Tower, most of its office squares lighted. Cleaning was going on there, like anywhere. But the Eiffel Tower was still absent from where he thought it should be. Lost in the snow. Possibly closed—though now would be the time to visit it, when the City of Light was lighted. He would certainly go back there when all this was over.

Only a few cars trafficked along rue Froidevaux. Not that it was so late—midnight—but no one wanted to drive through snow in Paris. A police car motored slowly past, its blue light flashing, bound for no emergency. Someone on a motor scooter parked at the curb and came straight inside the hotel. Someone who'd made all the racket yesterday, he thought. The night shift.

He watched a small man appear from the right on foot, possibly from rue Boulard, a man with what looked like a bedroll or a sleeping bag slung to his shoulders, a man in boots, with a long coat, capless. He crossed rue Froidevaux, through the line of sycamores, and walked down the cemetery wall until he was almost lost from sight halfway between the yellow circles of streetlamp lights. He stopped, lit a cigarette, exhaled smoke, turned and looked up and down the mostly empty street, then deliberately stepped to the wall, adjusted his bedroll higher on his shoulders, gave a last look around, and very efficiently but still deliberately scaled the wall and slipped down out of sight to the other side.

Matthews put his nose close to the frosted glass and stared out into the cemetery garden, so jammed with white stone slabs and prim little burial chapels as to appear full, though yesterday of course a place had been found for one more. That grave—in the clutter of others and in the snow and darkness—he could no longer find.

He waited for the man to reappear, searched all along the quadrant of what he thought was the Jewish section, near the man's entry point. But there was no one. The man had come in secretly and then disappeared. Though no doubt he was staying near the wall's interior shadow. There would be a guard inside, a patrol against this very sort of violation—fines exacted.

But there was a movement then, a flicker of darker shadow among the pale, flat monuments. A zig and a zag. Matthews almost didn't catch it, since it came far to the right of where the intruder had intruded, in a remoter corner of the cemetery, just inside the wall where rue Froidevaux intersected with a smaller, nameless street. It was only a flicker, a slight interruption in the snowlight. But it showed again, and then Matthews could see the man—or perhaps another man with a sleeping bag on his back. And he was darting and crouching, then quickly slipping behind a burial vault, then hurrying out the other side and ducking again, falling once, or so it seemed, then scrabbling on hands and knees to regain his footing and casting himself first this way, then that, as if something, something Matthews couldn't see, was dogging him, trying to drive him out of the place, or worse.

Matthews watched, his nose to the frosted pane, until the man had darted and skittered and cowered along the cemetery wall almost to the point of invisibility in the snow and dark. But then, all at once, the man halted before one of the steep, peaked-roof mausoleums, no different from a hundred others. He turned and, as he had outside the wall, looked one way and then the other, then he carefully opened the heavy grated gate, stepped inside, closed the door and was visible no more.

"What time is it in California?" Helen said. She was in the bathroom still, standing at the little mirror, examining herself. He hadn't heard the door open.

"I don't know," he said. "Why?"

"I thought you were standing there thinking about your wife and daughter."

"No," Matthews said, facing her across the cold, newly neatened room. "I was watching a man break into the cemetery."

"That's a switch. Most people want to break out." Helen had on pink, silky pajamas with dark piping, apparel he'd never seen her wear. Usually she slept naked. She brought her face close to the bathroom mirror and opened her mouth to see inside it. "Mmmmm-mm," she said.

Matthews wanted to be agreeable if that's what she wanted. He felt sorry for her. He thought he should feel sorry for both of them.

"I'd like to make love," Helen said, still scrutinizing herself up close, "but I'm too tired."

"That's all right."

"Take a rain check," she said. "Or a snow check."

"Okay," Matthews said.

"I put on pj's so you wouldn't have to see all my ugly bruises." She sighed at her image. "There's others."

"That's okay," he said. Somewhere in the sky outside, he could hear the rumbling and high whistle of a big jet settling out of the snowy night. Some oddity in the wind must've brought such sounds in. But if he looked, he knew he'd see nothing. He and Helen could be most anywhere.

"I would've liked to go dancing," she said. "I *am* a very good dancer. We've never danced. We should've, one time at least."

"Can't we dance later?"

"Oh. Maybe," she said. "You know what I said about eras? Whatever it was Bea didn't like. That was right, though, wasn't it? There aren't any eras. There's just one time, all together."

"I never thought about it," Matthews said, the jet rumbling on at a distance, lower and lower.

Helen walked out of the bathroom in her bare feet and came to the window where Matthews was and looked out. She smelled warm and fragrant. The bottom strands of her hair were damp. And he felt happy at that moment just to put his arm around her bony shoulders and draw her close to him. "I'm going through the change of life. Plus I have cancer," Helen said without inflection. "You'd think one of those would give me a break." She didn't return Matthews' embrace, didn't seem to notice it, just gazed into the stilly floating drama of snow. She was merely beside him here, no more.

But he felt, for that instant, stunned. And if she hadn't been in his arm's protection, he thought, he would've shouted out. A complaint. An objection. Some recounting of votes. How could anything else be important now? His worries, his hopes, his travails in life? Everything gave way to what Helen had just said. She could even have said something less important to her, and it would still have banished his concerns in a heartbeat. What was that quality? he wondered. A flair for the dramatic? An attitude that brooked no resistance? A certainty above other certainties? Whatever it was, he lacked it, definitely lacked it, at least in the quantities she possessed it.

But the result was to make him feel fond toward her, fonder than he'd felt in the entire year he'd known her, even at first, when she'd been his student and they'd fucked in his old house on Hickory Lane, and it was all excitation and sweating and plunging efforts. He liked her more now than he no doubt ever would. She set things in proper perspective regarding importance and unimportance, created a priority using her own life—a standard. And in all the ways he had wanted not to be at the center of things, he was not now, and what he felt was relief.

"Look, there's one little Christmas tree." She was gazing at the high apartment window across rue Froidevaux. "Weren't we supposed to make up a song? Christmas in Paris, da-dee-da, da-dee-da-da. You were going to write the words."

"I'll do it tomorrow," Matthews said. The dark little triangle of the tree, its orange and red and green lights twinkling through the snow and night, was perfectly outlined in the apartment window four floors up. To look at it provided a moment of purest pleasure.

"I think you're afraid of me. But for another reason now," Helen said.

"No, you're wrong," Matthews said with certainty. "I'm not afraid of you at all." He pulled her closer, felt the silk over her shoulders, took in the warm and slightly pungent aroma of her body. He could've made love to her now. It would've been easy.

"Then what do you feel?" she said. "About me, I mean."

"I love you," Matthews said. "That's how I feel."

"Oh, don't bring that into this," Helen said. He could feel her go limp, as if he'd insulted her. "Dream up something else. Think of some better words. Those weren't supposed to be in our deal."

"Then I don't know what else to say," Matthews said, and he didn't know.

"Well, then don't say anything," Helen said. "Share the happy moments in silence. Leave words out of it."

"I'm supposed to be good at words."

"I know," Helen said, smiling at him thinly. "You can't be good every time, I guess." She kissed him on the cheek, had a quick look back at the snowy night, then took herself to bed.

IN THE NIGHT, Matthews slept deeply again, a sleep that knew nothing, a sleep like death. Though after a time he knew he was asleep and wanted only to stay. He was aware of Helen leaving the bed, dropping something on the bathroom floor, saying something, possibly a laugh, then finding the bed again.

He slept until he needed to use the toilet and got up. But when he'd finished he put his face to the little bathroom window, which gave onto the air shaft. The snow, he saw, had stopped, and moonlight again was bright. Everything joined at the backs of the buildings, and some draft of air was making a flap of tin or steel rattle softly below. Across the open space he could see a lighted apartment, where four people—young French people, of course, two women, two men—were sitting on couches, talking and smoking cigarettes and drinking beers out of glasses. The light inside was yellow, and the room next to the sitting room was lighted also. There was a bed there with coats laid on top, and on the side opposite was a bright kitchen, with a window box of what might've been red geraniums. What time was it? he wondered. These people were talking so late. Or possibly he hadn't slept long, only deeply. He was sure, though, that soon he would see one pair depart and the other two begin straightening the house and preparing for bed. It would be satisfying to watch them, and not to see them undress or make love or argue or bicker or embrace, but just to watch them do the ordinary things, go about life as always. It would be so telling to see that. Over the years, he felt certain, others had done what he was doing: watched—perhaps watched these very people—and stolen about these strange rooms at late, undetermined hours, feeling desolate. Elated. Angry. Bewildered. Then taken some satisfaction to bed again. He shared this experience. Probably even with Langston Hughes—he didn't know why he'd thought of him—but with many others. They had all done this, in Paris, in this very bathroom. You only had to be here to share it.

Walking back into the dark sleeping room, he felt, in fact, elated and didn't want to go to bed again, though he was cold. An unusual spicy, meaty cooking smell came from somewhere. He thought he heard a voice laughing and the snap of shuffled cards. The room had moonlight in it, and the air was light and luminous. He sat in the chair and stared up at the Arab art, then stood and looked more closely—at the camels, the oasis, the men sitting talking. It all fit. The drawings were subtler than he'd realized. He had thought of this room as a pit, a hole, a cheap and dingy last-ditch. But he felt better about it. He could stay here. If Helen went on, or went home, he could take the room for a month. Things could change. The hotel would take on another character under other circumstances. He could provide a table and write here, though he had nothing in mind to write (Madame de Grenelle might prove important for this). Though there was no way to know until you tried. He'd seen photos of the rooms of famous artists— almost always in Paris—and they were all worse than the Nouvelle Métropole. Worse by a multiple of four. Yet in retrospect they seemed perfect, each a place you'd want to be, the only room that this novel or that poem could ever have been conceived in. You trusted your instincts. That was all. He tried to think of the line that ran through his head from time to time. Where was it from? He couldn't remember the line now, or who had written it.

He looked at Helen, sleeping. He came close, leaned over her, put an ear near her face to learn if she was there still, heard her breath, brief and shallow. She took pills. They could take you away. He would need to find a doctor tomorrow. There would be some numbers to look up in a book.

She was wrong, he thought, to keep him from disclosing his love. That had been what he felt and should've been allowed to say. Love was never inappropriate; it hurt nothing. It was not, of course, the spiritual thing she'd asked for, nothing like that. If he'd said "love" then, she'd have burst out laughing.

Somewhere down in the street a loud sound erupted, a pop, but a pop that was also a boom, like nothing he'd exactly heard before. He sat again, very still, waiting for other noises, following noise, his thoughts interrupted.

Helen lay as she had, on her side, though her eyes were open. She was staring at him, just seeing him.

"Why are you awake?" he said softly. He got down on his knees by her and touched her face, touched her cheek, which was cool.

"What are you doing?" she said without moving, almost inaudibly, then sighed

"Just sitting," he said.

"Tomorrow seems like an odd day, doesn't it?"

"It'll be fine. Don't worry about tomorrow," he said.

"Are you sleeping?" She closed her eyes.

"Yes," Matthews said. "I am."

"You should," she said, and slipped to sleep again in just that fragile moment.

Matthews sat back and waited a moment, listening for more noises out in the street. A siren or a horn blowing, something to add a rhythm to the other noise, the boom. He heard a car move down the snowy street, skid briefly, its brakes applied, and drive on. And then he came to bed, thinking as he crawled in from the bottom, along the cold plaster wall, that he would never sleep now, since his heart was pounding, and because in truth the day to come would likely be, as Helen said, a strange day.

WHEN HE AWOKE it was ten-thirty. Light through the window was brighter than he'd expected. A stalk of yellow angled across the tiles to his shirt, where it lay from the night before.

He put his trousers on and went to the window. There would be an entirely new view of Paris, he thought. The room wasn't as chilled. He had slept well and long.

And he was correct. The snow from the night had all but gone. A few irregular patches remained in the cemetery and on a parked car or two in the street. But it seemed spring suddenly, the sycamore trunks damp and darkened, the ground soaked, a light fog rising off the gravestones as the sun found them, making the cemetery a park. Of course, there was no sign of the man who'd slept in the tomb. He couldn't distinguish which one it had been, and thought it might've been a dream. He'd drunk too much. Even Rex and Beatrice seemed figmentary—bad dreams one ought just as well relinquish.

Helen lay perfectly still, her head under her pillow, no sign of breathing in the covers. For the second time—or was it the third—he leaned to listen. Her breathing was strong and deep. She could sleep until afternoon. She was weak, he thought. Rest would be her ally.

But what was he to do until then? Read one of her police mysteries. Sitting by Helen's bed reading while the city warmed and turned (perhaps only briefly) more agreeable would be the wrong thing. Too much like a hospital: wanting to be there when the patient woke up from the surgery. There wasn't any surgery; there wasn't anything. It was possible Helen *was* only jet-lagged. Or that because she was experiencing the change of life she exaggerated her symptoms. Something involuntary. That had happened to his mother and driven his father crazy. Then one day it had stopped. He didn't *know* if Helen had cancer or was experiencing pain. You only knew such things with proof, had seen the results. There were the bruises, but they could have simple explanations—not that she was lying.

But to let her sleep in hopes she'd feel better after, that's what he'd want if he were Helen. Until then, he could walk out into the Paris streets alone, for the first time, and experience the city the way you should. Close up. Unmediated.

In thirty minutes he was showered and dressed, had found the Fodor's, drawn the curtains closed across the bright morning and left a note for Helen, which he stuck to the bathroom mirror with toothpaste. *H. I'll be back by 1:00. Don't wear yourself out. We'll have a boat ride. Love, C.*

ON RUE FROIDEVAUX the morning *was* like spring, the light watery and dense, a new warm seam in the breeze that felt foreign and impermanent but saved the day. He had it in mind to walk in any direction until he found some kind of toy store, a fancy French version where there were precious objects unimaginable to American children, and there buy a Christmas present for Lelia. He'd loaded off boxes full of obvious American toys weeks ago. All from Ohio, from a mall. But something special from France could turn out to be perfect. The gift that made all the difference. He didn't know if Lelia knew he was in France, if he'd told her he was going when they'd talked the last time, after Thanksgiving.

Consulting the Fodor's map, he made a plan to walk to the Boulevard Raspail, go left and stay on beyond the Boulevard du Montparnasse—famous streets from his map research for *The Predicament*—then angle down rue Vavin to the Jardin du Luxembourg. Someplace along these storied streets, he was confident he'd find the store he wanted, after which he would try another plan, which would bring him back to the Nouvelle Métropole by one to look in on Helen. This might dictate a doctor visit, although he hoped not.

He wondered if she had a copy of his book stowed away. He'd meant to make a brief search of her suitcase when he was straightening the room and she was in the bathroom. But it had slipped his mind. Though truthfully, he didn't care now. Even if portraits made people look better than they ever could be, they still didn't like the idea. Biographies were full of these feuds. Helen, however, was capable of understanding that a character was just a character, a contrivance of words—practically total invention—not some transformation of a real person to the page. Real people would always have the tendency to be themselves and not as moldable as characters should be for important discoveries to occur. (This was certainly one of the problems with *The Predicament*.) Real people were always harder.

In Helen's current state, of course, it was difficult to know how she'd take it; it was possible that instead of getting furious, she might just laugh it off or even be flattered. The truth was that no one should get involved with a writer if she (or he) didn't want to show up in a book. Try a carpenter or a locksmith or an implement salesmen, and rest easy.

In the meantime he felt better about everything. And walking up the wide, congested Boulevard Raspail—a legendary street he knew almost nothing specific about, bound for some unknown destination, with little language available, no idea about currency, distances or cardinal points—made him feel a small but enlivened part of a wider, not a narrower, experience. Helen dominated life, shoved other interests aside, visualized her own interests clearly and assumed his were the same. And not that he even blamed her. He respected her for it. If his life had been narrow, the blame was his, especially given how charged he now felt as he crossed Montparnasse by Le Dôme, where Lenin and Trotsky had eaten lunch and where, he now remembered from teaching, the great Harry Crowder sang a song by Samuel Beckett in 1930. If he found his way here later and could figure out how to order *soupe de poisson* in French, he decided, he'd lunch at Le Dôme himself.

The best thing to say about Helen was that he wasn't adequate to her needs and demands, due to needs and demands of his own, and that he should let things go on as they now would, then quietly part company with her once they were home. He'd felt the very same—that he'd barely escaped with his life—when he left behind being a professor. He'd have taken the blame for that, too, if he'd gotten trapped there. Helen was nothing like as serious a threat. At day's end, Helen was a nice woman.

Something, without doubt, was changing in his life now, and changing for the better. The fact that he didn't mind being "lost" and alone in Paris was just one small scrap of the evidence. Blumberg's comment that nobody knew him here, which had seemed at the time (two days ago) like a great dark shadow on its way to blotting out the sun, seemed perfectly fine today. You recognized changes in yourself, he believed, not by how others felt about you, but by how you felt about yourself. And instead of worrying about how he couldn't convert experience in Paris to be applicable to Ohio, it might now be possible to convert himself to whatever went on in Paris—something he'd never have dreamed possible when he was teaching the African-American Novel at Wilmot College.

All of which made his planned visit with Madame de Grenelle even more crucial, since the translation of *The Predicament* seemed like the first move toward converting himself into someone available to take on more of life. That was undoubtedly why black artists had flocked to Paris: because in the process of removing themselves from the center of terrible events at home, they'd found ways to let more of life in and, in so doing, disappeared but became visible to themselves at the same time. "Paris welcomed the Negro writers." That was the phrase he'd read in textbooks, was certainly a phrase he'd repeated over the years, accepted without giving it a thought or without believing he had anything in common with Negro writers. Perhaps, though, Paris could open its arms to Charley Matthews. He wasn't spoiled to want that now. Many stranger things had happened.

Bending off Raspail and down onto narrow rue Bréa, he without once looking walked straight to the toy store he'd sought, a narrow shop window on a block of expensive-looking jewelry stores and second-rate galleries featuring Tibetan art. SI J'ÉTAIS PLUS JEUNE, the sign said.

Inside the shop, which specialized in toys made in Switzerland, he discovered a bewildering variety of wonderful possibilities, everything ridiculously costly and probably nothing able to be sent as far as California with any hope of arriving unbroken before New Year's. Possibly it would be better to buy something small, cart it home and save it for later—for Lelia's birthday in March.

Though that wouldn't do. Something *had* to arrive from Paris, whether she knew he was here or not, and he had to get it there in time for Christmas—a week away. Expense shouldn't enter into the equation.

He continued cruising the shop, examining exquisitely carved mahogany sailboats and handmade train sets in several different sizes and shiny enamel color schemes; lavish bear, lion and llama replicas made—at least it looked like—from cashmere and real jewels; and meticulously detailed puppet-show stages with silk puppets that actually spoke in French, German or Italian, using some tiny computer. He wanted to ask the young shopgirl (who was obviously a bored fashion model) what the store might contain that was small and portable and unique and that a six-year-old girl living in the South Bay would like and for which price was no concern. The clerk, he realized, would know English, as well as French, German and Italian, and probably Swedish and Dutch and Croat, but he felt he should speak to her in French, as Helen would've. Except he didn't know how even to begin such a conversation. What he wanted was hopelessly tangled up in unknown tenses and indecipherable idiomatic expressions and implicit French comprehensions, and worst of all with French numbers—large numbers, which the French purposefully complicated and for which he didn't know any of the names above twenty. *Vingt.*

The sales clerk stayed perched, legs crossed, on a high-tech-looking metal stool, reading *Elle* and wearing a preposterously short red leather skirt. And when he'd gone uncomfortably past her station by the cash register for the third time, he simply stopped and looked at her, smiled pitiably, shook his head and for some reason made a circular motion with his upraised index finger, by which he meant to indicate there were more things to admire and buy here than he could choose from, so that he was going to depart and possibly come back later. The young woman, however, looked up, smiled at him, closed her magazine and said in a shockingly American midwestern voice, "If there's anything I can help you with, just ask. I'm not very busy, as you can see."

At the end of ten minutes, Matthews had made his wishes, qualms and time restrictions known to the young woman, who was Canadian and who knew all about shipping, wrapping, customs declarations and valuation limits on packages sent to America. She even found, by looking in a book, the exact category of gift recommended for six-year-old French girls, from which Matthews chose a bright-yellow wall tablet made of plastic that allowed for the leaving of written messages, and from which messages could both be erased and electronically retrieved by pushing a red button on the side. He wasn't positive Lelia would like this, since she was reportedly better at math than at writing; but she could do math on it if she wanted to, and it wasn't American and had French phrases—*Hallo? On y va? Ça va bien? N'est-ce pas?*—worked into the yellow plastic border, along with molded images of the Eiffel Tower, the Arc de Triomphe, the Bastille, the Panthéon, a bridge of some kind: everything but Napoleon's tomb.

This, the clerk promised, would be carefully wrapped, insured against breakage and delivered by courier to Penny's house in Palomar Park on or before Christmas Eve. The entire cost was less than a thousand francs, which Matthews put on his credit card. He also inserted inside the box a handwritten note. *Dear Sweetheart, You and I will spend next Christmas together in Paris, n'est-ce pas? On y va. Voilà. Dad.*

As a result of his successful transaction, when he walked back out into rue Bréa, where the slant, late-morning sunlight on cobblestone pavement felt even warmer than earlier, as if December might just as easily give way straight to spring, he sensed the whole day had been saved, and he was even more free than ever to do exactly as he pleased. Paris wasn't menacing; he'd been right yesterday. And he could operate in it more or less on his own, just as he thought he'd be able to, even though it annoyed him not to know enough words to ask directions, or to understand if any were offered. He would need to stick to the simple, familiar touristic objectives (buying a newspaper, ordering coffee, reading a taxi meter), though this impasse would improve soon enough. But language or no language, he could go wherever he chose—even if he could only order coffee when he got there. The best idea was to treat Paris like a place he knew and felt comfortable, no matter how resistant and exotic it might turn out to be. He decided he'd buy flowers for Helen and let that be his first completely French transaction. A flower stall would come along the same way the toy shop had.

At the bottom of rue Bréa, he turned left toward what the Fodor's indicated would be the Luxembourg Gardens, hoping to take a walk on the sunny lawns, watch children maneuver their small boats in the lagoon (Helen had talked about this) and eventually cross to the Panthéon and angle down to the Sorbonne, while gradually making his way, if he could find it, to the St.-Sulpice church and rue du Vieux-Colombier, where the famous Club 21 had once been located, and where Sidney Bechet and Hot Lips Page played in the fifties. Why not go there, he decided, after all the hours logged yakking about places and people he never knew? He had no idea why the place stayed in his mind or what he hoped to see. Probably it would just be a boarded-up hole-in-the-wall—something else that existed only in a book. Though not *his* book. He'd made no references to any black clubs in *The Predicament*. They had nothing to do with his female character's—Greta's—ill-fated stay. Plus he knew nothing about jazz and didn't much care.

Sending a present off to Lelia had put Penny back in his mind—an unwelcome visitor. He realized that after Penny left, no matter how he felt at the time, or how many novels her leaving might've ignited, or how deep the trenches of despondence that might've cut down through his life, his assumption had always been that at some point he would simply "switch off." Switch *off* from Penny and *on* to something or somebody else. That's what he assumed people did if life was to go on. Airline-crash survivors, emigrants, exiles of war—they all drew for themselves, or had drawn for them, a line of demarcation they crossed once but then never stepped back over again.

Now, though, clearheaded for the first time in days, he realized that this assumption about lines of demarcation might not be entirely realistic; that succeeding as an exile was possibly a slower, more lingering process and could be one that never got completed before you died (children

made it much more difficult). And though sometimes he
nonchalantly thought it didn't matter if he and Penny got
divorced or never did, or if he sometimes felt as if Penny
had gone down in a jetliner and would never be heard
from, neither of those was true, so that stronger measures
needed to be taken to bring about the desired result. Divorce, in other words. He'd been reluctant or casual or
inattentive about it up to now. But no more. Divorce
would be his first official act upon arriving back in Ohio. If
Penny thought she wanted a divorce from him, she
couldn't conceive of the divorce he'd set in motion starting
day one. He and Penny would be "switched off" by Febru-
ary, and that was a promise.

This had to do, he understood, with wanting not to be
the center of things, with wanting to get lost in events, with
conceivably even fitting into the normalcy of another country—though normalcy, of course, was foolish to think
about. Look around (he said this unexpectedly out loud).
He could never *fit in* in Paris. Except that was no reason you
couldn't, with the right set of motivations, *be* here, even live
here, find an apartment, learn the streets and enough of the
language to follow directions. If you couldn't totally switch
off, or switch on, you could make clear and decisive moves
to produce at least some desired results. You could have part
of what you wanted.

He reached what he thought on the map should be rue
d'Assas, with the Luxembourg directly across the street.
But instead he found a different street, rue Notre-Dame-
des-Champs, and ahead of him was not the great garden
with the seventeenth-century palace built by the Médicis,
but once again the Boulevard Raspail, a part of it he hadn't
been on. Though the Luxembourg Gardens still had to be
on his right. He should simply take the first street that way,

even though that meant going back out onto Raspail, clogged now with spewing, honking traffic, stalled in both directions. It was smart, he felt, to be on foot.

The first street off the congested boulevard turned out to be rue Huysmans, which began in the right way until it split into two separate streets, with the one Matthews hoped to take to the Luxembourg blocked to pedestrian traffic by some kind of police action. Several white police vehicles with blue flashers, and even more white police motorcycles, with their helmeted riders sporting machine guns and black flak vests, were congregated around a small bareheaded man seated in the middle of the paved street, his hands raised behind his neck. A few French passersby stood watching down the short street, though a young policeman, also wearing a black flak jacket and black helmet, was using his machine gun to motion pedestrians onto the narrow street Matthews hadn't wanted to go on, rue Duguay-Trouin. Staring down at the man seated in the street, he wondered if there could be a connection between this event and the popping sounds—gun noises—he'd heard last night. Probably there was.

Something seemed familiar about rue Duguay-Trouin, which he reluctantly started down, following the policeman's indecipherable order and wave of his machine gun. He of course had never been on this street in his life. It was only one block long and ended bluntly in a busy, wide avenue Matthews assumed was Boulevard Raspail again.

On both cramped and shadowed sides rue Duguay-Trouin was a solid establishment of not terribly old, sand-colored apartment buildings with set-back, modernized glass entries giving onto courtyards where Matthews could see coldly sparse flower gardens and a few parked cars. It was a street that had been revitalized, unlike rue Froidevaux.

No cars were parked along the curb, and only a couple of overcoated pedestrians were on the sidewalk, walking dogs, and the street was sunless and therefore colder than when he exited the toy store. A few crusts of last night's snow had survived in the concrete crevices of the building fronts, and the whole aspect of the street was slightly inhospitable. He couldn't imagine why rue Duguay-Trouin would seem familiar—possibly some reference in some novel he once taught, or a house where James Baldwin or James Jones or Henry James had lived and done God only knows what, and which someone had to record and pretend to be fascinated by. He was happy to forget it.

But when he'd walked almost to the end of the street, where it entered the lighter-skied, wider street at a large, crowded intersection, his eyes happened to fall on the number 4 and another small brass plaque, inscribed with *Éditions des Châtaigniers*. His eyes passed over the plaque once, unalerted, but then returned. Éditions des Châtaigniers. No. 4 rue Duguay-Trouin. 75006 Paris. This was his publisher. It was only a small shock.

From the pavement he gazed up at the building's tan stone facade. Four floors, with a rank of little balustraded windows near the top, and above that a skimpy level of dormered ateliers with chimneys and what looked like geranium boxes. The offices might be one of the ateliers, he thought. Undoubtedly the whole operation was more modest than one might imagine. Yet it was satisfying to realize that Paris was a sufficiently small and knowable place that he should simply happen accidentally by his publishers on his second day.

Here, of course, was where he'd have met François Blumberg for a brief but solidifying conversation before adjourning up to Le Dôme or La Coupole for a long, memorable lunch that might've lasted until dark and where a staunch friendship could've been forged, ending with him strolling the Boulevard du Montparnasse back toward the hotel (a better hotel, in this revised version), smoking a Cuban cigar as the evening traffic thickened and the yellow lights of the brasseries and tiny bookstores and exclusive side-street restaurants began to warm the evening sky. Those had been his private thoughts, and they had been wonderful thoughts. He'd told no one, because no one would've cared except possibly his parents, who wouldn't have understood. *Châtaignier*—he'd looked it up—meant chestnut tree.

Yet here it was. At least. And he felt, in fact, certified in this small contact, closed though the offices were for the holidays. He was this near now and would someday most assuredly come nearer—when someone knew him in Paris.

He stepped over to the glassed-in arched entrance of No. 4 and peered down the interior passageway to a small bricked courtyard, where one car was parked and a man was sweeping snow, like fallen leaves, toward a drain grate, using a handmade broom with enormous straw bristles. The man paid him no attention and after a moment passed out of sight.

Beside the glass door was a brass panel with numbered buttons 1 to 10 and lettered buttons up to *E.* No names were listed, as there would've been in the States. You needed a code even to gain entry. France was a much more private place than America, he thought, but also strangely freer. The French knew the difference between privacy and intimacy.

He looked up again at the building's steep facade— smooth buff-colored stone ending in a remarkably blue sky. He checked back up rue Duguay-Trouin. Only a

blond woman with a small Brittany spaniel on a leash
stood talking to the policeman with the machine gun.
They were shaking their heads as if in disagreement. Muf-
fled traffic noise hummed from the other direction, on the
avenue.

Just for the touch, he wanted to push the brass buttons.
Nothing, of course, would happen; though he could get
lucky and ring the publishing office. He quickly pushed *C*
for Châtaigner, then his own birth date, 3-22-59, then
waited, staring into the shadowy passageway toward the
parked car and where snow crust was heaped on the drain.
He didn't expect anyone to turn up. C-3-22-59 meant
nothing. Yet he wouldn't have been surprised if someone—
a young secretary or a pretty but overworked assistant
editor—had suddenly rounded the corner, smiling, a little
out of breath, not recognizing him but happy to let him
in, bring him up to the offices. In his working out of these
fugitive possibilities he would speak French, just like in
his dream; the assistant would be charmed by him, eye
him provocatively, and he would later buy her dinner
and (again) walk in the evening down the Boulevard du
Montparnasse.

Only nothing happened.

Matthews stood outside the door, looking in, his hands
in his trench-coat pockets, his presence making no reflection in the glass. He had the sudden sensation he was
smiling; if he could've seen his face, it would've worn an almost beatific smile, which would certainly be inappropriate if someone should appear. He studied the panel again,
shiny and cold. Impenetrable. He firmly pushed F-1-7-8-9,
then waited for some sound, a faint, distant buzz of entry.
He looked back at the policeman at the top of the street,
where he now stood alone, staring Matthews' way. No buzz

sounded. And he simply turned and walked away from his publisher's door, hoping not to seem suspicious.

The Jardin du Luxembourg seemed like a lost opportunity now. The large, congested street at the end of rue Duguay-Trouin turned out to be rue d'Assas, but on his Fodor's plan, rue Duguay-Trouin didn't even appear, so that he wasn't sure where the park was but didn't now care if he walked its spacious lawns or under its chestnut trees. It would be there when he came back to Paris. The Sorbonne too. The Panthéon, the same. He'd never seen them. He couldn't be said to have missed them.

He didn't, however, feel absolutely certain what to do now. Helen would've gone for the guillotine site, a boat ride, possibly the Louvre. But on his own he lacked curiosity for these. A boat ride would be cold. The Louvre had the Japanese. (Most Parisians, he guessed, had never set foot inside the Louvre and couldn't tell you where the Sorbonne was. Most Americans, of course, never saw the Grand Canyon or the Empire State Building.) He believed he could probably find his way with the map to St.-Sulpice and the remains of 21 rue Vieux-Colombier, and then, if there was time, take a walk along St.-Germain for the experience. And he could also, along the way, find a public phone to make a call he'd assumed he wouldn't have the chance to make but now did—a flight of fancy, a single indulgence.

In his last three bleak years of Wilmot College (he couldn't actually remember the date, except Bush was the President), he had allowed himself a brief excursion outside his marriage. This was acknowledged to be nothing lasting, just a sudden careening together of two human beings in otherwise unexpressed and unexamined need (several of these careenings occurred in his Mazda hatchback, a time or two on his cold office floor, once in his bed at home, once in hers). She, in this instance, was Margie McDermott, wife of a professor in the history department, and a woman who was quietly going crazy in eastern Ohio, not so different, Matthews understood, from how Penny felt not long afterwards and probably with the same justice.

With Margie McDermott, the liaison had ended just as it had begun—undramatically though suddenly, and without a great deal of comment. One day they met in a sub shop in the next river town down from Wilmot, decided it was all over and that they were both headed straight for big, big trouble if they didn't cease right then. They looked toward each other across a raised Formica table, proclaimed they were both better served by marriage than by adultery and smart as whips for knowing it so soon. At the end of a brief lunch they got in their separate cars and drove away in opposite directions, feeling—Matthews had been certain—immensely relieved to have dodged the bullets they'd dodged.

In six months, of course, Margie had abandoned her husband, Parnell, and in a year Penny had abandoned Matthews. If they'd only recognized that likelihood, Matthews had often thought, they could at least have kept doing what they'd been doing and enjoyed life a little longer before the curtain slammed down on both their acts.

Margie McDermott had gone directly to Paris, leaving her three children stranded in Ohio with her husband. It turned out she had a former boyfriend from Oberlin who survived in Paris as a painter, someone she had not been in touch with for years but who'd told her she could always come to him if times got tough—which they were. Margie moved in with Lyle and his girlfriend, Brigitte, for six months, tried all kinds of jobs, searched for an apartment, studied French, borrowed money from Parnell, plus some from Parnell's parents, and at long last and after several false starts and tragedies found a job working as a receptionist for American Express, making four hundred dollars a week.

All this Margie had written to Matthews—in a letter that came out of the blue to his new address on the woodsy east edge of Wilmot. He had no idea how she'd found him or why she wanted to be in touch or explain her situation at any length. They had never passed another word once their cars had departed the sub shop on the Marietta highway in nineteen ninety-something. Once or twice he'd seen Parnell at the farmers' market on Saturday morning, looking forlorn and deviled, surrounded by unhappy kids who all, it seemed to Matthews, looked like the absent Margie and not a bit like Parnell.

In Margie's letter, though, had been an invitation that Matthews seek her out should he ever find himself in Paris. She could, her letter said, now cook an excellent *coq-au-vin*, and she had always felt "totally sorry" she'd never "in the midst of all that crazy time" cooked him "a proper meal" Matthews could "sit down to and eat like a civilized human being." She'd enclosed an address and a phone number. "Mine is a poor flat in a very chic neighborhood. The 6th Arrondissement." He had never responded.

He *had*, however, tried to picture Margie McDermott, who'd been a thin, small-boned, sallow-faced, delicately pretty brunette who wore corduroy skirts and blue stockings and always seemed passive and accepting and slightly defeated by life but who apparently wasn't at all. (You could never predict these things.) He'd pictured her first in Ohio and then in Paris—in settings he could only make up. But

it wasn't, he'd decided, an improbable transition to accept:
Ohio to Paris. Though he'd imagined that a difficult, somewhat straitened existence as a receptionist at American Express, instead of as the unhappy, adulterous wife of a history
professor and mother of three, would probably work out to
accentuate Margie's sallow and defeated sides rather than
the adventurous, no-holds-barred, narrow-eyed, nobody's-
fool aspects she'd set free in the back of his Mazda.

In any event, he had thought while planning the trip
that it was worth a phone call, possibly even a brief visit,
though he'd imagined he'd never get out of Helen's sight
long enough, in which case it wouldn't matter. He had no
idea why he might want to see Margie McDermott, since
he hadn't wanted to see her since the last time. His only
thought was that he wanted to see her simply because he
could, and because this was Paris, and visiting a woman in
Paris, even a woman he didn't much want to see, had never
happened to him in all of life.

The rue d'Assas, at its intersection with the rue de Vaugirard, offered an obvious turning and an invitation to
wander back toward the Luxembourg and resume a rem-
nant of his original scheme. But he had lost the taste for
sightseeing and felt more purposeful to find a phone and
call Margie McDermott, who must live somewhere quite
close by, though he couldn't find her street—rue de
Canivet, or possibly Canivel—in the Fodor's. Perhaps it
was too small to show up.

He made straight out for the busy commercial avenue,
which was rue de Rennes, which he *could* see on the map,
leading toward St.-Sulpice or close at least to a connecting
street, which seemed in fact to be rue du Vieux-Colombier,
where the famous club was and where he was sure he'd find
a phone.

Now was the beginning of the last weekend before Christmas, and the warmer weather and sudden sunshine had pushed Parisians out onto the damp sidewalks, crowding around the windows of stores where there must've been sales in progress and standing in line for buses to take them somewhere else, where there were even better bargains. He wondered if here was the true center of Paris, the official downtown recognized by all, or if Paris never had a downtown and was actually just a series of villages connected over time by commerce—like London. These were facts he'd eventually know. It could be that *downtown* was an American idea, something the French would all laugh at if they knew what he was thinking as he plowed along the crowded sidewalk. Ahead of him, down the long, descending avenue (sloping toward the Seine, he was sure), was St.-Germain-des-Prés and, he'd deduced, the Deux Magots, the Brasserie Lipp, the Café de Flore—one of the great confluences of Europe. There was no more famous place. Descartes was buried in the church. It would have to be the center of something.

At the corner of rue de Mézières he found a public phone outside a *tabac,* where workingmen stood at a long bar having coffees and smoking cigarettes. This phone accepted no coins, but Helen's travel agent had thought ahead and supplied two phone cards for emergencies, and she'd given him one at the Pittsburgh airport.

The card clocked up fifty crisp little units of something on the pale-green coin box window. Rue de Mézières had begun funneling a damp, bristling wind, and looking straight into it, Matthews could see one pale rounded tower of what must've been the St.-Sulpice church. It was colder, he felt, nearer the river—just like everywhere else.

He had no idea what to expect by calling, and it was tempting just to forget the whole idea. There wouldn't be time to see Margie unless she happened to live a half block away from where he was standing—which was of course possible. On the other hand, Margie could be different now. What he'd finally found uninteresting and going-nowhere about her in an Ohio college town (and no doubt she'd found the same about him) might be changed in Paris. Something locked away due to circumstance, that inhibited everyone's view of everything and everybody, might have opened up here. All kinds of things were now possible. At the very least, they could restore contact (she *had* written him), have coffee at the Deux Magots or step right inside the *tabac,* maybe set a plan in motion for his eventual return. Or in five minutes she could appear, breathless, expectant, wearing little other than a green cloth coat. After which they could hurry back to her "poor flat," and he wouldn't return to the Nouvelle Métropole until after dark, and possibly never. This, of course, wasn't feasible, given Helen's condition. But there'd been a moment, leaving the toy store, when he'd thought about not coming back, just having a long lunch alone, buying the cigar he'd imagined and setting off on a very, very long walk.

Margie's number was written in her cramped little bird scrawl on a scrap of paper in his wallet. The phone rang once, twice, three times, then Margie McDermott suddenly answered. *"Oui, c'est Mar-gee,"* Margie said, in a nasally girl-ish voice that sounded like a French chambermaid.

"Hi, Margie, it's Charley Matthews," he said, unexpect-edly light-headed, so that he almost put the phone down and walked away. Cavernous before him was now the un-happy need of explaining to Margie McDermott who he was. The words "Wilmot College," "Ohio," "Remember me?"—even his own name—were flat, metallic, about to be bitter. He looked around at the line of men at the smoky bar, drinking coffee and quietly talking. He wished he could speak French. That would be perfect. English was the wrong language for this sort of maneuvering. "Charley Matthews," he said again, wretchedly. "Remember me from Ohio?" He felt the same smile again involuntarily stretch to the corners of his mouth.

"Sure," Margie said brightly, French accent blessedly abandoned. "How are you, Charley? Are you in Ohio?"

"No," Matthews said. "I'm not." Though suddenly he didn't want to be in Paris. The sound of Margie's voice, small and waxy and drab, caused all the sound reasons they'd brought their interlude to a close—how long ago was it?—to throng up in his ears like a loud machine hum. "I'm actually in Pittsburgh," he said.

"You *are?*" Margie said. "What are you doing there?" She laughed an odd little laugh, as if Pittsburgh was the strangest place on the face of the earth to be. It annoyed him.

"It doesn't matter," Matthews said. "I was just thinking about you. I guess it's pretty odd. You sent me your number, though. Remember?"

"Oh, right. I sure did," Margie said. And then there was silence, or at least there was no talking on their line. All around was Paris street noise, but street noise was the same—unless a police siren started up on rue de Rennes. They might even hear the same siren if she lived close by. He would need to cover the mouthpiece. "Are you coming over here?" Margie said.

"Oh, I don't know," Matthews said, looking warily out at rue de Rennes, where cars and buses and scooters were hurtling past. He put his hand by the mouthpiece, ready to cover it. "Maybe someday. You never can tell."

There was another silence then. It was barely after six in Pittsburgh, he thought.

"Are you still teaching?" Margie said.

"No," Matthews said. "I'm not. I quit."

"Did you and Penny get divorced? Seems like Parnell said that."

"Not yet," he said. "But soon." The bristly wind gusted up in his face. "How's the weather in Paris?"

"It's been very cold," she said. "But it's a little warmer today. It's pretty nice. Parnell moved over here with the children. We're living together again. It's a lot better."

"Great," Matthews said, picturing Parnell looking lost, hauling her three look-alike kids around the farmers' market in Wilmot. It occurred to him he might look like Parnell right now. Cold, unattached, vaguely stupid. What forces brought about such an unwished-for moment? He could probably ask Parnell about it and learn something.

"So, did you just call up to say hi?" Margie said perkily.

"Yeah," Matthews said. "I'm at a pay phone."

"Is it cold where you are? Pittsburgh's cold now, isn't it?"

"It's windy. It's probably about the same as Paris." Matthews fixed his eyes on the blunt tower of St.-Sulpice, two blocks away. There was a flower stall in the church plaza. People were lined up there for Christmas flowers.

A third, even longer silence occurred between him and Margie McDermott. He closed his eyes, and in that instant there *were* three thousand miles separating them. He *was* in Pittsburgh. He *had* called her on a lark. He'd only wanted to hear her voice and imagine the possibility of something exceptional taking place. When he opened his eyes he wished he'd see Pittsburgh.

"Charley, is something the matter?" Margie said. "Are you okay?"

"Sure, I'm fine," Matthews said. "We just have a bad connection. There's an echo."

"You sound fine on this end," she said.

"I'm happy to hear your voice, Margie." The little unit counter was somehow down to forty.

"I am too, Charley. We didn't do anything too bad, did we?"

"No. No way. We did great."

"And we were smart to get out when we did, weren't we?"

Matthews didn't know if Margie meant out of their marriages, their affair or just Ohio.

"We were," he said.

"I'd like to see you," Margie said unexpectedly.

"Me, too," Matthews lied.

"Anything's possible, I guess. You know? If you come to Paris you should call me. Okay? Parnell travels a lot now. He's in sales. The kids go to school. We could probably find a little time."

"I'd like that," Matthews said.

"Me, too," Margie said.

He assumed she was lying and that she knew she was and that he was, and it didn't matter. "I guess I'd better take off," he said. "I've got to drive back down to Wilmot tonight. I mean this morning."

"Keep my number, okay?" Margie said.

"Oh, for sure, I will," he said.

"A big hug for you, Charley. Till next time."

"A big hug for you," Matthews said. "A big hug." Then he hung up.

SOMEHOW IT HAD gotten to be one o'clock. *Soupe de poisson* was on his mind. The Parisians were all heading to lunch now, jamming the restaurants around St.-Germain. Probably he should've had lunch with Margie, since he was hungry and hadn't eaten since Clancy's. Though how could he eat lunch with Margie if he couldn't quite stand the sound of her voice? Plus he was in Pittsburgh, not just down the street, cold and getting colder. He thought again about eating alone, buying a *Herald Tribune*. But since the restaurants were all full, the waiters would be in a hurry and testy. His French wouldn't hold up, and lunch would degenerate into bad-willed bickering and misunderstanding—the horror stories people talked about.

He'd been gone much longer than his note to Helen promised. She would be awake and wondering and possibly sicker. On the other hand, she might feel much better and be ready for some excitement. They could eat lunch together. It seemed strange now to have imagined not walking back, just leaving Helen in the hotel.

He thought he should start back.

The metro would be the quickest route to rue Froidevaux. The metro went everywhere. But pausing in front of the *tabac,* which was itself filling up, he couldn't find Froidevaux on Fodor's metro plan. The Montparnasse cemetery would be a good landmark, but it wasn't on the map, and he couldn't think of the name Helen had told him was the right stop. Possibly it was Denfert-Rochereau, though it might've been Mouton Duvernet, each of which he could see, each of which sounded right. But if he was wrong, or got on an express or on a train going the wrong direction, he could end up at the airport. It was risky.

Best, he thought, to walk back up rue de Rennes, away from the river, and look for a taxi at Montparnasse station, or else hoof it all the way to Boulevard Raspail and refind the lion statue, after which he'd recognize things. One way or another, it was thirty minutes. He knew Paris that well.

This trip, he thought, hiking up the cold avenue, was supposed to have been about one thing but had become about something else: a version of sick bay. Nobody's idea of fun. Helen was probably going to become a problem he didn't know how to solve. Terminate the trip, certainly, if serious medical issues arose. Maybe he could phone Rex and Beatrice, if Helen had their number. Or just show up at the hospital, the way people did at home now. English would be spoken in hospitals.

Oxford was out now. He hadn't thought about Oxford in two days. He'd looked forward to realizing—certifying was the better word—the idyll he'd esteemed all these years. The "sweet City with her dreaming spires." It was Matthew Arnold. He'd been offered encouragement fifteen years ago, written his essay on "Mont Blanc," stressing similarities with Thoreau but casting doubt on Shelley's view of the physical world as animate. It had won a minor college prize. But that had been that. He hadn't made it to Oxford the first time. This would be the second.

Reaching the conflux with Montparnasse, he saw across to the taxi queue by the station, where he and Helen had waited to go to the Invalides the day before. French trains must arrive in clusters, he thought, since thirty people were lined up with their suitcases. Only one taxi was angling off the avenue for a pickup. He would be there all day, when at the most he had a twenty-minute walk. He could call the room, but that would take more time, and Helen might still be asleep.

Without quite meaning to, he'd jettisoned the Club 21 and St.-Germain. When he came back to Paris, it would all

be different; when his book was published—the book
Helen could've been lying in bed reading while he tramped
the streets. The next time, he'd be alone. His orientation to
the city would change. For one thing, the squalid Nouvelle
Métropole wouldn't be the epicenter. Probably he wouldn't
be able to find it, whereas now it was "home." Next time
he would stay nearer St.-Sulpice and the Luxembourg—
the heart of Paris.

Thinking of Helen at that moment reading *The Predicament* in their cramped, smelly little room made him feel,
oddly, not like the writer of that book, not even like a
writer at all—far from how he'd imagined feeling when he
thought about occupying the same room for a month, expecting to create something there. Though it might be a
positive sign not to think of yourself as a writer, or not to
think of yourself much at all. Only phonies went around
thinking of themselves as being this or that. Self-regard was
the enemy.

In any case, he could never write about Paris—the *real*
Paris. He would never know enough. It could simply season him, call up an effect, color his views. He would never,
for instance, think of Christmas again in the crude, gaudy
American way. Paris had been added. It was possible even
to increase your brainpower with the additions of unusual
experience. Most people, he'd read, operated on one-
sixteenth of their brain's ability. But what happened if
they began operating on an eighth? The world would
change overnight. Great writers, the same article had said,
operated on a fourth.

The granite lion was dead ahead now, in the roundabout on Boulevard Raspail. Denfert-Rochereau was
entering from the left. That would've been the metro stop.

In the median strip on rue Froidevaux, children were playing Ping-Pong on green concrete tables, two on a side. Occasional flurries of ragged wind deflected the balls off the table, but the children retrieved them and began playing again immediately—their serves bouncing high over the low concrete barriers that served as nets. They were laughing and jabbering: *"Allez! Allez! Sup-er, sup-er!"*

He wondered what had happened to the man last night, the man who'd slept in the burial vault in his bedroll. Along the cemetery wall he could see reddish, leafless treetops. Was the same man there every night, or had that been his first time to scale the wall and seek that shelter? You wouldn't come back from that decline, Matthews thought.

In the sparsely furnished lobby of the Nouvelle Métropole, an Indian or possibly a Pakistani man approached him the moment he entered through the glass doors. It was as though the man had been waiting for him. He wasn't sure he'd seen this man before. Possibly when they'd checked in. A manager. The man wore a dark-blue suit, a white shirt and a dark-green tie; his black hair was neatly parted and combed. He smiled hesitantly, and his mouth showed a good amount of dark gums. He seemed, Matthews thought, concerned about something—how long they were staying, or some problems with a credit card; matters Matthews had already worked out with the other hotel personnel but that obviously hadn't been transmitted to this man. Everything was settled. He would see Madame de Grenelle in two days, and then, if Helen was well enough, they would leave.

"There is a problem," the Indian manager said in English, coming straight up to him and standing close, as if he expected to whisper. Though he spoke too loud. "A serious problem," he said. Matthews had already prepared an answer in French, about credit cards.

"What sort of serious problem?" he said. A younger Indian man stood alone behind the reception, his hands on the counter. He was staring at Matthews and also seemed concerned.

"The woman in forty-one," the manager said, and cut his eyes toward the reception. "I'm sorry. You are in forty-one? Is this true?" The corners of his smooth brown mouth twitched slightly. He might've been suppressing a smile. What had Helen done that was funny?

"That's my wife," Matthews said. "She's jet-lagged. If you'd like to clean the room, we'll go out for lunch."

"I'm sorry," the Indian manager said, and brought his two hands together at his waist and clasped them and blinked. His mouth twitched again, so that he could only repeat himself. "I'm sorry," he said again.

"What about?" Matthews said. "What are you sorry about? What's happening?" He looked at the manager, blinked his eyes too, took a breath, let it out, then waited to learn whatever the problem was, whatever would be next, the next inconvenience he'd need to divert from its present course onto a better one. It would be something simple. These things were the same—never easy, but simple. Nothing was ever easy. He was sure of that, if he wasn't sure of anything else.

And then the man began to explain what the problem was about.

THEIR ROOM smelled a way it hadn't smelled before. The curtains and the window had been opened, the air inside was cold, but still it smelled different. Not like death, but a clean, astringent odor, as though the room had been gone over, scrubbed and put right at some point. Outside somewhere, a dog was barking, a slow, determined barking—something the dog saw but didn't recognize. A mystery. Something that didn't fit into its regular world.

Their luggage was still stacked where he'd put it when they'd come back last night. Nothing was very different in the room. The Arab pictures were the same. The fluorescent light had been turned on. An empty bottle of Bombay gin had been added. Several—possibly four in all—clear plastic freezer bags, empty. A glass from the bathroom, also empty. An ashtray with two cigarettes stubbed out. But mostly neat. Had they scrubbed the room? he wondered. Who'd opened the window? He realized he felt slightly faint.

Helen lay on her side, her right hand open under her cheek, her left hand lost beneath the covers. She was wearing at least her pale-pink pajama top with dark piping. Her glasses were on the table beside the plastic freezer bags and his note. She was very, very pale, her features fixed. Her thick hair wasn't disarranged. Her bottom lip seemed to be tucked in under the top, her teeth undoubtedly resting on it. It was an attitude of sleep.

In the hallway outside he heard the elevator door open, then whispers. A woman's whisper and a man's. Suddenly a young Indian woman came into the doorway, one of the maids, in a loose-fitting, beltless seersucker dress. A large girl. She leaned in, looked at the bed, gasped, then disappeared. In a moment, the elevator closed.

On the night table were two white envelopes. One marked: *Mgt—Hotel Nouvelle Métropole SEULEMENT!*

He sat in the green chair and opened this immediately. In it was a folded piece of white notepaper on which was written: *My fate is my responsibility. Mr. Matthews is not my husband*. It was signed: *Helen Carmichael*. Her passport was enclosed.

The other envelope was marked: *Mr. Matthews*. In it was a similar piece of folded notepaper, on which he read these things:

My last thoughts . . .

I'm hurrying. I don't want you to come back and find me. *Alive!* Death is my little secret. I would like to stay in France. Please try for that. I really just don't fit anymore. Among the living, I mean. It's really no more complicated than that. (This stuff already seems to be working!)

I think a good life is supposed to be to die knowing nothing. Or maybe it's to die knowing nobody. Anyway, I've almost succeeded at both of them.

"Only in paradise is death banned from claiming the weak." This is a saying I've been saving. I forget where I heard it. Maybe TV. This stuff *is* working.

We were never in love. Don't misunderstand that. It will make all this trouble much easier. A cancer cell is just one organism proliferated. I thought of it being like a novel representing all of life and we had that in common. But it's not. It's not a metaphor.

Don't open the other envelope. Please! Goodbye. Good luck.

Affectionately,
Helen

HE COULD SEE both towers now: the Montparnasse and the Eiffel, though they were cut off by lowering clouds. Only their bottom halves were visible. He had thought, of course, that they would both make it home. And yet this had taken so little, so little time, only a small amount of planning. He didn't see how he could've been gone long enough. He'd said he loved her the night before and meant it, and she had said no to that. But if they weren't in love, he thought, what were they? And what was the spiritual component she'd wanted, the thing that to his discredit he couldn't think of? He had let her down.

He wondered if Helen had been reading his book. There was no sign to indicate that, on the bed table or on the floor. On the bed, anywhere. Probably that was all meant as a joke. Someone was jogging around the cemetery wall, clockwise. A woman in a bright-yellow running outfit. He didn't believe she could be French. The French were different: their gait; their pace; the distance they kept and didn't keep. A Frenchwoman would never run around a cemetery in a bright-yellow outfit.

Clouds were causing darkness to arrive early. The dog had stopped barking. A clock was chiming. The Christmas tree in the high window across rue Froidevaux shone coldly in the late day. Again he heard the shuffling card sounds through the wall.

"YOUR WIFE. I'm very sorry," the manager said. They were waiting. The people who were coming had decided to take their time.

"She wasn't my wife," Matthews said. "But—but I knew her very well." He had stammered. It shocked him. This was the first time in years. He had stammered as a child, experienced other difficulties, hadn't learned things very fast, but had overcome it.

"Of course," the Indian man said, and made the little gasping sound, the quick intake of breath, which signified, in this instance, he guessed, sympathy.

That was what marriage meant, Matthews thought: what you did at the very end. What you thought, how you felt, what you said. Your responsibilities were different then. He realized suddenly that he had forgotten to buy flowers. He had said to himself that he would and then hadn't. It was another error, and the thought of it made his heart suddenly race.

Outside in the afternoon air, swifts skittered among the rooftops and chimneys and out into the space above the cemetery. He was very hungry. He hadn't eaten since last night. Later on, he thought, he would have to find a place, someplace nearby, take his chances with the French, eat his dinner alone.

HIS ONLY OTHER trip to Europe had been to Spain. To Madrid, he said. He had been fifteen. Nineteen seventy-four. A youth group. They had stayed near the Parque del Buen Retiro and the Prado and walked and walked and walked, was what he remembered. For some of it he was sick, of course. But on the last day he was forced by others to attend the bullfight. Against his will entirely. They had ridden the subway to the stadium and sat in the sun in front of a legion of old Spaniards who were drunk on wine. All men. Sandwiches were passed around. In all, six bulls were killed, though none of them cleanly. Most, he remembered, didn't seem to want to fight at all. Often they just stood, observing what was happening to them. He'd hated it, he told her, had tried to leave. But everyone—his school friends—insisted he stay. He would never see it again. People threw cushions, eventually.

"Yes," Madame de Grenelle said. She had lived in the south, she said. A city called Perpignan. She had been taken herself.

Outside, children were chasing pigeons with switches in a little park. They were near Parc Montsouris. She shared a house with another woman, a pale stone row house built in the twenties, with creaking, shiny parquet floors and tall windows at both ends of the long downstairs study. At either end there seemed to be a park. On the walls were photographs, black-and-whites, showing what he thought were African women seated on the ground, weaving baskets in a dirty village, or washing clothes in a thick river, or holding babies to their breasts. All stared languidly at the camera. He had brought flowers, purple anemones.

Madame de Grenelle was of mixed race. That's all he could tell. She was tall and willowy, with dyed black hair, a flat nose, large hands and pale-blue eyes. Possibly, he thought, she was Berber—because of her eyes, and because she wore a long, thick caftan that was maroon with blue and purple octagon designs. It seemed to him Moroccan. Her father had been a professor of English in Toulouse.

"Translators have no lives of our own," she said in amusement. "We live off others' lives. Sometimes nicely." She smiled. They were seated in chairs in the middle of the long room, where the least light reached from outside. She was fifty, he thought. She smoked American cigarettes. Chesterfields. She'd put his flowers in a vase on a table beside them. He didn't know how to answer her. "Your book has the ring of actuality about it," she went on. "It's fascinating."

He didn't know if she meant it was true or simply seemed true. He chose the latter and simply said, "Good."

"It is your story, I think. The predicament."

"No," Matthews lied.

"No?" she said, and smiled at him in a penetrating way.

"I wanted it to *seem* true," he said.

"I see," she said. His book lay on the table beside his flowers. " 'Predicament' does not exist in French." She smoked her cigarette. "Often, of course, you learn what your book is about after you write it. Sometimes after someone translates it and tells you."

"It could be," Matthews said. "I can believe that."

"Your book will be better in French, I think," she said. "It's humorous. It needs to be humorous. In English it's not so much. Don't you think so?"

"I didn't think it was humorous," he said, and thought about the street names he'd made up. The Paris parts.

"Well. An artist's mind senses a logic where none exists. Yet often it's left incomplete. It's difficult. Only great geniuses can finish what they invent. In French, we say . . ." And she said something then that Matthews didn't understand but didn't try. "Do you speak French?" She smiled politely.

"Just enough to misunderstand everything," he said, and tried to smile back.

"It doesn't matter," Madame de Grenelle said, and paused. "So. It is not quite finished in English. Because you cannot rely on the speaker. The *I* who was jilted. All the way throughout, one is never certain if he can be taken seriously at all. It is not entirely understandable in that way. Don't you agree? Perhaps you don't. But perhaps he has murdered his wife, or this is all a long dream or a fantasy, a ruse—or there is another explanation. It is meant to be mocking."

"That could be true," Matthews said. "I think it could."

"The problem of reliance," she said, "is important. This is the part not finished. It would've been very, very difficult. Even for Flaubert . . ."

"I see," Matthews said.

"But in French, I can make perfectly clear that we are not to trust the speaker, though we try. That it's a satire, meant to be amusing. The French would expect this. It is how they see Americans."

"How?" he said. "How is it they see us?"

Madame de Grenelle smiled. "As silly," she said, "as not understanding very much. But, for that reason, interesting."

"I see," Matthews said.

"Yes," she said. "Though only to a point."

"I understand," Matthews said. "I think I understand that perfectly well."

"Then good," she said. "So. We can start."

ON THE STREET, rue Braque, he felt he could find the metro now, near where the taxi had left him on Boulevard Jourdan. A university was nearby. He could remember Denfert-Rochereau. Somehow, in the last days, he'd lost the Fodor's.

The children in the little park had quit chasing pigeons and were sitting in a row, all on one wooden bench, enjoying a winter picnic. It was warm again. He felt he should buy the cigar he had nearly bought two days before, on the day of Helen's death. He missed her, had thought of her a great deal, wished she hadn't suffered and could've felt more promise. She *had* fit in, he thought. That wasn't right. She should be here, but things needed to go on now. There was not so much left to do, a few details the embassy office had agreed to assist with. Helen would go home, of course. Burial was restricted to the French. A sister had been found. He would merely sign documents. All in all, it was not so complicated.

And then he would go on to Oxford, and afterwards—perhaps after New Year's—home. He had the feeling of having been in a long struggle. Though he sensed much of it was the foreignness, the beginning of a state of loneliness and longing which would be his if he stayed. It came directly behind all the feelings he liked. You could spend ten years in Paris, never do the same thing twice, but eventually longing and disquieting thoughts would take you over.

It had been a good talk, though it had not been easy to keep his book in perspective. Madame de Grenelle had mentioned Flaubert, and he'd tried to remember the first lines of *Madame Bovary*: someone arriving at a school, a foreigner. Were they famous lines?

But he had learned something. He had commenced a new era in his life. There *were* eras. That much was unquestionable. In two days it would be Christmas. They, he and Helen, had failed to make up a song. And yet, oddly, this would all be over by Christmas. He hadn't even written a letter to his parents. But in the time that remained here, he would. A long letter. And in his letter he would try as best he could, and with the many complications that would need detailing, to explain to them all that had happened to him here and what new ideas he had for the future.

THE SPORTSWRITER

'Ford is a masterful writer'
Raymond Carver

'A devastating chronicle of contemporary alienation'
New York Times

'Richard Ford's sportswriter is a rare bird in life and
nearly extinct in fiction'
Tobias Wolff

At dawn on Good Friday every year, Frank Bascombe
and his wife meet to pay their respects at the grave of
their firstborn. This year Frank plans to spend the
Easter weekend with a new girlfriend while on assign-
ment for his magazine. What might have been an
idyllic adventure becomes a succession of calamities
that extinguish almost all the carefully nourished
equilibrium of a man grappling with the failure of love
and the death of his son.

The end and the aftermath of a marriage, the
emotional dislocation and the discovery of a new life
while in the embrace of troubled memories of the old
have seldom been more harrowingly plotted. *The
Sportswriter* is also a wistful, very funny and always
human illumination of domestic and sexual anguish
through the story of Frank Bascombe, its hero, the
sportswriter.

Buy this book at www.bloomsbury.com/richardford

Independence Day

**Winner of the Pulitzer Prize and the
PEN/Faulkner Award**

'The best novel out of America in many years ...
simply a masterpiece'
John Banville, *Guardian*

'It is nothing less than the story of the 20th century
itself ... Eloquently, with awkward grace, in his
novels about an ordinary man, Ford has created
an extraordinary epic'
The Times

After the disintegration of his family, the ruin of his
career and an affair with a much younger woman,
Frank Bascombe decides that the surest route to a
'normal' American life is to become an estate agent in
Haddam, New Jersey. Frank blunders through the
suburban citadels of the Eastern Seaboard and avoids
engaging in life until the sudden, cataclysmic events of
a Fourth-of-July weekend with his son jolt him back.

The sequel to *The Sportswriter* and the first novel to
win the Pulitzer Prize and the PEN/Faulkner Award
in the same year, *Independence Day* is a landmark in
American Literature.

Buy this book at www.bloomsbury.com/richardford

The Lay of the Land

'Bascombe's voice remains one of the most generous
and wise in contemporary fiction, the honest
testimony of a pilgrim seeking the transcendent
in a decidedly mundane world'
Stephen Amidon, *Sunday Times*

With *The Sportswriter*, in 1985, Richard Ford began a
cycle of novels that ten years later – after *Independence
Day* won both the Pulitzer Prize and the PEN/
Faulkner Award – was hailed by *The Times* as 'an
extraordinary epic [that] is nothing less than the story
of the 20th century itself'.

Frank Bascombe's story resumes in the fall of 2000,
with the presidential election still hanging in the
balance and Thanksgiving looming before him with
all the perils of a post-nuclear family get-together.
He's now, at fifty-five, plying his trade as a real estate
agent on the Jersey shore and contending with health,
marital, and familial issues that have his full attention.
This is Richard Ford's first novel in more than a
decade: the funniest, most engaging and explosive
book he's written.

Buy this book at www.bloomsbury.com/richardford

A PIECE OF MY HEART

**'This is quality writing in the highest American
tradition of Faulkner, Hemingway and Steinbeck'**
The Times

'Superb ... Brutally real and at the same time haunting
... One of those rare surprises that come along every
few years'
Jim Harrison

Robard Hughes has raced across the country in pursuit
of a woman, and Sam Newell is hunting for the
missing part of himself. On an uncharted island on the
Mississippi, both these godless pilgrims find what they
have been searching for in an explosion of shocking
violence. The novel that launched the career of one of
America's late-twentieth-century masters, *A Piece of
My Heart* is a *tour de force* that does justice to Ford's
diverse literary gifts: his unerring eye for detail, his
pitch-perfect ear for dialogue, and his sharp understanding of human nature.

'I am enormously delighted to make the acquaintance
of this muscular American writer, whose glowering
prose, in hot mode or in cool, throbs with the weight
of the vast continent he lovingly embraces'
Independent

Buy this book at www.bloomsbury.com/richardford

WILDLIFE

'Every sentence Ford writes, illuminates ... His prose is strong, clear and satisfying, resonant with the bleak rhythms of unrewarded lives'
Sunday Times

'Ford's book observes the human animal with friendship, understanding, and an almost clinical detachment'
Independent on Sunday

In the autumn of 1960, Joe Brinson and his parents move to the edge of the Rocky Mountains to cash in on the promise of the American frontier, to seize a future as broad as the sweep of the Montana prairies. But when Joe's father leaves home to fight the forest fires that have raged since the summer, and his mother meets an older man, Joe finds his life changing too suddenly, blazing into unrecognisable pieces like the forests surrounding them.

'Ford writes carefully and with simplicity that is not deceptive but extremely difficult to achieve, about powerless, uninformed people and their surroundings, in close-up'
Victoria Glendinning, *The Times*

'What is satisfying in *Wildlife* is its density. This is proper storytelling, lean and taut. And it is real, grown-up life. Ford captures perfectly the loneliness that can only be had in families'
New Statesman

Buy this book at www.bloomsbury.com/richardford

THE ULTIMATE GOOD LUCK

'His prose has a taut, cinematic quality that
bathes his story with the same hot, mercilessly
white light that scorches Mexico'
New York Times

'Ford's taut, compelling prose is as piercingly clear as
a police siren. No other storyteller writes about the
alienated and uncommitted with such mastery'
Sunday Times

Harry Quinn and his girlfriend Rae head to Oaxaca,
Mexico, to spring Rae's brother Sunny from jail
and protect him from the sinister drug dealer he is
suspected of having double-crossed. But instead of
a simple jailbreak, Harry and Rae fall into a nightmarish series of entanglements with expat whores and
Zapotec Indians. The Cocaine Era's answer to
Graham Greene, this exquisitely choreographed novel
tracks Rae's and Harry's inexorable descent into the
Mexican underworld, where only a stroke of ultimate
good luck can keep them alive.

'So hard-boiled and tough that it might have been
written on the back of a trench coat. A grand *Maltese
Falcon* of a novel'
Stanley Elkin

Buy this book at www.bloomsbury.com/richardford

A Multitude of Sins

'Ford's sheer mastery of the short-story form
is jaw-dropping'
Guardian

'Ten sexy, grown-up stories about marriage and
adultery, passion and infidelity, disappointment and revenge.
Ford is a smooth master of his art'
Financial Times

With perhaps his fiercest intensity to date, Richard Ford, America's most unflinching chronicler of modern life, is drawn to amorous relationships inside, out and to the sides of marriage. In these extraordinary stories all human relations, our entire sense of right and wrong, are put into vivid and unforgettable play.

Rock Springs

'A collection of stunning impact, which marks Ford's
arrival at the pinnacle of his craft'
Sunday Times

'These are beautifully imagined and crafted stories. By turns
heart rending and wickedly funny – and just plain wicked.
Richard Ford is a born storyteller with an inimitable lyric
voice – and *Rock Springs* is the poetry of realism'
Joyce Carol Oates

The stories in this celebrated collection are about ordinary women and children. Unemployed, on the way back to prison, marriages in tatters, they confront their fates with hard-won optimism and flashes of insight.

Buy this book at www.bloomsbury.com/richardford